D0435835

Also by Akemi Dawn Bowman

Starfish

Summer
Bird Blue

Summer Bird Blue

AKEMI DAWN BOWMAN

SIMON PULSE
New York   London   Toronto   Sydney   New Delhi

This book is a work of fiction. Any references to historical events, real people, or real places are used fictitiously. Other names, characters, places, and events are products of the author's imagination, and any resemblance to actual events or places or persons, living or dead, is entirely coincidental.

SIMON PULSE

An imprint of Simon & Schuster Children's Publishing Division

1230 Avenue of the Americas, New York, New York 10020

First Simon Pulse hardcover edition September 2018

Text copyright © 2018 by Akemi Dawn Bowman

Jacket design and illustration by Sarah Creech copyright © 2018 by Simon & Schuster, Inc.

Jacket ocean photographs copyright © 2018 by ChrisVanLennepPhoto/Getty Images

All rights reserved, including the right of reproduction in whole or in part in any form.

SIMON PULSE and colophon are registered trademarks of Simon & Schuster, Inc.

For information about special discounts for bulk purchases, please contact Simon & Schuster Special Sales at 1-866-506-1949 or business@simonandschuster.com.

The Simon & Schuster Speakers Bureau can bring authors to your live event.

For more information or to book an event contact the Simon & Schuster Speakers Bureau at 1-866-248-3049 or visit our website at www.simonspeakers.com.

Interior designed by Tom Daly

The text of this book was set in Adobe Caslon Pro.

Manufactured in the United States of America

2 4 6 8 10 9 7 5 3 1

Library of Congress Cataloging-in-Publication Data

Names: Bowman, Akemi Dawn, author.

Title: Summer bird blue / Akemi Dawn Bowman.

Description: First Simon Pulse hardcover edition. | New York : Simon Pulse, 2018. | Summary: After her sister and songwriting partner, Lea, dies in an automobile accident, seventeen-year-old Rumi is sent to Hawaii with an aunt she barely knows while she and her mother grieve separately.

Identifiers: LCCN 2017048136 (print) | LCCN 2017058959 (eBook) | ISBN 9781481487771 (eBook) | ISBN 9781481487757 (hardcover)

Subjects: | CYAC: Sisters—Fiction. | Mothers and daughters—Fiction. | Death—Fiction. | Grief—Fiction. | Composers—Fiction. | Aunts—Fiction. | Hawaii—Fiction.

Classification: LCC PZ7.1.B6873 (eBook) | LCC PZ7.1.B6873 Sum 2018 (print) | DDC [Fic]—dc23

LC record available at https://lccn.loc.gov/2017048136

NEWPORT PUBLIC LIBRARY
NEWPORT, OREGON 97365

For Shaine and Oliver,
I love you more than all the stars in the sky

CHAPTER ONE

Summer."

"Bird."

"Blue."

Lea's face lights up like every star in the sky just turned on at once. "I love it."

Mom looks over her shoulder, the arch in her brow a mix of curiosity and amusement. She's heard us play this game a thousand times, but she still doesn't fully understand it.

I don't blame her. Most people think Lea and I are two of the weirdest people in the universe when we're writing songs.

"What does a bird have to do with summer or blue?" Mom asks.

Lea and I speak at the exact same time, our voices colliding against each other's like cymbals.

"It doesn't have to make sense."

"You're interrupting our vibe."

Mom laughs. Her eyes meet mine in the rearview mirror. "I

think 'black' would've given you more options. Shama thrush are beautiful songbirds, you know."

I glance at Lea and make a face. "What is she talking about?" I whisper.

"No idea," Lea whispers back. "I think she's just making up words."

Mom lets out a mock groan. "Fine. I'll just sit here quietly, the unpaid taxi driver whose daughters won't talk to her."

I laugh. Lea leans forward and plants a kiss on Mom's freckled cheek, their faces blending together like a blur of bronze skin and curls the color of burnt coffee.

My hair isn't wild like theirs—it's long and straight, probably because I'm not wild at all. They're the ones who go on all the roller coasters, sing in public, and dance to every song on the radio.

I'm more of a sideline kind of girl. I live vicariously through them.

Mom tilts her head back and purses her lips. "What about you, Rumi? Got a kiss for your mom?"

"I'm good," I say, rolling my eyes as Lea settles back next to me. It's not that I don't love my mother, but I'm not really the affectionate type. I'd blame it on the fact that I'm going to be a senior this fall, but Lea is going to be a sophomore and she still hasn't outgrown Mom's hugs.

Maybe it's because Lea is a way nicer person than I am. It makes sense—she's a giggler. And people who giggle are either incredibly annoying or so over-the-top nice you feel obligated to forgive them for it.

There's nobody in the world who would call Lea annoying. Not even me, and I'm usually annoyed by most things with faces.

Mom lets out a gentle sigh. "I'll try not to take it personally."

You know how some people have resting bitch face? I have relaxed jerk voice. Lea insists this is a real thing. She says I always sound like I'm barking instead of talking. So to compensate, I use the sandwich method.

A compliment, followed by my real thoughts, followed by a compliment. It was Lea's idea I sarcastically agreed to go along with, but for some reason it's kind of stuck.

"Your hair smells like flowers. Kissing makes me feel like you're violating my personal space. I like your lip gloss."

Lea coughs her laughter into the back of her hand. Mom looks at me with half-hearted disapproval.

There's a journal sitting in the space between Lea and me. It's sky blue and covered in tiny white stars, with an *R* and an *L* drawn on the cover in black Sharpie.

I pick it up, splitting the book open with my thumb, and flip through pages and pages of lyrics Lea and I have been working on all year. They were all inspired by three words, too. It's our game—to think of the first three things that come to us and write a song about them.

Some of them are funny. "Love String Macaroni." "House Ghost Marshmallow."

Some of them are dark. "Earth Blood Iron." "Lost Wings Ice."

But they are all us—Lea and me—and that counts for a lot.

I write "Summer Bird Blue" on a new page and tap the end of my pen against the lined paper.

Lea sniffs beside me. She pats her hand against her thigh, a beat that reminds me of a song we once wrote about a boy who still doesn't know she exists. "Every summer I remember what it's like," she starts to sing.

I close my eyes. "To feel the warmth against my skin."

"You know just how to take the sun away," she continues.

"And it's winter when I look at you again." I peel my eyes open and find Lea smiling at me.

Something rushes through my body, as if my blood has been replaced with starlight. I feel like magic, and wonder, and pure happiness. And when I look at Lea, my fifteen-year-old sister who glows and shimmers and is everything good that I'm not, I know she feels the same way.

Music is what makes up the single soul we share. I don't think I'll ever find another person in the entire world who understands me the way Lea does. We're the only two people in the universe who speak our language.

Lea throws me a thumbs-up. "I like it."

"I can't wait to get back to my piano," I say.

Mom slows the car down. Another red light. She looks up at us in the mirror. "But where's the blue bird? I thought you were singing about a blue bird?"

We talk over each other again, like sisters with the same thought but different words.

"God, Mom, let it die."

"You don't get us at all."

And then the three of us are laughing, and pretty soon it's just one loud sound that harmonizes together. Mom, Lea, and me. The song of our family.

The light turns green up ahead, and Mom pulls away, still smiling.

It's hard to explain what I see next. Nothing at first, and then something so dark and big that it shields all the light from the window. But I do hear the sounds.

A crash, like every chime and timpani and gong colliding all at once.

Shattering glass, like stars exploding into dust.

A crunch, like bone and stone and metal and so many awful things moving in directions they shouldn't be.

A breath.

A word.

And then complete and utter silence.

CHAPTER TWO

'm cradling my arm in a cast when the doctor tells us Lea is dead. Mom's in a chair next to me, her fingers digging into the hospital bed, her eyes dull like all the light has gone out of them.

I try to say so many words. *It's not true. You're wrong. She's alive. You don't know what you're talking about. You're lying. I don't believe you.*

But I can't say anything. The words for what I'm feeling don't exist.

I'm in bed when Aunty Ani knocks on my door to say we're going to be late for Lea's funeral.

I roll onto my side and wait for her to leave. Funerals are for saying good-bye.

I'm not ready to say good-bye. I'm ready to wake up from this horrible bad dream.

* * *

I'm looking into my mother's eyes for the first time in days when I tell her about Lea's final word.

Rumi.

My name, right before she died.

I ask Mom if it means anything—if she thinks Lea knew how much I loved her.

"I loved her too," Mom says, and her words fly toward me like I'm under attack. I'm arguing with her before I can stop myself, yelling about how I loved Lea more and that Mom never loved me enough. I don't know why I say it, or when loving Lea became a competition. Maybe I was just looking for reassurance. Maybe I needed my mother to comfort me because my sister is gone and the world feels empty and cold and hard.

Mom doesn't defend herself, or correct me, or tell me how horrible I'm being. She leaves the room.

She leaves *me*.

I'm sitting in Lea's bed when I hear Aunty Ani yelling at Mom over the phone.

"You need to come home," she shouts. "You still have a daughter, you know."

I'm lying on the bathroom floor the first time I realize I'm really, truly alone. Mom hasn't spoken in weeks. Lea is in a hole six feet under the ground. And Aunty Ani still feels like a stranger.

It's just me.

*　*　*

I'm hunched over a toilet, the sick heaving from my throat, when I realize I haven't cried yet.

I don't know what I'm supposed to feel in order to cry. All I know is that there's a giant key lodged in my stomach, and it's turning and twisting and tightening, making it hard to breathe.

The only way to make it stop is to throw up, and even then it's just temporary.

I'm sitting at the kitchen table eating toast when Aunty Ani sits down next to me. She wants me to come and stay with her for a while. She says it's because Mom needs time to grieve on her own. She says it's only for the summer, but I don't think a few months is enough time to heal the emptiness Mom has become.

She's a shell. A ghost. I think her soul climbed into the coffin with Lea.

I wish mine had done the same. Because at least then I wouldn't feel so left behind.

I'm sitting on a plane when I realize I haven't seen Lea's guitar in a month. I'm worried Mom hid it, or worse, got rid of it. I'm mad at myself for not checking before I left. I'm angry at Aunty Ani for making me leave my home to fly halfway across the Pacific Ocean. I'm even angrier at Mom for forgetting to keep at least half of her soul for me. And I'm furious the people who cleaned up the accident never found our journal.

I feel like I hate everyone. Every single person left in this entire awful world.

But at least I finally feel something.

And I'm somewhere above the clouds, curled up in the window seat trying to find Lea in my own reflection, when I remember I once promised Lea three wishes—three wishes to make up for trying to ruin Christmas once, when we were kids. And I remember that I still owe Lea one last wish.

The wish I promised her and still failed to give her, because I was too stubborn and selfish to listen.

And I know I have to make it up to her. Because Lea deserves her third wish—she deserves a sister who would've kept her promise.

It doesn't take me long to think of what Lea would ask for. Because I know Lea just as well as she knew me.

She'd want me to finish "Summer Bird Blue."

And somehow, even though I feel lost and alone and so unbelievably angry, I know I need to find my way back to the music— to find the words to bring our song to life—so that I can make up for all the ways I failed her.

A wish is a wish, after all.

Summer

CHAPTER THREE

It's dark when the plane lands at Honolulu International Airport. By the time Aunty Ani and I get our suitcases off the carousel, all the shops and restaurants are closed.

Aunty Ani offers to take my bags, but I shake my head and pull the straps of my backpack so it tightens against me. I don't know why I'm so protective about a worn-out bag, but I guess in some ways it feels like the only armor I have. And with Aunty Ani looking at me like she feels unbelievably sorry for me, I need it.

We step through the doors and walk down an outdoor walkway. The air is warm and a little sticky, and I can tell already that two-thirds of the clothes I packed aren't going to be any good for this kind of weather. Sunshine in Washington is a lot like the people in my life—great when they're there, but also completely fickle and unreliable.

I don't have the greatest track record for people sticking around. I used to think Lea and Mom were my only examples of real stability, but—well, I'm in Hawaii with an aunt I rarely see and about ten thousand holes in my heart.

"You feeling okay?" Aunty Ani eventually asks, maybe because she feels like she's supposed to. She's wearing jean shorts and a red sleeveless top that hugs her curves. I always thought Mom had the darkest skin of our family, but maybe that's because Aunty Ani was never around to compare her to. She looks like someone who's spent her lifetime under the sun.

I listen to the rolling wheels of my suitcase and try to think of something to say that has nothing to do with feelings. "This airport smells like flowers."

"Could be the pikake," she replies with a hurried, hopeful voice. "Or maybe you smell gardenia." She makes it sound like a question—like there's room for me to keep talking about the flowers or the airport or whatever I want just as long as I keep talking about *something*.

But I don't say anything else. I don't really care about flowers, and I'm not good at pretending I care about things when I don't.

Lea was good at that. She was smiley and kind and she'd encourage people to talk for as long as they wanted if it's what made them happy.

I'm the easily irritated one she'd sometimes pinch behind the arm because she was always trying to remind me to stop scowling.

Aunty Ani opens the trunk of her car, and I tuck my suitcase and backpack away. She shifts them around so hers can fit too, and when she shuts the door, I feel vulnerable.

"You probably hungry, yeah?" She climbs into the driver's seat and starts the engine.

I climb in the passenger's side. A string of white shells hangs from the rearview mirror with a handful of tiny characters dangling from the end. A black cat. A turtle. A Totoro.

I clear my throat. "I'm fine. I ate on the plane."

"Oh, but airplane food junk." She looks at me and smiles, showing off the slight gap between her front teeth. "I know one place still stay open. They have ono kine fish tacos. You like try?"

"No, thanks. I'm not hungry," I say, planting my chin on my fist and staring out the window.

Aunty Ani lives in Kailua, and she tells me it's a little bit of a drive to get to the east side of the island. I pay a little attention to the street names at the start, but they're hard for me to pronounce, and by the time we get onto the freeway, I lose interest in everything but the curve of my nose in my reflection, which reminds me of my sister.

It's good that it's so dark. I can imagine her face better in the dark, because in the daylight we were related but far from similar. I used to like our differences. Now I wish there weren't so many of them.

We turn off on a road called Mokapu Boulevard, and then we're turning left and right and left and right and I feel like we're in a maze I'll never be able to find my way out of. Eventually she makes a turn down a steep hill that curves into a small cul-de-sac, where three houses sit in an almost-triangle at the bottom.

They look gray in the darkness, and the only one with the porch lights still on is the one in the middle. There's an open garage on the left side held up by white wooden stilts, and the house is surrounded by a chain-link fence, bushes, and trees too dark to make out, with white steps leading up to the front door.

Aunty Ani pulls the car onto the driveway and turns off the engine. She tilts her head and gives me another encouraging smile. It doesn't work because she's not Lea. With a sigh, she says, "I'll leave the door unlocked. Come inside when you're ready, okay?"

She thinks I'm weak or breakable or tender-hearted. I've never had anyone look at me that way before—I've always been the strong one. The tough one. The one with the dead sister who still hasn't cried. What does Aunty Ani see that I don't?

She goes inside the house, and I sit in the car for what feels like an hour.

My first time visiting my aunt in Hawaii shouldn't have been alone. Lea should have been here. Mom should have been here. I feel like they both left me behind. Or rather, they both forced me ahead.

I don't want to do this by myself.

I'm not ready for Hawaii.

Something inside my gut aches, like there's iron in there being knotted over and over again. It makes my skin hurt. My face hurt. My throat hurt.

I scream, just to get it all out. I scream and scream and scream.

And then my eyes are shut tight and I feel like I have no control over myself anymore, but I can still hear myself screaming from somewhere miles and miles away.

When I finally take a breath, I open my eyes and see two

lights—one from the house on the left and one from the house on the right.

When I look up at the windows, I see two men staring down at me. The one on the left is young—maybe my age—and he's wearing a tank top with both his arms planted on the windowsill. He's lean, with dark spiky hair and a deep tan. In the other window is an old man with gray hair combed back like he belongs in a Gene Kelly movie and big heavy bags under his eyes that pull his face down. They both watch me, not like they've seen a girl screaming, but like they've seen something that simply needs to be seen.

My gaze shifts from one to the other and back again, like my eyes are the *ticktock* of a clock, and I'm watching them like they're the ones who have the problem, not me.

I hate the way they're staring at me even more than I hate the way Aunty Ani stares at me. Because they don't seem to care if I'm strong or weak, broken or whole. They just seem *interested*, and somehow that feels much, much worse.

And just like that, I build a mental wall, one hundred bricks at a time, like I'm creating armor out of my own frustration.

When I feel nothing again, I get out of the car and go inside.

CHAPTER FOUR

wake up to what feels like an actual earthquake, and when I roll over and open my eyes, I see Aunty Ani shaking the mattress with her foot.

She's holding a basket of laundry with both hands, and there's a sheen of sweat across her forehead, like she's been running around the house all morning. "You ready fo' get up?" I can't tell if she's trying to smile or catch her breath, and then I wonder if it's the chores that are making her sweat or the anxiety of—well, *me*.

Because I'm no longer Rumi Seto, the girl who believed she'd conquer the world armed with a piano and her best friend at her side. I've turned into someone else—someone unstable. I've run out of reasons to wake up every morning. I've become a corrupted version of myself—a version everyone seems to think is on the brink of self-destruction.

So, knowing all that, why is Aunty Ani trying to get me out of bed so early?

I roll back the other way and pull the sheet up to my neck. "My sister is dead. My mom abandoned me. I'm allowed to sleep in if I want to."

"I don't think—" she starts, but something changes her mind. Maybe she thinks it's too early to argue with me. "It's three o'clock," she says, except she pronounces it "tree," and now I remember where I am.

I press my fingertips against my eyelids and try to imagine a time when I didn't feel like I ran face-first into a wall of concrete. Aunty Ani moves to my window and pulls the blinds open before cracking the window a few inches. The warm afternoon breeze spills through the room, making everything smell like outside. Like flowers and fruit trees and freshly turned soil. It's strange and foreign, and it makes me think of where Lea is buried, and that makes me sick.

No matter how much dirt and rock and earth there is for me to dig up, I'll never be able to reach her. Not really. Because we don't exist in the same world anymore. I don't know how to hang on to someone who doesn't exist in the same world as me. I'm not sure I understand what any of it means.

Aunty Ani looks into the laundry basket, probably realizing she's completely unequipped to deal with someone like me. Maybe she thought being family would be enough, but family doesn't mean the same thing to me as it did a month ago.

"I go make you something fo' eat," she says at last, hurrying back out of the room before I can object.

I try to go back to sleep, but then it's too warm and I can smell the aroma of food sifting through the hallway like a scented lure.

I'm sticky and hungry, and by three thirty it makes sense to get out of bed.

I find Aunty Ani in the kitchen, stirring something in a pot and adjusting the fire until the flame is barely visible.

She brings her eyes to me briefly and smiles like she's holding back. "You like eat some saimin?"

I let myself fall into a chair, pressing my hand against my cheek to hold up the weight of me I can't seem to shake. "For breakfast?" I grimace.

"Oh, you have to wake up breakfast time if you like fo' eat breakfast." Aunty Ani gives me a gentle smile and scoops a huge portion of noodles into a bowl and places it on the table. Half a hard-boiled egg and a few slices of bright pink and white fishcake float in the broth.

The food triggers a memory. It tugs my chest like something heavy and metal is pulling at my sternum. A queasiness rolls around my stomach, and I clench my fingers as tight as I can to try to steady myself, my fingers cutting crescent moons in my palms.

It happens a lot these days—the aggressive force of memories coming back to me—and I don't know how to stop them. I wish I could, because my memories no longer feel like nostalgia. They're either dreams or nightmares, and—if I'm being honest—most of them feel more like the latter.

But when a memory clicks into my brain like a gear being forced, I have no control over it. The scene just plays out, taking control of my consciousness, forcing me to remember things that are painful and beautiful and horrible all at once.

A memory

The pan sizzles, and a dollop of butter turns from pale yellow to a rich gold so quickly Lea jumps away from the stove, scared she might get burned.

"That's way too much butter," I say from the table. I do that a lot—comment from the background, the way people do when they're watching one of those singing talent shows from their couch. *"Not the best song choice," "He's so pitchy," "What is with those dancers?"* Lea hates it—no, scratch that, *everyone* hates it. But I can't help myself. I'm a commentator.

Lea points the spatula at me. "Stop backseat-driving my breakfast."

I shrug. "Fine, but I'll make my own eggs."

She rolls her eyes and pours the bowl of gooey egg and milk into the pan. "One day you're going to miss my cooking."

I snort, turning back to my notebook. The top line says "Flicker Stairs Statue." With a heavy sigh, I say, "I think we made this one too hard. I feel like I'm writing a poem for Edgar Allan Poe."

Lea giggles, stirring the eggs around with the tip of the spatula. She laughs the way Mom does—like they breathe in pixie dust and float on clouds. I don't laugh like that, and I absolutely do not giggle. "I think it should be a love song," she says.

"You think everything should be a love song. You're the only person I know who actually thinks Valentine's Day is a romantic holiday and not a giant marketing scam."

She looks at me and shakes her head, like I'm the one who doesn't know anything about anything. Maybe she's right, or maybe I simply see the world differently than she does, like I'm looking from the outside in. I'm not the kind of person who falls for cheesy cards and bargain chocolate boxes. I'm not really the kind of person who falls in love with anything, if it isn't my piano and a blank sheet of music.

Love at our age? Pointless.

I hum a melody off the top of my head, tapping my pen to the beat. Lea hums along too, scratching at the pan with the spatula, before letting her notes fall in perfect harmony to mine. A few minutes later, she scoops the eggs onto two plates and sets them on the table.

"Okay, stove is all yours," she says.

I stand up just as Mom walks into the kitchen. Her hair is in a neat ponytail, and she's wearing a red shirt with khaki pants. There's a white name badge with a Target logo in the corner pinned on the left side of her chest that says "Mamo."

I take a breath, feeling my heart break a little bit when Lea's face lights up.

"Mom, I made you break—" she starts.

"I'm so sorry, honey. I'm already running late. Rumi, did you take my keys?" Mom is rummaging through her purse, her breathing rapid.

"They're on the counter," I say.

"I thought you were off today," Lea says, her voice breaking at the end.

Mom forces a grateful smile toward me and swipes her keys from the counter. She tries to smile at Lea too, but her eyes are darting everywhere. "They cut my hours at the bar, so I need the extra shifts. I love you guys. Make sure you lock the door if you go anywhere. Oh, and please remember to turn off the lights before you go to bed. Our electric bill is going to be the death of me." She blows two kisses into the air like she's flinging them at us and zooms out the door like she's on roller skates. We listen to the car engine start and the tires roll away.

Lea's eyes fall to the floor, and she twists her mouth like she's trying not to cry.

I tap my fingers against the back of the chair, looking at Lea and thinking about how much I hate seeing her so sad.

I sit back down at the table and pull one of the plates toward me, shoveling scrambled eggs into my mouth and staring off into space like it's not a big deal at all.

A few seconds later, Lea sits down across from me

NEWPORT PUBLIC LIBRARY
NEWPORT, OREGON 97365

and picks at the other plate with her fork, both of us chewing in silence.

When our eyes finally meet again, Lea's smiling warily. "Do you still think there's too much butter?"

I force myself to swallow. "I like your eyeshadow today. I feel like I'm eating neon-colored mucus. Thanks for cooking." Sandwich method, tried and tested.

Lea laughs so hard she starts to cough, and I shake my head and keep eating, letting a smile grow on my face too.

"Thanks, Rumi," she says after she calms down a little.

I nod, letting my fork fall against the edge of the plate. "She'll remember, you know. Sometime today she'll remember, and she's going to feel horrible about it."

"I don't want her to feel horrible about it."

"I know. But she will anyway."

Lea chews the edge of her bottom lip, still fighting the tears she doesn't want to come. Eventually she nods at me like she understands—like she *has* to understand, because not understanding would only make Mom's life harder, and she works harder than anyone we know.

We finish eating, put our plates in the sink, and when we're both standing near the doorway waiting for the other person to walk through first, I wrap my arm around Lea's shoulder and press my head against hers.

NEWPORT PUBLIC LIBRARY
NEWPORT, OREGON 97365

"Happy birthday," I say.

She blinks away her tears and smiles back instead.

Mom did a lot of things she felt bad about later, but none of them were ever on purpose. None of them were intentional.

Leaving me in Hawaii to grieve alone? Because she needed time to herself? Time without me?

That's not an accident.

But I know Mom, and one day she's going to feel bad about it. She's going to regret leaving me alone when my heart is broken and I'm missing my sister. And the truth is, I *want* her to feel bad about it. It shouldn't be as easy as apologizing and moving on.

Because it's not easy for me.

I'm not sure I'll ever be ready to forgive her.

I watch the steam rising from the broth for a long time, swirling the noodles around with chopsticks I'm out of practice with. Eventually I slide the bowl a few inches away from me like it's something foul and rotten.

Standing up more aggressively than I mean to, I say, "I'm going for a walk." I slide my shoes on and throw myself out the front door before Aunty Ani has time to object. The screen door rattles shut behind me, the noise echoing through the small cul-de-sac.

I take a quick look around. Hawaii is different in the daylight. Brighter, but softer somehow too. And none of the houses are gray at all—Aunty Ani's is more of an olive green, and the other two are painted a deep cream and surrounded by vegetation.

The only thing that's dull and gray and dark in Hawaii is me.

There's no color left in my soul, just like there's no music left in there either. How am I supposed to finish writing a song for Lea when I feel like my heart has been carved out of my chest and the empty, hollow space is all that's left?

What if music doesn't belong to me anymore, the way Lea doesn't belong to this world?

My stomach churns. No—I *have* to give Lea her wish. I can't let her down. Not again.

When I turn to my left, I notice the old man from last night standing in his front yard. His thumb is pressed to the end of a hose pipe, and a spray of water covers the row of flowering plants in front of him. His eyes, heavy with time, watch me the way someone watches a fly trapped between blinds and a windowpane—like he knows the struggle ahead of me, even if I don't see it myself.

"You goin' break da screen door you slam 'em around li'dat," he says suddenly, his accent much heavier than Aunty Ani's and his thumb never leaving the hose. There's a small black dog at his heels, yapping at the sky and the ground and everything in between.

I feel my entire body recoil, and the man watches me like he's watching a chessboard. He notices too much. I don't like it.

"It's a door," I reply tersely.

"Not *your* door," he replies with just enough grit in his voice. The yapping continues, but he doesn't seem fazed.

"Mind your own business," I say, heart racing.

"You da one stay outside my house—yelling, slamming da

door, and acting all lolo. Huh!" He snorts. "If you no like talk to me, den stop making all kine humbug fo' everybody."

My eyes dart back and forth. I know I shouldn't engage. Not even Lea would need to point that out. There is no version of this scenario where getting into an argument with an elderly man is a good idea.

But Lea is dead. So who am I to do any kind of rational decision making?

I don't even bother with the sandwich method. "If you care so much about keeping the neighborhood quiet, then try shutting your annoying dog up," I spit angrily, balling my fists like I'm trying to crush his glare within my fingers.

He watches me, twisting his mouth like he's chewing on tobacco. And then—without the least bit of warning—he turns the hose on me.

I let out a sharp yelp as the cold water collides with my body. I raise my hands to protect my face, but it's already too late. My hair is stuck to the sides of my temples, my clothes feel like they weigh an extra twenty pounds, and there's a giant puddle beneath my feet. I'm completely soaked.

"What the *hell*?" I sputter when he finally aims the water back toward his plants.

My voice startles the small dog, causing the yapping to temporarily stop. The black mutt retreats behind its owner and lowers its head cautiously. Because I'm no longer a stranger—I'm the girl who just became archenemies with an eighty-year-old.

"Dat's to cool off," he says with a straight, emotionless face.

"You realize you just committed assault," I growl, angrily wiping the water away from my eyes. I don't know if it's my blood boiling at one thousand degrees or the sun, but even though I've just been hosed down like a pair of muddy boots, my skin feels like it's on fire.

He turns away, waving the green hose back and forth over his small garden.

"I could call the cops," I try again.

He looks at me, nostrils flared, but he doesn't say anything.

"What, now you're going to ignore me?" The racing inside my chest grows. I feel like the veins in the side of my head are going to explode. "After you ruined my clothes? Because I slammed a door?"

"You, you too much noise," he says stiffly.

"You have issues!" I shout, spinning around and marching back into my aunt's house like I have a plan.

I don't. I barely know where I am.

I slam the door—again—and find Aunty Ani with her arms crossed near the window. She eyes me from head to toe and tilts her head slightly, her gaze disapproving.

"Please no make humbug with the neighbor. He no care fo' teenagers," she says.

"Are you kidding me?" My mouth hangs open, and I motion toward my clothes. "Look at this. He tried to drown me. I'm not *humbugging* anyone." My shoulders start shaking. It's probably because I'm wet and cold, but I don't really feel it. Maybe when you have too much emotion raging inside of you, you feel hot all the time.

"Mr. Watanabe is your elder," she says calmly, like she's talking to a small child. "You have to talk to him with respect."

The fire swirls inside me. "I don't care how old he is. I don't need to respect anyone who doesn't deserve it."

Aunty Ani sighs like a balloon slowly releasing air. I don't think she's irritated with me—she doesn't know what to *do* with me.

I'm not her daughter. We're only family by blood. And I just lost my best friend—my sister—who is never coming back no matter how many doors I slam. Neither one of us was trained to deal with a situation like this.

Aunty Ani's eyes fall to the fresh puddle appearing on the wooden floor. "Go change clothes. We can talk after, yeah?"

I look down. I'm wearing a T-shirt from a One Direction concert and a ripped pair of white jeans. They're Lea's. I stopped wearing my own clothes weeks ago.

I shake my head, the drenched strands of my hair flopping against my cheeks. "I don't want to change, and I don't want to talk. I'll dry off outside."

I find a chair at the back of the house, lean back so the sun lands on every inch of my face, and force myself back to sleep so I don't have to spend another minute *awake*.

CHAPTER FIVE

I think the people who invented smartphones never bothered to think about what it would be like for people in mourning. Or maybe they did know, and they didn't care.

The first few weeks after Lea died, my phone was constantly buzzing. You know those epic battle scenes in movies when entire armies rush at the screen like a stampede of amped-up adrenaline? That's what my phone was like, but in the form of notifications. Text messages, phone calls, e-mails, social media. A never-ending slew of "I'm sorry" and "Are you okay?" and "My condolences."

Except the battle eventually came to an end. The stampede passed. And it didn't end in a trickle either, the way I thought it would—it just stopped, maybe a week or two after it happened. Like Lea's death didn't matter anymore. Like it was old news.

There was so much noise, and then there was silence. But both of them were constant reminders that Lea was gone.

A few of my friends tried to keep in contact. Alice tried the hardest, which was both surprising and completely expected. Surprising because Alice stopped caring about my feelings around the same time she hooked up with Caleb, and completely expected because, well, it's Alice, who feeds off melodrama and gossip, and what could be more gossipy than knowing someone who recently died?

Other people tried to reach out too—maybe to make sure I was still alive—but I don't really know what I'm supposed to say to people anymore. *I'm not okay, and I probably never will be. I don't want to die, but I want to be in the same place she is. I'm not sure where to go from here.*

It's too heavy for normal people. It's even too heavy for me, not that I'm really all that normal.

I look down at my phone. No missed calls. No text messages. No notifications. And not a single word from Mom.

What's the point of even having a phone?

I march to the bathroom, lift the toilet seat, and drop the cell phone into the water like it's a penny in a mall fountain.

It doesn't make me feel better, but at least I don't have to be *reminded* anymore.

An engine rumbles outside the bathroom window. I peer through the blinds and see the boy from next door lifting a cooler onto the back of a pickup truck.

Normally I wouldn't care. Boys and trucks and coolers are about as foreign to me as people who think the best music is the stuff on the radio.

But I can hear it, somewhere between the laughing and the engine. I can hear *the song*.

The last song Lea and I listened to. Just before we got in the car with Mom. Just before we started to write our own song. Just before she died.

Something sharp hits my chest, like my heart is turning into ice. I feel dizzy and cold and far, far away.

I can feel her. I can *see* her. The way she sings with her mouth barely open, the way she taps her hand against her knee, the way she rests her head on my shoulder because sometimes it was the best way to say, "I get you, and you get me, and let's never change."

But it did change.

My head feels empty and full all at once, and before I know it, I'm standing at the edge of the driveway, lured by the song that will only ever remind me of my lost sister, and looking straight into the eyes of the boy from the window.

They're a dark, smooth brown. Most people I know have flecks of other colors around the irises—bits of gold or green or blue. But his are completely unblemished, like two perfect chocolate coins.

He grins with too much cleverness for his own good. "Hey, hapa girl. I was wondering if I'd see you again." His black hair hangs across his left eyebrow like he just rolled out of bed.

I look in the back of the truck. Next to the cooler are two surfboards—one with an oversized green gecko and the other covered in blue and green swirls. There's another guy sitting in the driver's seat, his hair in tidy curls at the top and fading into his skin by the time they reach his ears. He watches me—they both do—waiting for me to reply.

Ignoring them, I stare straight through the window until my eyes find the car stereo.

The guitar sounds like dripping caramel. The singer's voice sounds like he's singing in a room full of wood and fire, with a midnight breeze rolling through the open windows. Because to Lea and me, music wasn't only about sounds. Music was scenery and smells and tastes and magic, too.

But it doesn't feel like magic anymore—it feels like I'm being haunted.

Something punches me in the chest, and I feel my heart explode like icicles splintering in a thousand different directions. It's painful. More painful than I could've ever imagined. I don't know how something as beautiful and important as music could suddenly feel so empty and cruel.

Music used to be life and hope and everything happy. Now it's full of ghosts.

"That song," I start to say, but the rest of the words don't come to me.

The boy looks over his shoulder at his friend, who shrugs casually and grabs a baseball cap from his lap, spins it around, and snaps it against his head like a magnet.

"Dat's my sistah's iPod," his friend says. "I neva heard half da stuff before."

The boy from next door turns back to me, the happy creases next to his eyes never disappearing even when his smile tucks itself away. "Yeah, me neither. I like it, though. You know who sings this one?"

I try to push their faces out of my mind because I feel Lea slipping away. I hold my breath, like I'm trying to hold on to her. Like inside my heart is a pair of hands that are grabbing and reaching for any sliver of her left in the world, because they want to hold on to *something* of her.

I can feel her, somehow—even if she is buried in a graveyard in Washington State, hundreds of miles away from me. Music has always made me feel closer to Lea. I guess even death couldn't change that.

Except it's painful now, to think about Lea and to feel close to her. Which means listening to music is painful too.

Something strange and wiry creeps into my thoughts, like a slithery creature whispering things that just can't be true.

You don't deserve her. You never did. Maybe you don't deserve music, either.

My chest aches. And aches. And aches.

I can't take it anymore. Losing Lea feels like there's a knife forever twisting in my heart. It feels like walking up a stairway that never ends, and every new step gets harder and harder to climb. It feels like floating through space with no way of getting home.

It feels hopeless.

And losing music, too? It feels like someone has taken all the oxygen out of the world. It feels like I'll never be able to breathe again.

Having her close to me is too painful—so I let Lea go. I let her ghost slip away.

Another song starts—something upbeat and full of clever rhymes. The guy in the baseball cap points to the stereo. "Dis mo' like it," he says, bobbing his head around like it's floating in the water.

I let everything inside me escape like a heavy breath tumbling out of my mouth. It's too much—the loss of Lea, the loss of music.

The loss of Mom.

The boy in front of me cups a hand over his eyes like he's blocking out the sun. He doesn't seem bothered I'm not answering any of his questions, but he's also not ready to give up. "We headed fo' Palekaiko Bay. You like go?" he asks, breaking through my frustration. He has two matching dimples right in the center of his cheeks like a baby doll, but black sideburns that trail to the bottoms of his earlobes. He's like a man-baby. It's confusing.

"What?" I blink. I'm having a hard time concentrating.

"I t'ink she no can understan' your pidgin, brah." His friend leans out the window and cups a hand around the sides of his mouth. "He—like—know—if—you—like—hang—wit'—us . . . today," he says, drawing out each word like there's too much noise in between us.

My new neighbor pulls his face back and shakes his head, his eyes pinned over his shoulder. "Eh, genius, you still talking pidgin." He turns back to me and reaches out his hand. His forearms are dark and lean, but all muscle. "I'm Kai." There's a light behind his eyes—something more than just cleverness. It's something very much alive, like a gear constantly turning, or a wild crackle of electricity. Some people look like that—like their brains never take a break.

I used to look like that too, but now there isn't any light left. My brain has blue-screen-of-deathed.

His friend waves from the truck. "Gareth," he says, squinting like he's not sure if he really *wants* to be introduced to me.

Kai and Gareth have nearly identical tans—a deep beige closer to Aunty Ani's than mine—but the similarities stop there. Gareth is still in the car, but even I can see he's huge. The driver's seat is pushed back an extra foot to make room for what are probably the longest legs known to man. And his shoulders are broad and his neck is wide, and even though he looks strong, I don't think it's exclusively muscle.

Kai lets his hand drop when I don't take it, but he doesn't seem fazed. He crosses his arms instead and raises his shoulders. "So whatchu think? You like go to the beach?"

"What? No. I've never met either of you before," I say, my voice flustered.

Gareth lets out an impatient breath and reaches out of the window to nudge Kai. His hand looks like a massive bear paw. "Eh, brah, she no like go. Come on—we already stay late."

Kai waves him off like he needs another few seconds. "Well, can you at least tell me your name?" he asks me. "I mean, we can see into each other's bedroom windows. We're practically roommates."

"You can see into my bedroom?"

"Well, sort of. When the blinds stay open."

"That's creepy."

"No it's not. You can see into mine, too."

"That's even more creepy."

He tilts his head back and laughs. "I'm not getting this across well. I just thought we could get to know each other. Since we're neighbors."

"It's not a requirement to be friends with your neighbors. Some of the happiest neighbors are complete and total strangers."

"Well, what if our mail ends up at the wrong house, or if you need to borrow sugar?"

"Nobody borrows sugar in real life."

"Have you ever *needed* to borrow sugar before?"

"No."

"Then how do you know?"

Gareth hangs his elbow out of the window and looks at me with a tired smile. "Please jus' go tell 'em your name, or tell 'em you not interested. Cuz dis uncomfortable fo' watch already."

"Rumi," I say, clearing my throat. "My name is Rumi. But we're not going to be friends. I'll be leaving soon, so there's no point." *Just for the summer.* That's what Aunty Ani told me. A couple of months for Mom to grieve without me getting in the way.

A couple of months where Mom doesn't have to be anyone's mom at all.

My throat tightens, but I try to ignore it.

Kai turns around and looks at Gareth, who shrugs at him and starts pushing buttons on the stereo.

The black dog suddenly appears, yapping a few yards behind me, demanding everyone's attention. Its ears fold over lazily, and its tail curls into a bush of fur against its back.

Gareth groans. "Lolo dog."

Kai leans down and claps his hands together urgently. "Howzit, Poi? You got out of the yard again, eh?" He wiggles his fingers above the ground. "Come on, come here."

The dog doesn't stop barking. The more Kai interacts with it, the more frantic the yapping becomes.

Gareth flinches. "You making 'em worse."

Kai sighs, standing back up. He runs his fingers through his black hair. "One day we'll be friends." And then he looks at me, a twinkle in his eyes, and I'm not sure if he's talking to the dog anymore.

I look over my shoulder at the neighbor's house. There's nobody in the yard, and the gate is shut.

The small mess of dark fur bounces up and down near my feet, catching my attention. "I don't know why you want to be friends with it. That dog has social problems, just like its owner."

"You met Uncle George?" Kai raises a dark eyebrow. It looks like a faded caterpillar.

"Are you guys related?" I pull my chin into my neck at the idea that I might be surrounded by the world's weirdest family.

Kai laughs. "Everyone is Uncle and Aunty in Hawaii, hapa."

I raise my eyebrows. "I'm not calling him 'uncle' anything. *Your* uncle George has anger issues. He sprayed me with a hose."

He laughs louder, looser. You know the saying about being made of rubber and insults bouncing off a person because they won't stick? I think Kai might be made of rubber. A *lot* of rubber.

Poi keeps barking below us like a fire alarm that won't turn off.

"The first time I saw you, you were screaming your head off in the driveway. What's that make you?" Kai looks at me curiously, his cheeks tight with humor.

"I guess I've got issues too."

"Yeah no, you guys all lolo." Gareth taps his fingers against the steering wheel impatiently. "Jerrod stay waiting fo' us at da beach, and da dog is giving me one migraine. Can we go already?"

"Okay, okay." Kai waves his hand at him before making his way around the truck and sliding into the passenger seat. When he's settled inside, he leans forward and stares at me through Gareth's open window. "Be nice to Poi. I spent two years trying to get her fo' like me. Please don't mess up my progress."

And then the truck crawls up the drive before peeling around the corner and disappearing from my sight.

I face Poi again, its shrill yaps pounding through the neighborhood street like an alarm clock in a nightmare. When I look up at Mr. Watanabe's house, I see him standing in his doorway, barefoot and dressed in shorts and a T-shirt. His hands are folded behind his back, and he's watching me like I'm the problem and not his annoying little dog.

I retreat to the house. I don't feel like fighting today.

When I'm sitting on my bed, I close my eyes and try to let the music back into my head—I picture the stereo. I picture Lea. I picture the rise and fall of the melody. I try to remember the lyrics we made up for "Summer Bird Blue." But every time I think I have it, the sharpness returns in my chest and the notes pull away from me like the tide moving back into the water.

Holding on to a melody is like trying to hold on to Lea—I can't do it. I'm too afraid of the pain that comes with it.

How am I supposed to keep a promise I can't even hold on to?

I wish Mom were here, and then I hate myself for missing her at all.

CHAPTER SIX

I can't sleep. My mind is racing with too many thoughts—about how painful music has become, and how I still haven't cried since Lea's death, and how Mom should be here.

I press my fingers to my temples, staring at the moonlight slipping through the parted blinds, and I wonder if I'm somehow responsible for all of this.

Maybe I'm too heartless to cry. It's not a secret I wasn't as good a sister to Lea as she was to me. And maybe Mom knows it too—maybe Mom is finding it hard to love me when it's just me on my own, because it's so much more obvious that I'm not as good as Lea.

I wonder, if Mom had been given the chance to choose which of her daughters she could save, if she would have picked Lea.

It's not hard to imagine her answer. Because even *I* would've picked Lea.

The knot in my throat starts to grow, until it's pushing at my neck like there's a rock wedged in there. But the tears don't come.

I don't feel like I'm trying to hold back, or like I'm making an effort not to cry. But I can't do it—I can't turn my rage and hurt and heartache into tears. It's like whatever is happening in my head isn't connecting with my body.

I think it's because the car accident broke me. Losing Lea *destroyed* me. And I'm not sure how to put myself back together again.

Is that why I can't cry? Because I'm no longer whole?

God, Mom, why aren't you here? I need your help.

And for the briefest second, I think about calling her. I think about waking her up in the middle of the night and forcing her to talk to me—to *listen* to me. Because I don't know if I can keep doing this alone. I don't think I should have to—not when I still have a mother and she still has a daughter. Lea would want us to be there for each other.

But the thought fizzles away as quickly as it came. Because I remember why I threw my phone in the toilet—I remember why it was upsetting to see my phone light up and have no notifications. No missed calls. No contact from Mom.

She could've gotten in touch, but chose not to. Because somehow being near me was *hurting* her. It was keeping her from grieving.

Because I hurt people, even when I don't want to. Even when I should know better.

A memory

Lea's room still smells like her. Like vanilla soap and flowery perfume. It's faint—fading, like her—but it's there. I take a breath and feel the sting in my eyes.

Mom's voice makes me jump. "You don't have to do that."

I scowl and snap my head toward her. I don't mean to, but it's just my natural reaction to being startled. I try to smooth my frown away, but it's too late. Mom's already seen it.

"I didn't mean to interrupt," she says quickly, taking a step back out of the room like she thinks I need the space.

She's given me enough of that. Doesn't she see how much I need her?

I push myself up from the carpet and away from Lea's dresser. The drawer is still half pulled out, and there are clothes all around my feet. "You can stay," I say firmly.

Mom nods twice, but remains in the doorway. "It might be a little soon for this," she offers, her eyes falling to the mash-up of T-shirts, tank tops, and jeans.

I realize what Mom thinks I'm doing, and my eyes widen in alarm. "I'm not going through her stuff to get rid of anything."

Mom's eyes are so tired and swollen. I've hardly seen her since we came back from the hospital. She's mostly been in her room, crying and avoiding me.

The crying I understand, but the avoiding? I can't really figure it out.

I keep talking because it's different around Mom.

She makes me nervous. For the first time in my life, I'm scared I'm going to say the wrong thing. And I don't want to hurt Mom when she's already hurting. "I'm trying to remember what she was wearing. Because I thought it was her yellow shirt, but now when I picture her in the car, she's wearing a blue tank top. And I don't know why I can't remember anymore—you'd think I'd never forget that—so I'm seeing what clothes are still here. Which shirt she left behind."

"I don't understand," Mom says, and I think she hides a shudder. "What's this for?"

"Because I'm worried I'm going to forget," I say urgently. "I can feel my memories slipping. They're fuzzier than they used to be. And if I can't even remember what shirt she was wearing the day she died, how am I going to remember the important stuff? The stuff that *means* something? So I need to make sure I have it right. I need to make sure I remember everything *right*."

"Rumi, I don't think we need to do this right now." Mom's gaze continues to leap around the room like she's following a house fly.

"Aren't you worried you're going to forget?" I ask hurriedly. The panic clambers up my throat. I start to feel dizzy. "There's so many things we didn't get to finish. Promises we didn't get to keep. Things we never got to do." I pause, the shame practically swallowing me whole. "Things I never apologized for. And I need to remember all of it—I need to remember her."

Mom crosses her arms and lifts her chin so she's staring up at the ceiling. The tears are slipping down her cheeks. "I just think it's too soon."

"What else am I supposed to be doing?" My voice echoes in my own head, but I'm not sure it reaches Mom.

She doesn't move. Doesn't say a word.

I swallow the lump in my throat. I shouldn't ask, but I do anyway. "Mom? Why won't you look at me anymore?"

Mom squeezes her eyes shut and more tears fall.

Something sharp and painful gnaws at my chest. "I know you can't face what happened to Lea, but can you at least face me? I'm still here. And I don't know what it is I'm supposed to be doing."

"I don't know either," Mom whispers into the ceiling. "I wish I did."

I look at the pile of clothes on the floor. "Lea would know. She always had the right answer—knew the right thing to say to make everything better. If I had died instead of her, she'd know exactly what to do."

I only half notice Mom flinch because I can't stop the words pouring out of me.

"She was easier to talk to and easier to love. She was just *better* than me, and I know that, and I wish I deserved her more. I wish I had appreciated her, and told her I'm sorry, and let her know she was the best fucking sister I could have ever asked for. But I can't tell her these things, because all I have left are memories. And I have to make sure they're right. I have to know that I haven't forgotten anything."

Mom's lips quiver. "But . . . why?"

"Because I have to remember all the times I was horrible to her, and all the times I wasn't. Because the more I think about it, the more I worry I was a really bad sister to her. I think I spent more time being angry and jealous and petty than I did just loving her. And I did love her—I loved her more than anyone could've loved her. But I don't think I showed it enough when she was alive, and I don't know how I'm ever going to make that up to her. So I need to know—I need to know how much I owe her. I need to know if I failed as a sister."

Mom chokes out a breath and sucks the air back in like she's afraid to let her real feelings show. "You didn't fail her, Rumi. She loved you, *so much*."

"I know she loved me. I'm just not sure she knows that I loved her." I shake my head and try to find Mom's eyes. "She said my name right before she died. It—it felt like she was trying to save me."

The color drains from Mom's face. "What?" I think her voice cracks, but it's so quiet I can hardly hear her.

"I heard her say my name. And I know it doesn't make any sense, but it's the *way* she said it. Like she was choosing me, or trading her life for mine. And I don't know how I'm ever supposed to repay that kind of love. How do I ever show my gratitude? How do I make sure I don't waste my life, so that she won't have wasted hers?"

For a moment, Mom looks like she's on another planet. And then her eyes snap to mine for the first time in days, and something feral takes control of her face. "I loved her too, you know. If I could give my life to keep her alive, I would in a heartbeat."

I don't know why Mom's words hurt so much, but they do. Maybe because I'm the only daughter left, and she's still telling me how much she loves Lea instead of telling me she loves me, too. Maybe it's because I poured my heart out to her, and instead of comforting me she's telling me she'd rather die to make everything better than just be my mom.

Maybe it's because my jealousy of Lea and my fear that Mom loved her better all feel like they're coming true.

And I snap.

"You might've loved Lea, but not as much as I did. You weren't around enough to know her the way I knew her. And I'm sorry you lost your favorite daughter, but I'm still here. I might be too much like Dad, but right now I'm *still here*. So maybe you're the one who's more like him, because you're the one abandoning me. You're the one telling me you'd rather trade places with Lea than stay here and be my mother. You're choosing Lea over me, like you've always chosen Lea over me, and right now I hate you for it."

I don't know how I get through it all without crying, but I've been getting through a lot without crying these days.

Mom looks back at me with a red face and streaming tears that she just can't stop. But she doesn't say a word, and eventually she turns away like she doesn't want anything to do with me.

Thinking about Mom and where she is—safe in Washington, in our home, in our old life—makes me angry.

It's not fair that she sent me to Hawaii so that she could have time to grieve. So that she could find a way to say good-bye to Lea. What about my grief? My good-byes? Am I just supposed to put my feelings on hold while Mom figures out hers?

She sent me to a different state, without my piano or my friends or anything at all that's the least bit familiar to me.

I don't care if she's struggling to grieve—at least she's *home*.

I push myself up and let my legs dangle over the edge of the bed. I squeeze the sheet between my fingers and release all the air through my nose, but it doesn't quell the thunder in my chest. It grows and grows like a monster, and I'm not sure I'm going to be able to stop it.

I don't want to talk to her. I hate her for leaving me. I hate her for being so selfish. I hate her for not choosing me when I'm all she has left.

I hate her.

I hate her.

I hate her.

The shrill yapping from next door breaks my thoughts. I lift my chin, my body still shaking, and turn my ear toward the window.

The barking echoes through the neighborhood. And even though I should probably be grateful for the distraction from my thoughts about Mom, I can't stop the scowl that starts at my brow and ends in hard lines around my mouth.

I stomp through the hallway with as much rage as a person can have at midnight and step out onto the balcony at the back of the house. Aunty Ani says it's called a lanai in Hawaii, which sounds a lot prettier than "balcony," except Aunty Ani's view isn't some gorgeous beach with white sand and cerulean water. Her view is a mess of trees, a chain-link fence, and a forgotten project car in a neighbor's yard. I'm not sure it deserves to be called a lanai.

When I'm leaning against the railing, I can see Mr. Watanabe's window to the right. The lights are all turned off, but the television is still on. And somewhere below I can hear Poi trying her best to wake the entire world up.

"Shut your dog up!" I shout as my fingers close over the railing.

The barking continues.

"Seriously, it's twelve a.m. People are trying to sleep!"

Mr. Watanabe doesn't appear, but Poi's barking turns into a desperate whine.

I start to turn around, but Lea stops me. The Lea in my head, stuck somewhere between remembering and forgetting. The Lea it hurts so much to hold on to.

She wouldn't go back to bed—she'd find out what was wrong with the dog.

Because Lea was good that way. She worried about other people and other things. She'd be concerned about a dog getting through the fence and roaming the neighborhood unsupervised. She'd worry it might get stolen, or worse, hit by a car.

I can picture her here now, prodding me and telling me to go outside.

"It might be hurt," she'd say. "How would you feel if you were hurt and scared and all alone?"

I bite my lip. I'd say being hurt and scared and all alone probably feels like absolute shit. It would probably make you want to go to sleep forever, because sleep is the easiest escape.

Sighing, I make my way to the front door, slip on a pair of flip-flops—Aunty Ani says they're "slippahs" in Hawaii—and wander out into the street.

I find Poi near her own fence, whining and clawing at the closed gate she somehow managed to escape from.

"Seriously?" I ask. "What's the point of breaking out if you just want to be let back in?" I lift the handle, and Poi scurries back toward the house. Just as the gate falls shut, I hear a gruff voice.

"Whatchu doing in my yard?" Mr. Watanabe is standing behind his screen door, his face so worn and sullen I can't tell if he's been asleep or not.

I raise my hands in defense. "I wasn't in your yard. I'm only putting your dog back. She was in the street."

He stares back at me like he's angry, and I feel my heart start to pound again. It doesn't take much these days for the world to feel like it's closing in on me—like the world is attacking me. So I meet his anger with my own.

"You should be more careful. I mean, she could've been hit by a car or something. That's your friend, isn't it? You should care more about your friend. You should be making sure she doesn't die—that she doesn't end up alone, and scared, and lost in some place she doesn't recognize. You should take care of your family."

At first I don't know where it all comes from.

And then I realize maybe I do.

Mr. Watanabe doesn't say anything. He simply watches—*stares*.

I rub my eyes with my fingers, take a breath, and retreat into the house. I just want to go back to bed.

CHAPTER SEVEN

Aunty Ani points her chopsticks at the food in her Styrofoam to-go box. "You like try beef curry?"

"No thanks," I say. I rub the back of my knuckle against my eyebrow to get rid of some of the sweat pooling on my forehead. It's so hot, and Aunty Ani doesn't have air-conditioning, so we brought our lunch to the beach, hoping the breeze and the water would cool us down.

She shovels another chunk of rice and meat into her mouth and makes a noise. "Ono, you know," she says, speaking out of the side of her mostly closed mouth.

I eat another bite of macaroni salad and focus on the water creeping up on the beach. We're sitting beside a palm tree near the border, where the grass becomes a blanket of white sand. There are people in the ocean and people on the shore, but we're the only ones who seem to have a view of the entire beach.

I look over my shoulder, moving my hair to the other side so it stops blowing in my mouth while I eat. I can see Palekaiko Bay, which, as it turns out, is some kind of resort and not a bay at all. The lanai is painted a pale blue—it's almost the exact color of the sky—and there are a few people sitting in the dining area eating their lunch from a large buffet table, the smell of barbecue wafting toward us.

Aunty Ani follows my gaze. "You know, they're always hiring teenagers over the summer break. You could get one summer job. It might keep you busy—keep your mind off things."

I can't help the scowl that takes over my face. "I don't want a job. I don't want to be here at all." I want to be back in Washington with my piano, where everything felt unnatural and familiar all at the same time. Where it felt wrong not to see Lea everywhere. Where feeling nothing was starting to feel normal.

It's different in Hawaii. *I* feel different. I'm in a constant state of total and utter rage. I feel like the rest of me is on pause— like my soul took a vacation, so that it wouldn't have to deal with everything buried beneath my anger. And maybe that's self-preservation, but I can't write without my soul. I can't finish our song if all I can see is fire and red. If I try to reach for my words—for my feelings—I'm too afraid they'll burn me.

And I'm scared it means I won't be able to find my way back to the music ever again. I'm afraid my ability to write might have died with Lea.

Aunty Ani nods and it feels like a quick surrender. "It was only a suggestion. Thought you might like some pocket money."

"I don't need money. Mom left me plenty of it, remember?

Probably so she doesn't have to feel guilty about not being here," I say curtly.

Aunty Ani's body stiffens. She lets her to-go box fall into her lap, and she presses her lips together while she puts her sentence together in her head. "There isn't a person in the world who could love their child any more than your mother has loved you girls," Aunty Ani says suddenly. "She'd be here if she could. I hope you know that."

A memory

There are butterflies in my stomach. No, not butterflies. Wasps. Hundreds of wasps, stinging me from the inside, throwing themselves around my organs until I want to clutch my stomach and squeeze them still.

Lea's guitar is over her shoulder. She takes my hand. "I'm nervous too."

I tilt my head back and breathe through my nose. "I shouldn't be nervous. I'm never nervous." I look back at her seriously. "This is Mom's fault. Why did she have to tell me she was coming? I feel like I'm going to throw up."

Lea peeks behind the curtain. Amanda Meyers is still onstage singing a Katy Perry song. She's okay, but she got Kevin Harris and Robbie Garcia to be her backup dancers, and they're the best dancers in our junior high school. The auditorium sounds like a Justin Bieber concert.

"You don't need to worry. Mom still isn't here," Lea says.

"What?" I say, startled, leaning over her head and peering into the crowd. Lea's right. Mom's not here. I know because she spent all night making the most embarrassing sign in the world—a giant banner that said TEAM RUMI AND LEA, which doesn't make any sense because it's a middle school talent show. There aren't any "teams" because there aren't any winners. It's a glitzed-up assembly—a chance for students to show off and for parents to brag.

But the sign was at least five feet wide, with green and blue glitter and fuzzy cotton balls in every color of the rainbow surrounding each letter. I think Mom used an entire bottle of glue to finish it.

I don't see the sign, which means Mom isn't here. She wouldn't have left it at home, even though we told her repeatedly that her artwork was going to humiliate us, because that's kind of Mom's thing. She *likes* embarrassing us. I think it makes her feel like she's on the inside of one of our jokes, which she rarely is because she's rarely home.

Today's a big deal. It's the first time Mom has ever had the time off work to come and see us perform together. It's a big deal for her to be here. The *biggest* deal, even.

I pull away from the side of the stage, feeling the

wasps dropping one by one. It's not my stomach that hurts anymore—it's my heart.

"Maybe she forgot the sign?" Lea asks beside me, her finger tapping the drum of her guitar nervously.

I shake my head. We don't say anything else until Mrs. Hernandez calls our names and we set ourselves up in the middle of the stage. I take a place on the piano bench, and Lea perches herself on a stool and moves her fingers over the guitar strings.

The lights are really bright—almost painfully bright. And everything echoes. The squeak in Lea's stool, the man coughing in the audience, and the door slamming shut followed by the, "Oh, I'm sorry!" and the unexplainably loud shuffle that follows.

"*Psst.*" Lea is smiling at me.

When I look back out into the audience, I see Mom standing in the center of the aisle with her sign above her head, jumping up and down like she's cheering on a toddler learning to walk. She waves the sign back and forth, her mouth in such a huge, wide smile I actually start laughing on the stage.

She made it. She's late, and she almost missed it, but she made it.

Because when Mom makes a promise, she doesn't break it. And she promised she'd be here.

I look back at Lea. She nods at me, I smile at her, and I play the first notes of our song.

The mom I remember would never have abandoned me. But that mom had two daughters.

Is that the difference? Maybe Mom can't love me the same with Lea gone. Maybe being around me hurts her too much, because I'm sharp and brutally honest and easily annoyed. Aunty Ani says she needs time to grieve, but I think what she really needs is time away from me.

She lost her good daughter. Her kind, gentle, sweet girl who wasn't capable of hurting anyone. And maybe having Lea around made it easier to have *me* around.

Hawaii feels like a punishment, but I can't figure out if it's because I was a bad daughter or a bad sister.

Maybe I was both.

I drop my chopsticks into the container and let it fall onto the sand. "I'm going for a walk," I say stiffly.

Aunty Ani looks crushed from the inside out. It almost makes me feel guilty. "I was only trying—" she starts.

"I don't need you to try," I snap. I guess sometimes guilt isn't enough.

I move across the sand, stepping closer and closer to the water's edge until I feel the sea roll over my feet. I step over seaweed and broken bits of shell, going farther into the water until pretty soon my feet vanish and the ocean is up to my knees.

Lea would've loved it here. The ocean sounds like crescendos and diminuendos, and all the flowers and birds are so vibrant and colorful that I can hear flutes and piccolos just looking at them. And she'd love that—the music Hawaii offers. I think she'd feel at home.

She'd appreciate being here more than I do. More than I ever could, even if my soul weren't on pause. Because she loved life differently than I do. Her love was loud and colorful and so unbelievably hopeful.

It hurts so much to think about the life she doesn't get to have. It hurts more than thinking about the moment she lost it.

The moment she called my name.

And for a flicker of a second, I wonder if maybe the wrong sister died that day.

I'm shaking—either from memories or the cold—so I get out of the water as fast as I can and walk all the way to the rock wall before turning around again.

When I reach Aunty Ani she's standing with Kai and a woman I haven't seen before.

They smile at me when they see me—Aunty Ani doesn't.

"You must be Rumi," the woman says, stepping forward to give me a quick hug. She smells faintly of honeysuckles. When she pulls away she lifts her sunglasses. "How do you like Hawaii so far?"

I start to point out that I'm here against my will—that I'm only in Hawaii because my mom needed a vacation from being a parent. But I pinch myself on the back of the arm the way Lea would have, to tell me to shut up and be nice.

"It's hot here," I say thinly.

She nods. "I'm Sun. I live next door. You already met my son, Kai."

Kai lifts his chin. "Howzit?"

Aunty Ani doesn't look the least bit surprised, but tries to feign it all the same. "You two met already? That's good. Nice to have someone your own age fo' hang out with, yeah?"

"I guess," I say, looking around for the food I left on the ground because I suddenly see the benefit of having something to do other than make small talk with the very temporary neighbors.

If Sun notices my discomfort, she doesn't let it stop her from carrying on with the conversation. "Must be hard not knowing anybody around here. Come by the hotel anytime you like, okay?" She tilts her head toward Palekaiko Bay. "We have our own little beauty parlor. I was a beautician before I got into hotel management. I'll do your nails for free. A little 'Welcome to the neighborhood' present, yeah?"

"Thanks," I mumble.

Aunty Ani tries to shift the conversation away from me. "Looks like you got one full house today." She motions toward the reception area where the hotel guests are eating lunch.

"You know how it is in the summer," Sun says, setting her sunglasses back on the bridge of her nose. "I'm only taking a break because Ken's supposed to meet us for lunch. He has a half day today."

Aunty Ani asks whether Ken is going on deployment again, and halfway through Sun's explanation, Kai suddenly latches on to my wrist and pulls.

"I'm taking Rumi to the lookout," he says simply. Almost too simply for them to even notice we've left them.

He lets go of my hand before it starts to feel like it means anything at all, and we're halfway across the beach when I make a face at him.

"Your parents own a hotel?"

"No. My mom owns it. My dad is in the navy," he corrects.

"Divorced?"

"Nope. Just financially independent from each other."

"That kind of sounds like being divorced."

"Is that what happened to your parents? Divorce?"

I snort. "They were never married. My dad was free to go—and he did."

He sniffs the air like he's amused. "If it makes you feel any better, being married doesn't force anybody to stick around." He pauses. "My dad is going to cancel lunch today. My mom just doesn't know it yet."

"How do *you* know?"

"Because he always cancels."

I watch our feet press into the sand, leaving two matching trails behind us. "Sorry," I say.

"Sorry about what happened to you, too. Aunty Ani told my mom about the accident—I shouldn't have given you a hard time the other day," he says. It's quiet for two and half seconds, and suddenly he's pointing excitedly toward a trail of rocks leading out to the sea. "Look, look."

I follow his gaze to the water. Someone is standing at the edge of the rocks, their fishing rod in one hand and a small hammer-head shark in the other.

"The buggah big, eh?" Kai says.

The shark flicks its tail, its gills expanding slowly and its body looking pale, rubbery, and drier by the second.

I feel angry. God, why do I always feel so angry? "That's such bullshit."

Kai looks at me quizzically. "What is?"

"Life. I mean, you're a shark, you're supposed to be at the top of the food chain, and you're swimming around looking for some breakfast one morning and *BAM*. You have a hook through your mouth and your life is over. Because of some jerk with a fishing pole."

"Most people catch sharks by mistake," he offers. "He's probably goin' put it back."

I twist my face. We watch as the fisherman tosses the shark back into the ocean.

"See?" Kai shrugs. "Fixed."

"He's still got a hole in his mouth," I mutter under my breath. Besides, he's still going to die one day. The fisherman didn't save him—he disfigured him and prolonged the inevitable.

Kai leads me up a trail until we're at the top of a hill overlooking the ocean. There's so much blue and sun I start to wonder if my eyes are playing tricks on me. I know I should feel happy looking at so much beauty. I mean, they call it paradise for a reason, right? But I don't know what happiness is supposed to feel like anymore, and no amount of coconut trees and orange blossoms is going to change that.

Maybe when people die, the people they leave behind die, too.

Maybe all that's left is my physical body. Maybe that's what happened to Mom.

I wonder if we all died in the car that day, but Lea died completely, Mom died halfway, and maybe I'm struggling to find out where they went. It makes sense, I guess, that if you really loved someone and they died, that a little bit of you would die too.

But I don't understand why Mom is so much more lost than me. Does her not being able to function as well as me mean she loved Lea more than I did? Because that's impossible. I loved Lea the absolute most. I know she was Mom's daughter, but I mean, I'm her daughter too and look how easy it was for her to abandon me.

Or maybe Mom loves her more than she loves me.

And then the thought returns, but this time it's more than a flicker—it's a spotlight.

Maybe it *should've* been me who died and Lea who was left behind, because then Mom wouldn't be so sad. They'd get over it, the two of them, eventually, but they'd get over it together, which is better than the lone-wolf thing I'm dealing with right now.

Oh God. I think that's why Mom left me. Because she lost her favorite daughter.

Why am I thinking about this?

Why am I *letting* myself think about this?

Why did I wake up today at all?

"Anybody home?" Kai's voice sounds like a piano chord inside an empty church.

I snap out of my thoughts and see him waving a hand in front of my eyes.

"Did you hear me?" he asks.

"Huh?" I shift my weight to the other leg and cross my arms.

He nods to the ocean. "I said there's a sandbar out there. You like sea turtles?"

I blink at him, his kindness not registering the way he probably means it. "Why are you talking to me?" I can't think about being nice to him when all I'm thinking about now is my sister and my mom and the varying degrees of dead they both are.

I don't think I'm the right person to be in paradise right now.

Kai's face doesn't change. "Aunty Ani asked me tŏ hang out witchu. She said you're depressed."

"My sister died. Of course I'm fucking depressed," I snap. "What makes Aunty Ani think you're the person who can suddenly fix me? Because you own a hotel? Because your mom offered to paint my nails? Because you're some rich-kid-surfer-boy with father problems that I'm supposed to somehow relate to?"

"Eh?" He half rolls his eyes and steps away from me. "I was just offering fo' keep you company. I thought you'd want to get out of the house, that's all. I don't know what all that other stuff is you're talking about. Father problems? Rich surfer—wait, what was it you called me?"

"I don't need your help, and I don't want to be your friend." I turn away so fast I slip on the combination of rock and sand. My feet give way so quickly that I end up on my butt in seconds, a sharp pain hitting my tailbone.

When Kai reaches for me, I swat his arms away with both hands furiously. I shout something about leaving me alone, and it takes me all the way to the end of the path to realize he's laughing at me.

Like, *really* laughing at me. As if I'm some fan-favorite character out of a sitcom. As if injuring my tailbone is somehow hilarious.

I should hate him for laughing and for not caring or being sympathetic, but I don't. For some unexplainable reason, his complete disregard for my pain is having the opposite effect on me.

Everyone else is trying to coddle me. Everyone else is handling me with wool mittens, like I'm made of glass and dried flowers. Like they're afraid if they crush me, I won't be able to mend.

Kai is laughing like there's nothing different about us at all.

But still.

I'm not in the mood to be anyone's friend. And I'm certainly not going to make an exception for the boy next door.

CHAPTER EIGHT

It turns out that while sleep deprivation for an entire week is a form of torture, sleeping for an entire week just gives you a really bad headache.

Aside from waking up for food, bathroom breaks, nightmares, and the many times Poi decides to serenade me through the window, I've basically been living in bed, in the same pair of pajamas, with my hair knotted in a tight bun, because who cares about showering when my world is in pieces?

Apparently, Aunty Ani does care.

"You stink," she says sternly from the doorway.

I look up from the pillow. "I'm trying to sleep."

She lets out a noise of frustration. "You need fresh air. You need fo' move around."

"I need to be left alone."

She throws her hands up. "You can't live like this, Rumi. Not under my roof. Not anymore."

"Fine." I throw myself out of bed, my whole body shaking.

"Send me home, then. If you don't want me here, I'll leave. It wasn't my idea to come here in the first place."

Aunty Ani steps forward and grabs me so suddenly my heart jumps. "I want you here, you got that? *I want you here.*" Her eyes are so powerful. I don't think I've ever seen strength like that in Mom, even when Dad left all those years ago and she had to work day and night to keep our house.

I look away because right now strength makes me uncomfortable.

Aunty Ani pulls me into her chest and hugs me. "I'll never send you away, you understand? We're family—ohana." She tilts her head up to the ceiling. "But you need a shower. You smell like sour milk."

She's trying to show me she cares, but I'm still not sure I know what that means anymore. Lea not being here—*Mom* not being here—left a gaping hole in my chest. I'm numb. How do I fix that? Do I even want to fix it?

But I take a shower anyway, because at least if I'm clean I'll have another week of Aunty Ani leaving me alone. I stand under the water for a long time, staring at the colorful bottles of shampoo and soaps in the metal shower caddy and wondering if my skin could absorb enough water to become liquid and wash down the drain.

I sigh, pressing my fingers to my face and scratching my scalp like there's dirt and grime everywhere and how can I get it all off?

I lather soap all over myself, rinse it away, and start again. But I still feel like I'm covered in a layer of muck. I still don't feel like I have my skin back.

So I wash myself, over and over and over again, until the bottle is empty and now I'm just rubbing water into my pores like I'm trying to drown my flesh.

There's a knock at the bathroom door. "You all pau in there?" calls Aunty Ani. "Or are you trying fo' dry up the ocean?"

"I'll be right out," I call back, twisting the shower faucet and letting the water slowly fall away from me.

I still don't feel clean.

When I'm dressed again, I pull my hair into a wet bun and sneak outside while Aunty Ani is humming to herself in the kitchen.

It doesn't take me long to notice Kai in his driveway, his arms covered in soapy water and a yellow sponge in his hand. He's washing a car I haven't seen before—a blue Mustang convertible that looks like an old classic. Maybe something from the sixties.

Kai is kneeling near one of the wheels, sponging down one of the hubcaps with his earphones dangling in front of his bare chest. He catches me watching from the gate, and our eyes take a long time to move away from each other. When I'm looking at one of the plants nearby, its leaves trailing along the concrete like it's surrendering to the heat, I remember I decided not to be friends with Kai.

So staring at him is super weird. I don't know why I'm doing it.

He frees his right ear and scrunches his face at me. "How's your okole?"

"What?" I blink at him.

He nods toward me, his finger pointing below my waist, and I realize he's motioning toward my butt. "From when you got all bust up."

"You mean when you laughed at me for falling?" I glare at him, ignoring the sun.

He shrugs, grinning. "People fall down. You can either laugh or cry. Laughing makes it easier fo' get back up, though."

"You're weird," I say.

"You're lolo," he says.

We assess each other the way you do when you're little and it's your first day of a new school year. Like we're trying to figure out if the other person is nice or not. Like we're trying to figure out if the other person wants to be our friend.

Maybe it's because he doesn't treat me gently, or because he acts like he's forgotten I'm the girl with the dead sister altogether, but maybe I don't dislike Kai as much as I want to.

He holds up a sponge. "You here fo' help or fo' yell at me again?"

I help him wash the car. We don't look at each other, or say even a single word. We simply move around the car like ants on a mission, passing the bucket back and forth and staying out of each other's way.

When we're finished, Kai puts the empty bucket and sponges back in the garage and brings over two cans of guava juice from a nearby cooler. We sit on the step near his front gate, our knees inches apart, admiring our handiwork as the car gleams under the afternoon sun.

"Why did you call me a surfer?" he asks, his eyes rich with life.

"What do you mean?" I ask.

"The other day"—he shrugs—"you called me a rich surfer, or something like that."

"You had surfboards in the back of your truck. I just assumed."

"No, but the way you said it." He pauses. "Like you thought I was one spoiled brat or something."

"It didn't mean anything" is all I say.

"Mmm." He taps his finger against his can. "I'm not a jerk, you know."

"Okay."

"It matters to me that you don't think I am."

"I said 'okay.'"

He nods. Takes a long sip. "Aunty Ani says you're a musician?"

I wrap my fingers around my own can of juice and follow the lines in the concrete. "Maybe. I used to be. I don't know." I take a long sip too. My heart used to belong to melodies and lyrics—now I'm haunted by them. I'm not sure I can call myself a musician anymore.

"Gareth's sistah is in one band. They play sometimes at the Coconut Shack during open-mic nights. It's down the road from Palekaiko Bay. You like karaoke?" He pronounces it the Japanese way. Kah-rah-oh-kay, and he rolls the *r*.

I raise my shoulders and don't let them fall. He doesn't know how much music hurts me now, because he doesn't know how much I loved it before. He doesn't understand my loss—I'm not sure anyone besides Lea ever could.

And I've lost her, too.

"It's every Thursday night, if you like stop by sometime," he says. "We never miss it."

On paper it sounds great. A shirtless boy half inviting me to go to karaoke in Hawaii? Lea would've freaked out. She would have laughed and smiled so hard over this that she would've complained her face and stomach hurt. She lived for moments like this—the spontaneous ones. The ones that made her feel giddy and grown-up. The ones that usually involved boys.

But Lea isn't here anymore. How am I supposed to smile when Lea isn't here?

Besides, smiling about boys has never been my thing. It was hers.

The door opens from behind us, and a tall man with meticulously short hair and wearing an olive-green flight suit appears at the top step. Kai stands up so quickly that my body reacts before my brain does and I'm standing up too.

The man walks down the steps and stops in front of us. He looks so much like an older version of Kai it's almost scary. Except Kai has wild, mischievous eyes—there's nothing wild about the man in front of me. He looks hard and stern, like he's made up of chords that never break.

He's wearing a tan cap with gold pins on the sides. I catch sight of the name badge sewn over his chest. LCDR YAMADA.

He looks at me, then at Kai, and then at the car.

"I have to go back to work," he says abruptly.

I can practically feel the weight that pushes down on Kai's shoulders. It pushes against me, too.

"But you said I could borrow the car. You said if I washed it—" he starts.

Mr. Yamada interrupts him. "I said I have to work. Things come up."

Mrs. Yamada's voice sounds from behind the screen door. "Kai, you can borrow my car."

"He doesn't need anybody's car," Mr. Yamada snaps. "He can learn a good lesson here. Sometimes plans change. Besides, he spends too much time screwing around on the beach. He should be studying."

"Studying for what, Dad? School is over," Kai says irritably.

He and his father look at each other with so much fire I'm worried they'll erupt. Mrs. Yamada must be worried too, because she's suddenly between them with one hand on Kai's shoulder and a smile pointed toward her husband.

"Go on, you'll be late," she says, like a triangle signaling the end of a fight before it's even begun. "Kai knows not to stay out too late. It's only a barbecue with friends."

"Too much playing around, too many barbecues, too much time with friends." Mr. Yamada looks at me. "Don't you kids care about getting your future in order?"

I can't stop myself. "My sister died and my parents abandoned me. I kind of stopped caring about tomorrow."

Mrs. Yamada takes a quick breath. Kai raises a brow at me.

Mr. Yamada twists his mouth, his eyes calculating, observant. And then he looks at Kai. "I don't want you hanging out with this one. There's something wrong with her." He gets into his car without another word and drives away.

Mrs. Yamada widens her eyes and laughs before motioning for Kai to follow her and disappearing back into the house.

Kai shakes his head slowly, his face fighting a smile. "You

really are lolo." When he's halfway back inside, he looks over his shoulder. "I'll see you around, hapa."

It takes me a moment to collect myself, and eventually I retreat into my own house, alone and wondering why my mouth moves so much faster than my brain.

Maybe that's why I *am* alone—because I say things without thinking. I hurt people without thinking.

Maybe that's why I failed so horribly at being a sister—because I don't consider people's feelings. I just react.

My skin feels brittle, and I scratch at my arms like I'm trying to find a new layer of skin that isn't so ugly and worn. It was thick, once upon a time. Maybe too thick.

And maybe that's why Mom isn't here—she thinks I'm strong enough to do this alone.

I shouldn't hate her for not knowing me as well as Lea did, but I can't help it.

I failed as a sister and a daughter, but she failed as a mother, too.

CHAPTER NINE

I'm not prepared for this.

Lea's guitar stares up at me from the floor. It's covered in stickers—the oldest is a shimmery My Little Pony one, and the newest is a Pikachu face. Her hot pink guitar pick is still wedged between the strings and the fret board.

Mom must have sent it. Why else would it be sitting in the middle of Aunty Ani's living room like a long-lost relative showing up in the middle of a dinner party?

A memory

I shouldn't be jealous, but I am.

It's just a guitar. I already have a guitar, even if it isn't anywhere near as nice as Lea's. *And* I have my piano, which Babang bought me the year before she passed away, back when Lea wasn't interested in music. Back when I had music all to myself.

Lea forfeited her birthday present this year because she wanted a guitar for Christmas. A guitar *I* told her she should get, so that the two of us could be in a band. This isn't a surprise—it was inevitable.

So why am I so mad about it?

I didn't ask for a guitar, and I didn't give up my birthday present. I wanted a new planner for Christmas—a fancy one with my name on it and washi tape and stickers and gel pens and all the rest of it. Because I'm going to be in sixth grade next year. Everyone in sixth grade uses a planner. Or at least, that's what Bella Polednak told me, and she's in seventh grade so of course she's right.

And I got it—all of it—even the My Little Pony stickers that I wanted almost more than the planner itself.

It's not that I want Lea's guitar—I just don't want *her* to have it. Not anymore. Because all Mom's been asking all day is for Lea to play her more songs and sing her new melodies, and it's like they both forgot that I've been playing the piano for years. When I said we could start a band, it was going to be me and Lea, on our own.

Mom wasn't supposed to be a part of it. She wasn't supposed to start paying more attention to Lea. She wasn't supposed to suddenly be less interested in me.

I'm the musician.

Or, I was. Now I guess there's two of us, and I'm not sure I'm happy about it.

I listen for Mom and Lea at the door. They're in the kitchen getting dinner ready. Lea's guitar is sitting on her bed. Alone. Unwatched.

And I don't know why I do it. Maybe I'm just a jealous jerk. But I take one of my gel pens—the purple one, which is the darkest—and I draw a big, squiggly mark on Lea's guitar. Because now it's not perfect or new or cool. Now it's ruined.

I take a step back, push the cap on my pen, and look over the instrument like I'm hoping to admire my handiwork.

Except I don't feel pride or glee or even remotely better. I feel so much worse.

Something heavy forms in my throat, and before I can think, I'm running my thumb over the ink, trying to wipe it away. It smears deeper into the grain, a menacing blotch of meanness that erupted from inside me. I can't take this back. I can't erase it. I can't hide it.

I find my chair and wait for the inevitable.

When Lea comes into the room a few minutes later, she looks like she ran through the hallway. "We're making apple pie for dinner. Want to help make the shapes for the crust? I'm going to do a horse."

"Horses don't belong on an apple pie," I snap, my eyes burning because the guilt is already taking over.

She moves toward her bed, and my heart plummets into my stomach. I can't look at her. I squeeze my hands together and stare at my desk.

Lea lets out a noise. She sounds like an injured animal. And then it turns into a growl. "Rumi, what did you do?" she shouts.

I spin around and try to keep my face still. "What?"

Her brown eyes are filled with water. "You drew on my guitar!"

"No I didn't. I didn't do anything."

"You did, you liar. Look!" She points at the mark.

"That wasn't me."

"It was. It's *purple*."

"So what?"

"I don't have a purple anything, Rumi!"

And suddenly the two of us are screaming at each other. I keep telling her she's wrong, and then she calls me a liar, and I call her a liar for calling me a liar, and there's so much screaming and shouting that Mom has to come into the room to slice through the yelling.

"What is going on?" she demands, wide-eyed. "It's Christmas. There's no fighting on Christmas."

"She ruined my guitar!"

"I did not!"

"You did too!"

"I don't even care about your ugly guitar!"

The screaming picks right back up again, and

Mom moves between us and looks at the guitar.

I swallow the lump in my throat. She knows. She recognizes the purple, and all the denial in the world isn't going to convince Mom it magically appeared there.

"Lea, can you please go to the kitchen and check on the casserole?" Mom asks gently.

Lea is crying furiously. "But, Mom—"

"Now, please. I'll be there in a minute." Mom presses her hand against Lea's back and guides her out of the room. I can hear my sister wailing from the hall.

I sink into my chair, scowling. I wait for Mom to accuse me of defacing Lea's guitar. I wait for her to scold me, or to tell me how horrible I've been, or to tell me she knows I'm being jealous and cruel and that she's going to take my planner and everything else away because I don't deserve it.

Scowling is all I have left.

But she doesn't say any of those things. She looks at me with big eyes and a soft brow. "It's a real shame Lea's guitar is marked up, especially after she was so excited to get it. She'd been asking for more than a year to have a guitar. She thought if she had a guitar, you and her could have something in common. You know, because you always spend so much time on the piano. She thought if she got really good, you might want to start a band with her."

My lips are pressed so tightly together that I can

feel dimples forming all around my mouth.

Mom shrugs. "And it's too bad because what Lea really wanted for Christmas was that My Little Pony set. She only asked for a guitar because she thought you'd be happier if the two of you could have something to do together."

I feel wriggly and sick and like my skin is going to fall off, but I have to be still. I don't want Mom to see me fall apart. I'm too ashamed. Lea asked for the guitar because of me. To make *me* happy. And I ruined everything because I don't like sharing Mom, even though Lea has just as much right to her as I do.

I look at the floor instead.

Mom lets out a sigh and leaves the room, and as soon as the door shuts I start crying like I'm a broken sink.

I want to take it back, but I can't erase gel pen. When I stop crying, my eyes find her guitar. I can't erase this. There's no way to reverse the damage I've done. She'll always look at her guitar and know I tried to sabotage Christmas for her.

She'll always remember that I'm the worst sister ever.

I don't know what to do to make her forgive me.

I stare at the purple mark for a long time. I think of Lea making her horse pie crust. And then I turn around and look at my pile of new stickers.

When I bring the guitar to the kitchen, Lea is sitting at the table with Mom, cutting out the shapes in the dough. She looks at me, then the guitar, and her eyes start to flood again.

"Here," I say quickly, forcing the instrument toward her.

She takes the guitar and holds it to her body almost protectively, and then her eyes drop to the purple mark. It's covered by a big, shimmery sticker of Rainbow Dash.

Rainbow Dash isn't even Lea's favorite; she's mine, which is exactly why I picked it.

I don't have to explain it—Lea sees the sticker and knows what it means.

"This too," I say, thrusting a piece of paper under her nose.

She picks it up carefully and looks over the scribbled, glittery writing that reads:

This piece of paper is valid for three wishes to be used at any point in time, which I promise to carry out to the best of my ability because a wish is a wish.

I've never been very good at saying sorry, but this is me trying in my own way.

When Lea looks back up at me, her small face so tired, she says, "Want to help make the pie crust?"

I nod, pressing my lips together. "A horse?"

"A horse," she repeats. "Because horses like apples."

The Rainbow Dash sticker is the most faded of all of them, but it's still there, hiding the purple mark.

Aunty Ani stares at the guitar for a long time, probably deciding what she should say next. I'm not looking at the guitar anymore—I'm watching her face. I'm watching the care in her eyes, the consideration she's giving to her words. It's like watching someone dance with fire. I literally have no idea how she does it.

Words don't mull over in my head. They come out like vomit, harsh and abrupt. It was like that even before Lea died.

I'm not a sensitive person. Maybe I've always been cold. Maybe it's more noticeable now that she's gone.

"Why is this here?" I growl, my throat raw already.

Aunty Ani looks up, horrified. Not at the gesture, but because she didn't quite manage to find the right thing to say. "I'm sure your sistah would have wanted fo' you to have it."

"Why? So I can miss her more than I already do?" My shoulders are shaking. I don't feel anything but uncontrollable rage, and I'm running out of people to direct it at.

"I thought it would be good fo' you. So you could practice again," she offers.

Why doesn't anyone see what a terrible idea this was? To have Lea's guitar just show up one day, like how I want my mother to show up—like how I want Lea to show up—it feels like someone's stabbed me in the chest and is waving the knife around in front of me.

And maybe Aunty Ani couldn't have known what music is to me—what Lea's guitar being shipped here would mean to me—but Mom should have. More important, she should have brought it herself, if she cared at all, instead of shipping it across the Pacific Ocean like she shipped me away.

I pull my arms over my chest and squeeze my rib cage like I wish my body would collapse into itself. I shake my head to make the throbbing stop, but it only makes it worse.

Aunty Ani looks over at me from the table, frowning and tearful. "I'm trying really hard, Rumi. I thought getting you your guitar back was the right thing fo' do. I'm sorry if it wasn't."

"This is Lea's guitar," I say thinly. "It's not mine. It doesn't belong with me." I might've wanted to know it was safe, but I didn't want it *sent to Hawaii* like I've inherited my dead sister's prized possession.

Aunty Ani moves toward me and places her hands on my shoulders. "But maybe music could help you heal. Maybe if you spent the summer—"

I take a step back so her hand falls away from me. I don't want comfort. Not from her.

"No" is all I manage to say, and suddenly I'm in my room with my back pressed to the door and my eyes shut tight.

Music can't heal me. Music *hurts* me.

I spend the rest of the day in bed.

I don't know where Aunty Ani puts Lea's guitar, but I don't see it when I wake up the next day. And I don't ask, because the truth is I'd rather not know. Looking at it scares me. I've never seen a guitar so soundless before, like all the life was ripped out of it. There was no music left in it—just emptiness.

How could Lea's guitar end up that way? So hollow and void of life? How could her songs just end, like notes on a page that will never be played again?

It's too fucking sad. I can't take it.

I find Aunty Ani sitting at the table behind her laptop. She looks surprised to see me. I think it might be the earliest I've woken up since I got here.

"Are you hungry? You like me make you breakfast?" she asks eagerly, pretending yesterday's conversation didn't happen at all.

I shake my head. I don't want her to be nice to me.

She gets up anyway, rummages through the fridge, and comes back with a container of sliced mango. She sets it on the table and pulls out a chair. "Try eat a little bit, okay? I don't want you getting sick."

I slump into the chair and pick at the fruit with a fork. Aunty Ani is trying to hide the fact that she can't stop watching me, but I feel her eyes land on me over and over again. It's annoying.

After a while, she pushes the lid of her computer down and clears her throat. "I go back to work tomorrow. I used up all my vacation days."

"Okay," I say, the sweetness of the mango washing over my tongue.

"You'll be okay at home? On your own?"

I look up at her. She isn't asking if I can take care of myself—she's asking if I'm emotionally stable enough not to completely lose it.

"I'm sad, but I'm not suicidal," I say forcibly. "They don't always go hand in hand, you know."

Aunty Ani tightens her mouth. "I'm just saying, if you aren't ready fo'—"

"I'm fine, okay?" I stab another piece of mango. "Besides, Kai wants to show me Palekaiko Bay. I'm making friends." It's kind of the truth, I guess. Even if his dad did say we aren't allowed to hang out together.

"Oh. That's good," she says, and that's the end of our conversation.

At the hottest part of the afternoon, I move to the covered patio—the area beneath the world's saddest lanai—and lean back against a cushioned lawn chair with one of Aunty Ani's magazines in my lap. I'm not actually reading it—I'm trying to remember the lyrics Lea and I were working on. The last song we tried to write—the one I have to finish because it's the only thing I can think of to repay Lea for being a better sister than I ever was. I'm trying to rewrite every word, just as Lea thought of them, inside a magazine so it doesn't feel like I'm betraying Lea.

But it feels so much like betrayal that I can't keep my hand still.

Because I was never supposed to write songs alone. We were a team. We should still be a team.

Writing lyrics down in a notebook feels too real. It feels like cheating.

I bite the inside of my mouth, and tell myself this is what Lea would want and to stop making excuses to avoid facing reality forever.

She's not here anymore. Every time I write a song or play the piano or think up a new lyric, it will be me without Lea. I can't change that, but I can give her the song we started. I have to try.

I should try.

Because I owe her, and because it might be the only thing in this world I have any real control over.

My eyes fall back to the magazine. *In the summer*—no. *Every summer I think*—no. Why can't I remember it? What was the bird part? The blue part? Did we even make it that far?

God, why can't I remember the words?

I can only remember her word. Lea's last word.

Rumi.

But I'm not a song. Lea was the music—I was the page that collected all the notes together. I'm the part that doesn't change—the base that never moves. Lea was water, and magic, and emotion.

I need her to write. I need her to live.

I can't do this on my own.

When I look down at the magazine, the page is crumpled and half falling out of the binding. I've been squeezing it without realizing. Do I do that a lot nowadays? Do things without realizing? Sometimes I wonder if I'm really awake, or if this is all one really drawn-out nightmare.

I fling the magazine across the patio angrily.

My eyes catch sight of something wedged between the outdoor fridge and a chain-link fence that's being overtaken by grass and leaves.

A black guitar case. Lea's guitar case.

Something tugs at my rib cage, and I'm standing in front of the black case without realizing I even got out of my chair. I don't know what Aunty Ani was thinking, leaving it outside in the heat, but I guess she doesn't know anything about music or instruments.

I should be irritated. I *am* irritated. But I'm also distracted by the sight of Lea's guitar.

Nobody is watching. It's just me, and I can react however I want to—however I need to. Maybe looking at her guitar won't be so hard when I'm by myself. Mom needs to deal with her grief alone—maybe that's what I need too.

I lay it over the outdoor table and take a step back. It looks like a coffin. And what's inside is practically the same as a dead body, at least to me.

My fingers tremble as I lift the first clasp, and before I know it the case is open and the guitar is in my lap. I squeeze my left hand against the guitar's neck.

I miss it so much—the music. The magic. I miss how it used to make me feel—like I was *alive.*

I close my eyes, try to empty my thoughts, and strum my thumb against the strings.

The guitar is out of tune, and the sharpness of the chord jolts me back into the present.

What am I doing? Why am I playing my sister's guitar, hoping to feel alive again? What is *wrong* with me?

Lea isn't alive. She never will be again. I'm going to grow old without a sister—I'm going to live an entire lifetime without my best friend.

Playing her guitar—trying to feel alive again—it feels like I'm trying to move on. It feels selfish.

And being selfish is the reason I'll always hate myself for everything I did to Lea.

For everything I didn't do, too.

It's too soon.

It's way too soon.

By the time I'm back in the living room with my arms wrapped protectively around the black case, I'm breathing so heavily there's spit flying from my mouth.

"You can't leave this outside. It can't be out in the heat. It's a guitar, not some old piece of garbage!" The voice I'm using toward Aunty Ani isn't one I even recognize. It sounds cruel and vicious—when did I become those things?

I know my anger is misplaced, but I don't care. I'm full of steam and smoke and fire, and that kind of anger has to go somewhere.

Aunty Ani's eyes flit back and forth. She pinches her necklace, rolling the small shells between her fingers like she's nervous. "I'm sorry, Rumi. I didn't mean—"

"This is Lea's," I scream. "It's Lea's and it means something. You don't throw away things that mean something. You don't abandon them like they were never important to begin with!" My voice becomes hoarse quickly; it feels like I've been yelling for hours. And

85

maybe I have. But maybe it took everyone a long time to hear me.

Mom abandoned me. She left me to figure out how to say good-bye to Lea all by myself. I don't know how to do this—I don't know how to keep going. Lea's dead, and Mom should've been here with me, telling me how I'm supposed to deal with that. I needed her to not be broken. I needed her to pick me over Lea, for once in her life.

I don't know how to be all alone.

"Stop," Aunty Ani says suddenly, her hands balled up tight. "Stop speaking to me like this. I'm your family, and I'm trying to help."

The words that fly out of my mouth come from someplace so dark and poisonous that it sends chills up my arms. *"I don't have any family left!"*

I put Lea's guitar in my room, and at some point I'm puking into the toilet with my hair in one hand, wondering how I'm supposed to turn off this kind of pain.

CHAPTER TEN

For once it isn't Poi's barking that wakes me in the middle of the night—it's music.

I sit up in bed, squinting at the door and wondering what would possess my aunt to have a house party after the nuclear bomb that went off in her living room. When I open the door, the hallway is completely dark. Aunty Ani's door is shut tight. I pad carefully through the house, my feet sticking slightly to the floorboards, and I realize the music isn't coming from here—it's coming from Mr. Watanabe's.

Rolling my eyes, I slip on my shoes and walk over to his house, ready to pound on the door and tell him to turn his music off.

But when I reach the top step, I pause. I hear the strums of a guitar, like the ocean swirling against the sand. It sounds the way mango tastes—soft and sweet, and just enough warmth to make you feel calm. It's such a mellow sound, and before I know it, I'm sitting with my back against Mr. Watanabe's screen door with my eyes closed, my feet tapping to the beat of the music.

I almost forgot what this felt like—to be lost in the music. To hear a melody that doesn't break my heart over and over again.

Maybe it's the absence of lyrics, or maybe it's because the song has no connection to Lea, but either way it feels good. I've been so afraid that music was never going to be the same again that hearing something so beautiful and pure—it makes my entire body relax.

My heart, too.

I don't know how long I'm sitting there—a minute, an hour—but eventually the door opens, and Mr. Watanabe stares down at me like he knew I was there all along.

I jump up, straightening my pajama shirt. I open my mouth to tell him his music is too loud, that I can't sleep, that he needs to shut it off, but I can't. Because I don't want the music to stop.

He looks at me, opens the door even wider, and moves toward his living room.

I hesitate. Is this an invitation?

When Poi shows up yapping through the screen like she's eaten batteries for lunch, I pull the thin door open and step inside.

Mr. Watanabe's house smells like grass and old wood. I don't know how anyone's home could smell so much like a terrarium when there isn't a plant in sight. Maybe it's all the time he spends in his yard. Maybe the smell sticks to him, the way songs used to stick to Lea and me. Like they just couldn't leave us.

Poi sniffs at my feet, barking and barking like she wants the world to know she's found me.

"Is she going to stop?" I ask.

Mr. Watanabe is sitting in a deep red chair, an old record player near his right and a small table with a wooden box at his left. He doesn't say anything—he tilts his head back and closes his eyes, listening to the scratch of the vinyl beside him.

I sit on the floor and hold out my hand to Poi. She comes closer, running her whiskers along my fingers, and then jumps away again, yapping frantically, like she can't control herself.

Mr. Watanabe whistles once, and Poi skirts across the room and hops into his lap, content.

I roll my eyes. That dog has more things wrong with it than I do.

When the next song starts, I don't move from the floor. I listen to the mango guitar and breathe in the earthy room, and suddenly I'm lying flat on the wooden floor watching the ceiling fan spin around and around and around.

And for the first time in weeks, I don't feel like the floor has been pulled out from under me. I feel steady.

We listen to the entire record. When it ends, Mr. Watanabe looks at me and says, "You go home."

When I'm standing outside the front door, I turn back to him. "Can I come back tomorrow?"

Maybe it's a lot to ask of a stranger, but I don't care. I found something familiar in a world where nothing is the way I remember it.

The music that exists in Mr. Watanabe's house isn't haunted by Lea. I feel safe here, and I want to hold on to this feeling for as long as I can. For as long as Mr. Watanabe will let me.

I need music not to hurt anymore, and I'll visit Mr. Watanabe and his annoying dog every single day if that's what it takes.

His face is dry and covered in sunspots, and sometimes he looks like he's made of leather and not human skin. But after a very long silence, he blinks at me like someone at the other end of a job interview.

"Tomorrow" is all he says.

CHAPTER ELEVEN

A unty Ani leaves for work before I'm even out of bed. I'm glad—having her hovering around me all the time only reminds me of what Mom should be here doing, instead of vanishing from my life like she somehow became Dad.

It's not fair for people to grieve alone. The people who are left behind should stick together. They should *want* to stick together.

I try to think about lyrics for "Summer Bird Blue," but it feels unnatural, the same way losing Lea and being in Hawaii feel unnatural. Summers are supposed to be about having fun and enjoying some freedom before school starts again, but I don't feel free—I feel trapped and lost all at the same time, as if I woke up on a deserted island in the middle of the ocean and I can't remember how I got there.

Summer, Hawaii, the world—none of it makes sense without Lea.

I know I need to write this song, but I don't want to. I don't want to do any of this without my sister and without my mom.

It's not fucking fair.

I see Poi through the kitchen window, napping in the sunshine like she doesn't have any cares at all. Either that or all the barking might have actually worn her out.

I decide I don't want to wait until night to find out if Mr. Watanabe is going to play his record again. He said tomorrow, right? And it is tomorrow.

I knock on the door and set off the Poi alarm.

Mr. Watanabe appears and leaves the door open like he did last night.

When I step inside, I try to pet Poi. She runs around me a few times, looking like a giant rodent with too much hair, before scurrying onto the couch and growling under her breath.

I look at the empty record player and my heart sinks. "Where's the music?"

He looks at me with tired, dull eyes before pointing to the bottom shelf next to the couch. It's full of records, all neatly lined up against one another, their spines so worn away they appear fluffy. The rest of the shelves are covered in gold trinkets and a few photographs.

"Go, find one," he says.

I kneel down next to the shelf and pull the records halfway out one at a time, until I find something with a violin on the cover. I look up at him.

He makes a noise like he's disgusted and waves the record away. "Dat one no good. Try da uddah one."

I find a cover with a piano on it, and he gives a single nod.

I sit on the floor next to the record player while he writes something down at the kitchen table. We're silent; neither of us interested in talking. It's almost peaceful, even with Poi's sporadic noises erupting every few minutes from the couch.

The piano music is like vanilla lattes and sugar cookies. Cozy. Homely. God, I miss the feel of the keys beneath my hands so much.

I don't realize I'm mimicking the notes with my fingers against the wooden floor until I catch Mr. Watanabe staring at me, his nose dipped so his glasses fall right below his eyes. I pull my hands back and turn toward the speakers, biting my lip so I don't let myself get too comfortable again.

Later that night I see Aunty Ani. She doesn't ask for an apology, and I don't give her one. I think we're going to pretend nothing happened.

When she's in the shower, I sit on my bed with Lea's guitar in my lap, my back to the open window. I bring my hand to the strings, telling myself it's okay—that the notes don't have to be painful. They don't have to hurt.

Listening to music next door was easy—why can't this be too?

But as soon as I feel the pang in my chest, I let my hand fall back to the mattress. Maybe grieving Lea isn't supposed to be easy.

Right now it feels impossible.

I close my eyes and take a breath, focusing on something other than my thoughts. The flutter of nearby leaves on the fruit trees.

The chorus of tropical birds I've never seen before. I try to listen for Mr. Watanabe's music, but I can't hear it. Maybe he's like me—maybe some days he needs to be heard, but most of the time he'd rather be hidden.

"That's one big ukulele," Kai says.

I spin around. He's leaning into the window opposite mine. It's not far—I could easily throw something straight into his house if I wanted to, and I'm not even *remotely* athletic.

"It's a guitar," I say stiffly.

Kai laughs. "Yeah, I know that." He lifts his chin. "You play?"

I run my fingers over the stickers, some soft with age. "A little. But Lea was better. I was always the piano player."

"Can you play me something?" he asks, his fingers tapping against the windowsill.

I look at him seriously. He's so carefree, like he doesn't understand the gravity of losing a sister—*of death*—and how it's way too soon for me to even be thinking about playing an instrument again.

He smiles, his teeth white and his skin so tan, and I pull my eyes away before I forget what I'm trying to say. "No," I manage to get out, putting the guitar back in its case and leaning it against the wall. When I get back to my bed, Kai is still at the window.

"Hey, I have a question for you," he says.

"What's that?" I ask, and my nerves rumble to life.

"You like go to the beach tomorrow?" he asks with a smirk.

I stiffen. "Why did you have to start it off like that?"

"What do you mean?"

"The whole, 'I have a question for you.' Like you were about to ask me something important."

"It's not *un*important."

"Yeah, but you're making it weird when you say it like that. Like it's a date."

"Do you want it to be a date?"

"No," I practically bark.

He shrugs. "Okay, fine. You still like go?"

I make a face. "I thought your dad didn't want you hanging out with me."

"Eh." Kai waves a hand. "I'll act like you're all depressed about your sistah. He'll be fine."

"I *am* depressed about my sister," I say.

He shrugs. "Well, perfect then, yeah? I don't even have to lie."

I raise my eyebrows.

He laughs. "Come on. Goin' hurt my feeling if you say no."

"Your feeling? As in one?"

"I only have one left."

"You're so weird."

"I have da kine—low self-esteem."

"I seriously doubt that."

"No, it's true. I hate myself almost as much as you hate the entire world. We can try bond over that."

"You're making fun of me."

"Never, hapa." He's grinning wildly because he can't keep a straight face to save his life.

Still, I almost smile. *Almost.* "Okay, fine."

"Cool. Meet me downstairs tomorrow morning? At seven?"

"Seriously?" I say. "Seven in the morning?"

Kai laughs loudly, leaning away from the window. "Early bird catches the waves."

I start to point out that he never said anything about surfing, but then he's gone and it's just me, musicless and motherless and sisterless, but maybe no longer friendless.

And I feel like that means more than I want to admit.

CHAPTER TWELVE

The water is still strangely warm, even in the mornings. Not Jacuzzi warm, but when the only ocean you've ever been in is the one off the coast of Washington State, the water in Hawaii feels like a completely different species altogether.

Gareth starts throwing around lumps of food wrapped in plastic. When one of them hits me in the chest, I study it like someone would study a fruit they've never seen before. It looks like a slab of rice and some kind of meat, all wrapped up in seaweed.

"Spam musubi," Gareth says. "You eva try?"

"I've had Spam. My mom always cooks it with sugar and soy sauce. But I've never had it like this," I say.

I glance around at the rest of the group. There's Kai, Gareth, a girl named Hannah, who looks enviably perfect in a bikini, and her younger brother, Jerrod. They're all eating the seaweed wrap hungrily. I take a bite out of mine and meet Gareth's gaze with approval.

"Ono, yeah?" he says. "You like anuddah one?"

I shake my head and swallow. "One is fine. Thanks."

He nods, falling into the sand next to Jerrod, who seems to have a cell phone surgically fixed to his hands. Kai is talking to Hannah with so much animation, I'm not sure he understands what seven in the morning actually means.

He catches me looking at him and winks. I shake my head slowly. Low self-esteem. What a bunch of garbage.

It doesn't take me long to realize why Kai wanted to get here so early. They didn't come here just to surf; they've also borrowed a bunch of equipment from the hotel. Boogie boards, a paddle board, a small kayak—and they want to use them before the hotel guests begin renting everything out for the day.

I watch Hannah bundle up her curly hair in a high knot. She has pretty hazel eyes, dark, earthy skin, and freckles covering both her shoulders. She grabs one of the boogie boards and heads out into the water, Gareth following closely behind her with a surfboard.

Kai motions over his shoulder. "You like try surf?"

I shake my head. "I'm still half asleep. Contrary to what everyone seems to think about my morbidly depressing situation, I'm not looking for a way to check out early."

"Noted," he says, and makes his way to the ocean's edge with his own board just as Gareth dips his body below the water to miss an incoming wave.

Jerrod sits down next to me with a can of pineapple juice in one hand and his phone in the other. I watch him swipe his thumb against the screen, and a moment of frustration flashes across his face.

"No signal?" I ask tiredly.

He looks up at me like he's only just noticed I've stayed behind. "Did you know the Great Barrier Reef is dying? It's like eighteen million years old. How ridiculous is that? That you could live that long and still be at the mercy of mortality?" he asks.

Eighteen million years, eighteen years—it's all a travesty to me. Life is nothing more than a flame. It doesn't get to decide when it goes out—it's either time or an outside interference.

I shrug. "Pretty ridiculous, I guess. Why is it dying?"

"Bleaching or something. I'm still reading," he says, scrolling down the article.

I look out into the water. Gareth and Kai are farther back, the pair of them sitting on their boards like ducks in the water, waiting for the perfect wave. Hannah is still fairly close to shore, her arms swooping low in a strong paddle as the crest of water appears behind her.

Jerrod snaps a picture of something in the sand. Maybe a seashell. Maybe his own feet. "So, how long have you known Kai?"

I shrug. "A week, maybe? But I don't *know* him know him. He's mostly hanging out with me because my aunt told him to, and I think I'm mostly hanging out with him because his dad told me not to." It probably says a lot about who Kai and I are as people, to be honest.

Jerrod snorts loudly and stifles a laugh. "I don't blame you. His dad is a douche."

"Who's a what now?" Hannah says, dropping her yellow boogie board into the sand and reaching for her water bottle.

"Kai's dad," we both say at the same time.

She rolls her eyes. "Our dad used to be on the same squadron as him, and even he thinks Kai's dad is a jerk." She sits down next to me, patting at the dark brown knot on her head, which is starting to come undone. "You a military brat too?"

"No. I'm visiting my aunt for the summer," I say stiffly.

She nods and bites into one of the extra Spam musubis. "Where are you from?"

"Washington," I say.

It's strange how quickly the ability to converse with people comes back to me. People always compare picking up old hobbies to riding a bike, but it's different from that. Socializing is like getting out of bed after you've been sleeping for weeks. Which pretty much sums up my life since I've been here.

They tell me how they used to live in Everett and how Kai is lucky because he's never had to move—something about Palekaiko Bay being his mom's second child—and that their own dad is getting new orders next year and they're hoping to move to Italy. Hannah tells me how much she loves surfing but hates her school, and how everyone calls her "hapa" because her mom's Japanese and her dad's black and she's sick of hearing it. Jerrod interrupts to point out they're not really hapa anyway, and that if you google it, "hapa" is supposed to mean people who are half Hawaiian.

Hannah shrugs. "I think most people use it to mean half white and half Asian, but honestly? Every single person in our little group is half something, technically. Gareth is half Filipino and half Samoan. Kai is half Japanese and half Korean." She looks at me. "What are you mixed with?"

"My mom is half Japanese and half Hawaiian," I say.

"And your dad?" she asks.

"White. Irish, I think. We don't speak." I kick my heels into the sand.

"Sorry," she says.

"I'm not," I say, but I change the subject anyway. "Kai calls me 'hapa' all the time. Should I be offended?"

Hannah snort-laughs. "Some people don't like the word, but a lot of people embrace it. I guess it means something to their identity, whereas it doesn't for me. But if you don't like it, just tell Kai to shut up. He needs to hear it now and then. People with faces as pretty as his never hear it as much as they should."

As if on cue, Kai erupts with laughter. The three of us look out toward the ocean's edge, almost missing the moment Gareth concedes a wave to Kai, who pops his feet up on his board and stands just as the frothy water builds up around him.

For the briefest pause in time, the world seems to still. Kai's arms are spread wide like they're wings preparing for flight. His electric smile is as wild as ever, and his face has a kind of serenity I've never seen before. It's like he doesn't know what it means to be anxious or worried or nervous—he simply exists in the world. He accepts it, like a bird ready to fly no matter the weather.

And then time remembers itself. The wave moves—Kai moves—and for a moment he becomes sea and salt and shadow. It's kind of beautiful. And freeing.

I wish I could feel like that.

Kai emerges free of the wave, and suddenly he's whooping toward Gareth still out in the calm. I can't hear what Gareth shouts back, but whatever it is makes Kai laugh all the way to shore.

For about thirty seconds, I forget about Lea. Like, I really forget. I forget why I'm here, and how she died, and that she doesn't exist anymore. And I start to live—for thirty whole seconds—until I realize what a selfish asshole I am for forgetting about her so easily, and for hiding out here on the beach when I should be trying to finish our song.

Lea would've never forgotten about me so quickly. She always treated me like I was the most important person in her world—like she'd always have time for me. Like she'd always *make* time for me.

A memory

Mom's at work when I get home, which is good because I slam the front door so loud it practically makes the house shake. Or at least, it feels like it's shaking, probably because *I'm* shaking.

When I get to my room, I throw the door open and let my backpack plummet from my shoulder to the floor. The weight of the textbooks makes Lea jump. She looks at me from her bed, her eye shadow palette in one hand, an applicator in the other.

"What's wrong with you?" she asks. One eye is purple and shimmery and lined with black. The other is still bare. I don't know why she insists on applying makeup that way, one eye at a time, instead of doing it in stages like a normal person. Eye shadow, eyeliner, *then* mascara. It isn't rocket science.

"Nothing," I reply too fast.

She tilts her head to the side and makes a face. "Liar."

I sink into my bed, too angry to hold myself up. "I don't want to talk about it." My eyes follow the many outfits thrown around the room. "Are you going somewhere?"

"Marley's having a party at her house. Ben is going to be there." She widens her eyes like this is major news. And to her it is—she's had a crush on Ben all semester. Something about his green eyes and pouty lips.

I can't relate.

I groan. How is it possible that my fourteen-year-old sister has a more exciting social life than I do?

Lea places her eye shadow next to her but keeps the brush between her fingers. "Okay, I'm not going to finish getting ready until you tell me what's wrong. And for the record, hanging out with Benjamin Blythe is, like, the most important thing that will happen to me this entire year. So please don't make me late."

I roll my eyes and tuck my hair behind my ear. "They kissed, okay? And not by accident, like they got too drunk or their faces smashed into each other in the hallway. They actually *kissed*. On purpose."

She frowns and puts the brush down. "Caleb and Alice made out? Like, with *tongue*?"

"Of course with tongue. It's Caleb. He's been kissing girls with his lizard tongue since the fourth grade."

Lea gets up from her bed and finds a space next to me. "Well, this is good, right? You said it's been awkward since you turned him down. Maybe now it will go back to normal."

I blink at her. "I can't take you seriously when you look like half a clown."

She snorts and jabs me in the ribs.

I let out an agitated sigh. "I don't care that they're together, or whatever. I care that everything is changing. Everyone is moving on, and growing up, and I just feel so left behind."

Most other people my age have crushes—they're attracted to each other and have the urge to flirt. I don't feel anything like that—when I think about romance, I feel indifferent. When I see someone I think is physically attractive, I don't picture them naked or wonder what it's like to kiss them—I just see people who are aesthetically pleasing and could potentially make a good friend.

And it never used to feel like I was missing out on anything. I always felt like I was the way I'm supposed to be. But then high school started and suddenly everyone became so confident and knowledgeable about dating and sex and sexuality—and honestly? I've never felt more different in my entire life. I feel like the world is shouting at me to make decisions I'm not ready for.

I lift my shoulders. "I've tried to like boys. I've even wondered if I like girls—or *both*. But I don't like anybody. I can see when people are attractive, but I don't want to date them. I don't want to hold hands, or flirt, or . . . kiss. And I don't feel like I have fewer pieces than anyone else, or that I'm somehow less whole because I don't want to date. But I feel like I'm *supposed* to feel that way." I frown. "Does that make sense?"

Lea scrunches her nose at me and laughs. Of course it doesn't make sense to her—she's like Alice. They've been interested in boys since kindergarten.

Still, she shoves my knee with her hand and smiles. "It doesn't have to make sense to me. It just has to make sense to you."

"But it doesn't." I press my teeth against my bottom lip and shake my head. "That's the problem."

Lea trails her finger along the threads of my blanket, thinking. "Well, maybe it doesn't matter. Maybe you don't have to know everything about yourself right this second. Maybe you're still figuring it out."

"What if I never figure it out? What if I get to college and it takes me six years to pick a major, and three years after that I change my mind and have to start all over again? What if I think I don't want kids, and then when I'm fifty I think I made a mistake but it's too late?

Or what if I pick the wrong guy—or girl—and they end up leaving me with two kids and I have to get two jobs to be able to pay the bills?"

Lea relaxes her shoulders like she finally understands. "You're worried you're going to end up like *him*."

I make a face and take a deep breath through my nose. I didn't turn out like Dad on purpose. Sometimes I don't even understand how it's possible when he was never around. But I know what it feels like to not feel settled. I know what it feels like to feel confused about everything.

I'm my father's daughter whether I like it or not.

Whether Mom likes it or not.

And I hate that I can't make up my mind. I hate that understanding myself isn't as simple as doing a Google search on what I'm feeling. I hate that one moment I think I know who I am, and then the next moment I'm second-guessing myself and feeling like a fraud.

"What if I'm already like him? What if I spend my entire life feeling lost?"

What if me being so much like him is the reason Mom likes you better? What if it's the reason everyone *likes you better?*

I bite the inside of my cheek and keep the rest of my questions to myself.

Lea rests her head on my shoulder. "Well, then you can move in with me and we'll figure it out. Together. Preferably before you ever consider abandoning your children."

I lean back against my sister. She makes it so easy to like her. I wish it came that easily to me.

I start crying again without meaning to. Life comes so much easier to people like Lea and Alice. They know what they want, and they aren't afraid to go after it. They're so sure of themselves—so certain they aren't making mistakes.

Knowing myself should be the easiest thing I do in life, but somehow it feels like the hardest.

Lea doesn't rush me, or tell me I'm being silly. She sits with me, because she knows that's what I need.

When my breathing slows I pull away. "You should probably finish getting ready. I don't want you to be late for your party with Ben."

Lea jumps up from the bed, and I think she's going for her eye shadow palette, but instead she finds our lyric notebook and tosses it on the bed next to me.

"I'm not going anywhere. We have a song to write," she says.

"I'm fine. Honestly." I shrug. "You don't need to change your plans because of me."

"I'm not leaving you alone when you're upset. Mom's not home—you need me."

"Lea—" I start.

"Rock," she interrupts.

I smile. "Clown."

She giggles. "Sisters."

Lea was the most selfless person I ever knew. She would drop everything she was doing to make sure I was okay. She was thoughtful, and good, and so easy to love I can't understand why I was ever horrible to her.

And now she needs me—she needs me to finish our song—and I'm too weak and scared to find my way back to the music.

I'm letting her down *again*.

Maybe I deserve what's happening to me now. Maybe the universe is trying to teach me a lesson. Because even though Mom is selfish for leaving me alone, I've been selfish most of my life too.

I was selfish for not giving Lea her last wish. I was selfish for always wanting to keep Mom to myself. I was selfish for always quashing Lea's happiness, when all she ever did was try to make sure *I* was happy.

And I'm selfish for sitting here on the beach socializing with people like it's the most natural thing in the world. Like it's normal to talk to people. *Like my life is normal.*

I lost my sister. Nothing will ever be normal again.

The knots build in my stomach until they're pushing so hard against my heart that I feel like I'm going to pass out.

I stand up and dust the sand from my shorts. Lea's shorts. "I just remembered I have to help my aunt with something," I lie.

Jerrod looks up from his brightly lit screen. "Okay. See you."

Hannah squints up at me like she's only now noticing there's something wrong with me. "It was nice to meet you."

CHAPTER THIRTEEN

I start walking home, back up the path Kai drove us down, and find myself at a dead end filled with chickens and a couple of bizarrely calm stray cats.

I think I might be lost.

I turn back around, trying to keep the hills on my right because it's the only visual marking I can remember from the drive here, when I hear a car honk from behind me. I look up to see Kai in his mom's car. He pulls over and rolls down the window, his hair slicked back with salt water that still hasn't had time to dry.

He folds his arms over the top of the steering wheel and leans forward. "Do you know where you're going?"

I look around. There's blue sky and ocean to my left and a hill to my right that looks like someone sprinkled it with soft, green leaves. Nothing about this place looks familiar because nothing about it *is* familiar. This isn't my home. This is someone else's home—I've just been thrown into it because nobody knew what else to do with me.

Kai motions to the seat next to him. "Come on, don't be stubborn. I'll drive you home."

I slide into the passenger's seat, and the car climbs the rest of the hill and makes a quick right into a neighborhood.

"How come you're running away?" he asks, breaking the silence.

"I wasn't running away," I correct. "I just . . . shouldn't be at the beach right now. I have something to do." I open my mouth to explain that I have a song to write, and that if I don't figure out a way to make music hurt less, I'm going to be breaking my promise to my sister. I'm about to tell him that finding my way back to music feels like running into a forest that's dancing with wildfire. I'm about to tell him I keep finding ways to quit on our song, because I'm selfish and afraid and dying on the inside.

I close my mouth and swallow the words. Some things don't need to be said out loud.

"You feel weird being around people without your sistah?" Kai asks like it's the most casual thing in the world.

"Well, don't beat around the bush," I say dryly.

"I don't really know how to talk about dead people." He pauses. "Sorry, was that insensitive?"

"Very." I laugh, and it surprises me. "But I don't really care. I prefer it to what my aunt does, which is tiptoe around the subject like it's going to set me off."

I can hear the humor in his voice. "Will it? Set you off?"

"Almost definitely," I reply. And then I look at him for half a second. "So why does everyone hate your dad?"

Kai laughs. "'Cause he's unlikable. I can't even make excuses fo' him. We're like oil and water. It probably wouldn't be so bad if he'd been around my whole life, but he was stationed in Japan fo' most of my childhood. Now that he's back, I think he's trying to cram eighteen years of parenting into one. It's not really working."

"That sucks."

He shrugs. "It sucks about your sistah and mom, too."

I raise a brow.

"Sorry," he says sheepishly. "Sometimes things just come out of my mouth, you know?"

I settle into the seat. "Yeah. I do, actually." Maybe neither of us has the appropriate filters to deal with so much heaviness. I mean, it's not like they have a class in high school that teaches you how to cope with death. There isn't a handbook for it—it's like someone gives you the most difficult test in the world and expects you to pass on the first try.

Death is supposed to be natural, but it literally makes no sense. I don't understand how someone can exist one minute and be gone in the next. And why? Why is that it? What's the point of being good or brave or kind or hopeful when it just goes in a flash? Where's the meaning in that?

Kai taps his thumb against the wheel when we pull up at a red light. He's singing so quietly along to the radio that I can barely hear him, but it isn't terrible. In fact, it's kind of good. He sings completely in key.

"I didn't know you could sing," I say. I'd rather we kept

talking. It keeps my mind on something other than my pain.

Kai smirks. "Because you're still assuming I'm some spoiled jock with rich parents?"

"Yes, actually."

"I can sing because I like music. I've been in band since middle school."

My eyes widen.

"See? You shouldn't judge people so quickly," he points out.

"What do you play?"

"Percussion."

I laugh.

"Why is that funny?"

"You're a drummer. If you had told me you played the oboe or bassoon, I would've been surprised. But the snare drum? The xylophone? Come on. Percussionists are the jocks of the band room."

"Why do you hate jocks so much? And people you think have money?"

"I don't hate them. I think they're clichés, and I hate clichés."

He's quiet for a second. "It makes so much sense now."

"What does?"

"Why you're so mean to me all the time." His face breaks into a grin. "You hate that you might like the boy next door."

"That's the most ridiculous thing I've ever heard," I say through his laughter. "I'm not mean to you, first of all, and if I am it has nothing to do with you being a cliché. It's because I don't see the point in making friends when I'm going home soon."

"Yeah, well, I'm leaving too and I still like be your friend," Kai says.

"Where are you going?"

"My dad wants me to join the navy," he replies simply. "So I guess I'm leaving fo' boot camp at the end of the summer."

"That doesn't sound like it's your idea," I say.

He twists his jaw. "I don't really have a choice. My dad doesn't think parents should pay fo' their kids' college. He says they should learn how fo' work themselves." He shrugs. "Hawaii is expensive, you know? The military might be my only option."

"No it's not. There are always other options. Plenty of them," I say almost defensively. Kai has the whole world within his reach. He has options—more options than most. More options than Lea. "You don't have to pick the same career as your dad just because he told you to. You should do what makes you happy."

"You don't know my dad. He's never been proud of me before. I think we both *need* me to join the navy. Otherwise I'm not sure we'll ever have anything in common. Besides, it's not so bad. I can try get stationed here, do my four years, and then go to college." He raises his hand like this isn't a big deal. "Four years not the end of the world."

"But it's your life," I say. "You only get this one. Why would you throw it away? Why would you let your dad make you do something you don't want to do?" I feel the headache growing inside my skull, and Kai is looking at me like I'm spiraling out of reality. And maybe I am. Because a reality without my sister just isn't fair. She didn't deserve to die—she didn't deserve to leave this world before she even got a chance to experience it. "You don't know what's going to happen tomorrow. You could die. He could die. Why would you waste your life for someone else?"

"That's dark, hapa."

"Of course it's dark. Life is dark. It doesn't care about anyone. Yours just hasn't gone to shit yet. You should care about that." *You should appreciate having a life at all.*

"Are you okay?" Kai asks seriously, and I realize I'm shaking everywhere.

I shove my hands between my knees and stare out the window. "I'm fine."

My mind doesn't stop racing and my heart doesn't stop pounding, and the next time I look up we're in Kai's driveway and the engine is off.

"I'm sorry if I upset you. I don't take this stuff as seriously as you do. It's not a big deal to me," Kai says.

I don't know why, but I feel anger toward Kai. I hate that he doesn't care about his life enough to treasure it. I hate that he has a life he can just throw away.

Lea would've made the most of her life. She would've followed her dreams. She wanted to be a songwriter. She wanted to spend her life writing music with me. And Mom supported her because Lea was life and wonder and childhood excitement, and it was so fucking beautiful.

Lea wouldn't have wasted a single day. She would have lived her life like a star—burning bright and loud until she went out in one giant explosion that would change the world.

It's not fair. It's not fair she's dead when she deserved life so much more than someone like Kai. Someone like *me*. And I don't care if that's a horrible thing to say.

"Thanks for the ride," I say thinly, and I run away from Kai and his car and his wasted future.

CHAPTER FOURTEEN

Mr. Watanabe is outside digging a hole near the pavement. Poi is running around his yard chasing a lizard that's holed up behind some of the potted plants. When she sees me, she barks and runs to the edge of the grass, the sound as frantic as it always is.

"What are you doing?" I ask when I approach them.

Mr. Watanabe doesn't even glance my way. "Whatchu t'ink I doing?"

"Digging a hole." After a pause, I ask, "Why are you digging a hole?"

"You ask too much questions," he says, pressing his hand against his back when he straightens up.

"Do you want some help?" I offer. It's not because I'm trying to be kind—I'm just bored, and I'm avoiding Kai and Aunty Ani. My grouchy older neighbor is literally the only person in my life right now who isn't trying to force me to talk. Or feel something. Or *do* anything.

We both like the silence. We're a good match.

He points to the dirt. "Dig two more li'dis. Dea' and one ova dea'." He passes me the shovel and disappears into a nearby shed. When he comes back, he's carrying several wooden posts.

I shovel, Mr. Watanabe sets the posts, and Poi skids back and forth behind us like a tornado of hyperactivity. By the time the sun is setting, we're looking at a fence that encloses the grassy patch behind us. I think it's a dog run.

"Did Poi get out again?" I ask.

Mr. Watanabe grunts. "She like beef wit' da neighborhood cats."

"Beef?" I repeat.

He eyes me. "Scrap. Fight."

"Oh, right." I look around the yard. "Do you need help with anything else?"

He makes a face. "Too late. Time fo' eat."

I nod, and the heaviness comes back. I'm running out of distractions—I can feel it.

"You know how fo' cook chicken curry?" he asks.

"Yes," I lie.

"Okay," he says, not looking like he really believes me.

We go inside and he chops up vegetables while I stir the ingredients he leaves on the counter into a thick liquid. Then he boils rice and preps the chicken while I keep stirring the curry. At some point we both get distracted by the music playing in the background—the saddest guitar piece I've ever heard, like frozen berries and cold, herbal tea that's been left out for hours—and I'm not sure exactly how much of the food is burned, but when I stir again there's a layer of blackened curry that floats to the top in bits.

Mr. Watanabe makes a noise of disgust, but he serves the meal out anyway over a bed of sticky white rice.

We both eat the first couple of bites in complete silence, chewing carefully and staring at the table. But then he sets his chopsticks down and tilts his head back so he's looking down at me with his almost-black eyes.

"You no can make good curry," he says. "Dis terrible."

I put my chopsticks down too and frown. "The curry is fine. It's the chicken that tastes like garbage."

Mr. Watanabe explodes with a laugh that sounds like an elephant, and it's so loud and out of nowhere that I jump in my seat. When it ends, he's smiling with only the corner of his face.

"Okay. We have curry some uddah time." He stands up, taking both of the bowls with him.

Five minutes later, we're sitting on his couch eating coffee-flavored ice cream and listening to a ukulele player on vinyl with Poi sitting between us, asleep but still grumbling, and I'm wondering if Mr. Watanabe is my new best friend.

CHAPTER FIFTEEN

Aunty Ani makes eggs on rice for breakfast, and after we finish eating she asks me if I want to go to the mall with her.

"It's my day off," she says. "You like go shopping for summah clothes? Too hot fo' wear jeans all the time, yeah?"

I tug at the frayed bits of string hanging from the bottom of my shirt. *Lea's* shirt. I don't want to replace her things. She's not replaceable. "I was going to listen to records with Mr. Watanabe."

Aunty Ani tucks a strand of hair behind her ear. "I not so sure if you should be bothering the neighbor."

"I'm not bothering him," I snap.

She nods like she understands, but she doesn't. Nobody does. "It's just he's older, you know? He might not like you over there so much."

"Nobody else comes to visit him," I interject. "He's old. He's probably going to die soon. Maybe he doesn't want to be all alone right before he's going to die."

"Just because someone is older doesn't mean they're about to die," she argues. "I don't think you'd want someone saying those things about you when you get older."

"Well, it's the truth. People get old, and they die." I pause. "Sometimes they don't even get old. I'd be happy if I lasted long enough to call myself old."

"Rumi—" she starts.

"I'm not going to stop hanging out with him. He's my friend." My voice is wobbly and too loud.

She sighs. "I'd really like you to find something else fo' do. You can still hang out with him—but maybe not all the time. What about Kai? I thought you guys were getting along? I heard he goes to karaoke every week with his friends. Maybe you could go too? It might be fun to try singing again."

My eyes snap toward her, and she flinches. She doesn't get it— she doesn't understand how much music hurts me. Because music doesn't mean anything to her—it's just noise.

But to me music is just as important as the blood running through my veins. It gives me life, and it can take it away too.

I know I owe Lea a song, but I'm not ready to write again. I'm not ready to sing or play the guitar or experience what it's like to perform without my sister. It hurts too much. It feels like my heart is made of glass, but her death shattered it into a billion pieces. Trying to make it beat again is agonizing—I can feel every shard, every break.

I'd rather have my heart feel nothing at all than the pain that comes with writing music.

Aunty Ani takes a breath like she's ready to try again. She's as stubborn as I am. "How would you feel about maybe going to talk to someone? They have group therapy fo' people dealing with loss. It might be helpful."

"Hanging out with Mr. Watanabe *is* helpful." *Music doesn't hurt at his house,* I want to say. *It's the only place that's safe.* "I'd rather punch myself in the face repeatedly than go to group therapy," I say instead. I don't have anything against therapy, but I do have something against people. If I were going to share my feelings with anyone, it should be Lea and Mom—not a bunch of strangers.

I don't need to talk to anyone—I need to be left alone. Because alone is what Lea and Mom left me, and if I can't figure out a way to make sense of that, I'll be lost forever.

I don't have my family anymore. I don't have my music anymore.

I have a shattered heart and a haunted guitar.

And maybe I can't find a way to fix them, but I do need to find a way to live with them.

Because this is my life now.

"Why is it so hard fo' you to talk to anyone? It doesn't have fo' be me. But it's important you talk to *somebody.* You have to heal." She speaks with so much kindness and good intentions that if I weren't so angry I might actually appreciate it.

But I don't. Her words physically hurt me. "I don't have a cut, or a broken arm, or even a broken heart," I say, and I feel like there's a lump of rock and ash moving up and down my throat. I can hardly breathe. "Lea died. Her life was over in a blink. There was no warning. She wasn't old, or sick, or too sad to keep going.

She was here, and then she wasn't, and there's no healing from that. Because she was my entire world. I could live without so many things—without parents, without music, without my eyes or ears—but without my sister? How am I supposed to do that? How am I supposed to get better from that?"

Aunty Ani stands in front of me, tears streaming down her face and spit forming each time she tries to open her mouth. But I don't stop. The words keep pouring out of me, hard and unforgiving, and my eyes are as dry as they've ever been.

"Therapy isn't going to fix me. The boy next door isn't going to fix me. Singing isn't going to fix me. Even Mom being here wouldn't fix me. Because I don't want to be fixed. I don't want to heal from this. I want her back. I want Lea to be alive. So stop trying to make me talk about it, or make friends, or have fun on the beach, or go shopping at the mall. I'm coping, okay? I'm still here. But don't try to change the place I exist now, because besides a few shitty T-shirts and a guitar I can barely look at, the hole Lea left me is all I have to remember her by."

The sobs coming from my aunt border on wailing. But there's nothing inside me that's soft and warm. I can't comfort her. Lea was the sand, and I'm the rocks—when a wave washes you to shore, there's one you'll always prefer over the other.

She knew how to fix people. I know how to hurt them. Does it matter if it's not on purpose?

"And stop making excuses for Mom," I say evenly. "I hate her, and Lea would hate her for leaving me here too. And you can tell her I said that, because I know you talk to her, even if you don't tell me about it. I know because I still talk to Lea, and Lea is dead. Because that's how it is when you have a sister you love—you never stop talking to them, not ever, not even when they do something horrible, or stop breathing, or exist in some place you can't see. Because their ghost stays with you forever, and you spend the rest of your life trying to say all the things you wish you had said when they were alive. So, you tell Mom what I said—tell her she's an asshole for leaving me to figure all this out on my own. A world without Lea is hard enough, but making me spend the summer in a different state, away from my home and my friends and my piano and my *mother*? She might as well tell everyone both her daughters are dead, because she's not my mom anymore. She's just the woman who abandoned me on an island without even saying good-bye."

Aunty Ani sucks in her breath and holds it, her eyes darting back and forth like she wishes she could fix everything with words. And it would be so much easier if pain could be healed with the right words.

But it takes so much more than that.

And some things just aren't meant to heal. Some things are so horribly unfair that there's no coming back from that amount of pain.

I've lost everything. Music. Mom. Lea.

But I'm coping. This is me *coping*.

Bird

CHAPTER SIXTEEN

I'm flat on the wooden floor, my arms spread out, my palms faceup, and my legs close together. The record today sounds like the ocean—like I'm floating through the water on a raft, the waves carrying me up and down as the clouds morph above me into so many shapes I start to lose track of them.

It's like the ocean and fresh coffee and wood on the fire.

The vinyl record crackles to a stop. I open my eyes, watching the ceiling fan spin in circles. Poi is looking down at me, breathing so close to my face I can smell dog biscuits.

Go away, I mouth, but she pushes her nose against my chin and sniffs and sniffs until I have to push her with my hand.

I'm not sure she would've given up if it weren't for the noises outside. There's a car door followed by laughter. Probably Kai and Gareth, because God knows there's nothing happy coming from the other two houses on this miserable cul-de-sac.

Poi leaps over me and scurries outside, the barking at full volume.

I sit up and wipe my chin with the back of my hand. Mr. Watanabe is asleep in his chair, his arm draped lazily over his lap with his glasses still pinched between two fingers. I don't want to wake him up by digging through his record shelf, so I follow Poi outside.

The warm sun hits me in the face, and I scrunch my eyes to get a better view of the driveway two houses away. Kai is there, not with Gareth but with Hannah. They look like they've just come back from the beach. Hannah is wearing jean shorts and a turquoise bikini top, her curly hair knotted at the top of her head and a white flower over her right ear. Kai is carrying his surfboard from her truck into his garage. He's wearing red board shorts, sunglasses, and flip-flops, and his dark torso is completely bare.

"Hey, Rumi!" Hannah calls, waving from next to her truck.

My body goes stiff. Kai looks up, realizes I'm watching them, and raises a hand.

Great. Now he's going to think I was spying on him like a weirdo. He might even think it has something to do with him not wearing a shirt, and it definitely, definitely does *not*.

I reach the gate at the same time they do.

Kai makes a face and laughs. "Whatchu doing at Uncle George's house?"

"We're friends," I say.

"You friends with Uncle George?" he repeats, as if the very concept is completely unfathomable to him.

"It's not weird. We like the same music. We *get* each other," I say.

Kai holds up his hands like all I'm doing is proving his point.

Hannah nervously eyes Poi, who hasn't stopped yapping through the fence. "We're all heading over to the Coconut Shack for fish tacos. Want to come?"

"She won't want to come. We're not the right age group for her," Kai says, leaning his elbow against the fence. He's lean muscle from his shoulders to his feet, and he has the darkest eyelashes I've ever seen on a guy. God, he really is pretty. And he knows it too, which makes the whole thing so much more annoying.

I scrunch my nose. "Why do you have to be so obnoxious?"

He shrugs. "All I'm saying is I get it now—why you never hang out with us."

"What's that supposed to mean?" I challenge.

He starts pointing to his fingers one at a time like he's making a list. "You're always grouchy. You're obsessed with mortality. Your only friend is a geriatric." He looks at Hannah sympathetically. "She's a ninety-year-old trapped in a teenager's body."

Hannah shakes her head. "You're ridiculous. Besides, you didn't even let her answer." She turns to me. "Don't feel like you have to come just because he's trying to pull some reverse-psychology bullshit on you. But you're welcome to join us, okay?"

I look at Kai, who is smiling like a child who got his way, and it suddenly doesn't matter that I don't want to go with them. I just don't want him to be right. "Yeah," I say to Hannah. "I'll come."

"Cool." She grins and sticks her tongue out at Kai.

I look down at Poi. "*Stay*. I'll be back later." I have the urge to pat her on the head, but I don't think either of us has made up our mind whether we like the other or not, so I pull the gate shut behind me and get in the back of Hannah's truck.

The Coconut Shack sits across the road from the same beach that leads to Palekaiko Bay. It's made up of thick panels of wood, all painted with colorful graffiti. The front half of the restaurant is completely exposed to the outdoors, except for the pillars holding up the second floor. There are a handful of tall, skinny tables in all different colors, where people can eat, drink, and watch the surfers from only a hundred yards away.

When we get inside, Hannah leads us upstairs to the karaoke lounge. There's a huge open space with more seating, an empty stage, and a bar. We turn the corner and find a long hallway with a handful of private rooms.

One of the doors is already open, and when I step inside I see Gareth and Jerrod already sitting on one of the couches.

"Oh, howzit?" Gareth says, holding up his fist with his pinky and thumb sticking out—the shaka sign. He shakes it lightly before dropping his hand. "You hungry? We just ordered da jumbo plate."

Hannah falls onto the opposite couch and leans her head back. "My legs are seriously *aching* right now."

Kai pulls a T-shirt over his head—finally—and sits down in one of the single chairs. He picks up the menu at the table, except it's not for food—it's for music. "Did you guys turn in the list already?"

"Nah," Jerrod says, pushing a piece of paper toward him. "It's here."

I sit down, listening to them talk about surfing and leg cramps and song choices, until a man comes in with an enormous tray of appetizers. There's onion rings, fish tacos, jalapeño poppers, ham and cheese quesadillas, and some kind of meatball and pineapple combo pierced with toothpicks. Before the man leaves, Kai passes him the piece of paper.

Hannah spreads out her arms. "Someone please feed me. I'm too tired to move."

The flat-screen TV hanging on the wall lights up, and a few seconds later a song starts playing. Gareth leaps up and grabs a microphone from the wall.

The rest of us eat while he serenades the room with his own rendition of a Bruno Mars song. Jerrod sings next—an eighties hit I've heard a thousand times but can never remember the title of—and after that Kai sings a song in Korean, complete with a rap in the middle.

I'm not going to lie—it's the most attracted I've ever been to him.

Hannah finishes writing down some more song choices while Gareth and Kai duet a Fifth Harmony song, and she slides the paper toward me and points to the menu. "You can pick whatever you want. Just write the number code down."

"I don't sing," I say, pushing the paper back to her.

She shrugs. "Okay. Well, if you change your mind, the list is here."

Hannah sings an Adele song next, and she can't stay in key to save her life, but she's so theatrical and earnest that even though everyone is laughing at her she's still completely adorable.

I eat onion rings to keep myself busy, but I'm so entranced watching them sing along to the lyrics scrolling across the TV screen that after an hour of them prodding me to join in, I do.

I pick a song by Regina Spektor called "The Call" because it's one of the first songs Lea and I tried to play together. When we finally got the piano-guitar arrangement right, we didn't stop singing it for months. Years, actually.

I remember the very last time we sang it. We were in Lea's room, writing lyrics in our journal, both of us lying on our stomachs against her shaggy purple rug. There was a crunchy bit of fur from the time she knocked over an entire bottle of my nail polish. God, I was so mad at her that day. Why did I have to get so mad? I wasted hours being angry at her—hours I wish I had now—over a few dollars.

When the song came on that day, we looked at each other like everything in the world was falling perfectly into place. We sang and danced around like wood nymphs, spinning and twirling and jumping off the bed until Mom came into the room, yelled at us to be quiet, and then after very little coaxing she was spinning around and singing along with us.

Because that's how we were, the three of us. We loved each other. We made each other happy.

I'm singing without really thinking. I see Lea, sitting in the room, smiling and swaying and mouthing the words along with me. I can hear her guitar—the careful way she used to strum, like the guitar was made of sand and sugar and water and one wrong move would crumble it into a trillion tiny pieces. And her voice, so soft and doelike. Her voice was always prettier than mine. I sing with a scratchy rasp, like someone who's been in a room filled with smoke for years and sleeps on the grit of the earth. Lea's was angelic, like she was literally created from the clouds.

God, we were so different, but so exactly the same, too.

It hurts so much to see her. It feels like my heart is being ripped out of my chest all over again. My throat starts to swell, and my voice trails off into nothingness.

This . . . was a mistake.

It's too soon to sing alone.

I look at Lea's ghost and mouth the words without really thinking. *I need more time.*

She smiles like she understands, but I don't think she does. Because I don't know if there are enough hours in a lifetime to get used to her being gone.

I will never get used to performing without her.

I will never get used to singing solo.

I will never get used to not having a sister anymore.

My shoulders shake like there's an earthquake in my core. Every inch of me tenses up like I'm bracing for the room to split apart—for the earthquake inside me to be real. I imagine the room exploding to bits, with pieces of drywall and tile flying in every direction and the tremor of the earthquake breaking the building in half.

But all my rage stays bottled up inside me, with no way for it to get out.

I don't feel the microphone fall from my hand, but I do hear the *thud* and piercing shriek it makes when it hits the floor. I see someone get up—Kai, I think—but I'm pushing past him without really thinking.

"I'm sorry," I think I say. "I can't be here right now."

And this time Kai doesn't follow me home.

CHAPTER SEVENTEEN

The next time I visit Mr. Watanabe, he hands me a pair of gloves. We spend two hours weeding a strip of yard at the back of his house that looks like it's been neglected all summer.

Afterward we sit in the shade. I'm drenched in sweat and bits of grass; Mr. Watanabe looks like he's been sitting in front of a fan all day. Poi's ears perk up when Aunty Ani opens the gate, and she takes off sprinting like a hunting dog chasing a rabbit.

"Hello?" Aunty Ani calls, keeping a nervous eye on the hyperactive dog trailing behind her.

Mr. Watanabe nods and grunts simultaneously. "Howzit?"

"Sorry fo' interrupt, but, Rumi, you have one phone call," she says timidly.

When I look up at her, my face flushes, and in an instant all the effort I made to cool down in the shade goes away.

It was only a matter of time before Mom decided to get in touch. I knew it would happen eventually. She'd wake up from whatever haze she's been living in and try to check back into reality. And she'd want to talk to me—the daughter who's still alive—to say how she's ready to be a mother again.

But it doesn't work that way. You can't stop being a mom just because your heart is broken. There are rules. There are consequences, too.

"I don't want to talk to her," I say, grinding my teeth together. It shouldn't be this easy for her—to just call me up and have things go back to normal.

She left me, and she doesn't get to fix that with a phone call.

"She really wants to speak to you," Aunty Ani says quietly, her eyes flickering between Mr. Watanabe and me. "She loves you, and even though you're angry, there are things you need to hear, too. Please—just talk to her."

"No." I squeeze the armrests, and I can feel the wood pressing too deeply against my skin.

Mr. Watanabe lets out an irritable cry. "Go talk to your muddah," he spits. "We finish anuddah time."

And just like that, he kicks me out of his yard.

I trudge through the house and throw the phone to my ear roughly. "What do you want?" I snap.

It's quiet for three whole seconds. "Hi, Rumi," Mom says. It doesn't even sound like her. Her voice is like a room full of broken glass—unrecognizable. She isn't the mom I know. She isn't the mom I loved.

Her two words pierce me straight in the chest. My heart beats violently.

I don't want to forgive her. I want to fight.

"Did she tell you? Did she tell you I said you're an asshole?" I growl.

"Rumi!" Aunty Ani exclaims from behind me.

I ignore her. "I don't want to talk to you, okay? You aren't here. You haven't *been here* for months. I have nothing to say to you."

"I just—" Mom starts, her voice shaking worse than my shoulders.

"I don't care. I don't care if you needed time to heal, or if you needed to grieve without me getting in the way. I don't care if seeing me reminded you of Lea, or if you just wanted to be alone. Whatever your excuse is, it's not good enough. Because I wouldn't have left *you* alone." I pause, and then the heat reaches my voice. "And I don't think you would've left Lea alone if I had died instead of her."

"*Rumi!*" Aunty Ani shouts louder this time.

"I only wanted to   " Mom tries to find her words, but I cut them down like they're nothing more than weeds.

"It's true," I bark to anyone who is listening. "You think I don't feel things as much as Lea did, but I do, you know. I feel a lot. And you didn't care." I'm squeezing the phone so hard I almost wish it would burst into ten thousand slivers of plastic and that Mom would hear the explosion and know that's how I feel about her.

I don't care what she has to say because I know the truth: She never would've sent Lea away. She would've grieved with her and been there for her. She would've made sure Lea knew she was loved. She would've made sure Lea knew the accident wasn't her fault.

That Lea deserved to survive.

But Mom didn't tell me any of those things. She was too busy grieving over the loss of her favorite daughter.

I'm the daughter who survived. I'm the daughter who is still here.

And Mom didn't want me.

"I hate you. Don't call me again."

I click the phone off, throw it against the couch, and wander outside.

Aunty Ani doesn't come after me. She's probably too busy trying to call Mom back to comfort her, even though she deserves everything she's feeling and more.

I look over at Kai's house. I know the last time we saw each other I was running away from him—running away from the music. But I know Kai well enough to know he won't make me explain myself. He won't push for answers.

And I don't want to talk right now. I just want to be *somewhere else.*

I walk to his front door and knock four times.

His mom appears and pushes the screen out so she can see me better. "Are you looking for Kai?" She smiles, and for the first time I notice how pretty she is. Her makeup is perfect and so is her hair, and her nails look like they were polished and shaped within the last hour.

I nod, and she calls for him from over her shoulder. When she looks back at me, I feel like she wants to talk, but my lips are pressed together so tightly and I'm still so furious with Mom that

I don't think anyone would be brave enough to start a conversation with me right now.

Except for Kai.

He's already half smiling when he opens his mouth. "You look like you're ready to hit someone."

"Shut up. I'm in mourning," I say sourly.

"Are you the one who killed the buggah? You come here fo' one alibi?" Kai laughs.

"God, you really are insensitive."

"My gift to you." He pauses, his eyes twinkling. "Whatchu want anyway?"

I roll my eyes. "I want to go to the beach."

"What—now you asking me out on a date, hapa?" he asks.

"No," I correct. "I'm being neighborly. You said your dad is giving you a hard time about getting out of the house, and I'm practically a walking charity case. I'm doing you a favor."

"Mmm." He crosses his arms. "It kinda sounds like you the one asking fo' a favor."

"Look, do you want to go or not?"

"Is this how you talk to all your friends?" he asks.

I throw up my hands. "Forget it."

When I'm back on the sidewalk, he shouts, "Okay, okay, okay. I go get my keys."

Kai drives to the beach in his mom's car. After we park, we make our way to the sand before pulling our flip-flops off and gravitating toward the edge of the water.

"Thanks," I say after a moment. It comes out in one rushed,

heavy syllable. I clear my throat. "I didn't really want to be alone in the house."

I'm surprised when he doesn't smile. He simply breathes in the salty air. "No problem. But just fo' let you know . . ." His voice trails off for a moment, and when it returns, his crooked grin makes an appearance too. "I would've wanted to hang out witchu anyway. Even if my dad wasn't giving me a hard time about surfing."

I pin my eyes to the caramel-colored sand. I know I have to focus on some part of what he said, so I go with the part that isn't about me at all. "Aren't you eighteen? He can't really tell you what to do anymore. You can do whatever you want."

Kai makes a face, but I don't look closely enough to know if there's any disappointment in it. "I don't know how your parents raised you, but if I talked back to my dad like that he'd slap me upside the head." He lets out a breath, dragging his feet through the sand. "Nah, it's easier to keep the peace."

I bite the side of my tongue. I don't understand his passiveness. I don't understand why he doesn't have more fight in him. It's *his* life, after all. Not his dad's.

"What about you? You have college plans?" he asks.

"I still have one more year of high school," I say, and a lump starts to form in my throat. This past year was the first time Lea and I had been in the same school together since junior high. We didn't have any classes together, but that didn't matter. It felt like we were finally closer in age somehow. It felt like we were finally where we were supposed to be.

I don't want to go back next year and walk around the hallways where she won't be. I don't want to have to see her friends without her there. To pass by the locker that no longer belongs to her.

Sometimes I'm not sure if there is anywhere left in the world I can look where I won't see the empty spaces she left behind.

Maybe we shared too much together. Maybe that's why it's so hard to live without her—because everything I did, she did too.

I look out into the ocean. The horizon is aqua and white and so very far away. I couldn't reach it if I tried. And maybe that's what I need—something out of reach. Something that never belonged to Lea, so I can do something—anything—where I don't see her.

Maybe that's what I need to be able to write again—to play an instrument again. Maybe music is only painful because Lea's still too close to my heart. Maybe I need her out of my head, even if only for a little while. I need enough time to finish "Summer Bird Blue." Enough time to keep my promise and finally give her the wish I owe her.

If I never write another song after that, well, at least I won't have let her down one more time. I already did too much of that when she was alive.

"Hey, next time you guys are all going back to Palekaiko Bay, can I come too?" I ask suddenly.

He looks surprised. "So you *do* like hanging out with us."

"I . . . kind of want to go surfing." Lea's never been surfing before, and she's never been to Hawaii, which means she can't be out there—in the water, beyond the waves. She can't exist in the place Kai goes to be free.

I don't know what it means exactly, or what it is I'm trying to do. But it feels like the start of something.

He looks surprised. "You never told me you knew how fo' surf."

"Mm-hmm," I say, which implies I mean *Yes, I totally do*, even though I totally *do not*. But Lea never knew how to surf either, and right now that's the only thing I care about.

He rubs the back of his neck. "You're welcome anytime, hapa." And then he straightens up and grins with the corner of his mouth. "How about tomorrow?"

I look up at him with narrowed eyes. "Are you going to make me wake up at seven in the morning?"

Laughing harder, he says, "We know each other so well."

CHAPTER EIGHTEEN

Gareth's truck smells like vanilla air freshener. I settle in the back next to a recycled grocery bag of snacks. There's not a lot of legroom, so I feel like my knees are up to my chest.

Kai looks over his shoulder. "You got enough room back there?"

I nod.

Gareth meets my eyes in the rearview mirror but doesn't say anything. The three of us eat dried pineapple and granola bars in the truck. I breathe through my nose, the vanilla becoming less overpowering the longer I'm in the car. I'm nervous, and I don't know why.

Maybe it's suddenly dawning on me that Kai's going to find out I lied about knowing how to surf. But I mean, how hard is it to float around on a surfboard and then balance for a couple of seconds? I've already watched Kai and Gareth do it. The waves weren't twenty feet high and towering over them like something out of a movie. They were baby waves. I can do baby waves, right?

This will be good for you, I tell myself. *To try something new. To take a break from the nightmare you're living.*

Gareth pulls up in a parking space next to the sand. I help carry a small cooler while he and Kai carry their surfboards toward the beach. Using the blue box as a seat while the boys survey the water, I start rethinking my plan for coming here today.

My fingers dig into my ribs. I watch Kai and Gareth pull their shirts off and toss them onto the sand in a pile.

"You can head out wit' Kai first if you want," Gareth says, stretching his arms out sleepily.

I look at Kai. Half-naked Kai who's drinking out of a water bottle like he's in a Gatorade commercial.

I've never really been nervous in front of a guy before, but I am in front of Kai. And not because of his missing shirt, but because it's becoming more and more likely that he's going to find out I know nothing about surfing.

But I need this. I need to have something that doesn't feel like it belonged to Lea.

Baby waves, I repeat to myself. Maybe I need to watch them surf for a while longer. Maybe I need to build my confidence up.

I mean, I never told Kai I was an expert. I just want to try something new without having to point out to anyone that I'm trying something new.

I don't want anyone to know I'm doing this to escape from Lea.

"You guys go ahead," I say, trying to buy more time. "I'll wait for Hannah to get here." I shrug casually, when inside I feel like there are bugs rolling around in my stomach. I try to focus on the waves—on what I came here to do.

He shrugs, takes hold of his surfboard, and heads down to the water.

Kai paces nearby, his phone in his hand and a strange look in his eyes.

"You all right?" I ask.

He looks up and shoves his phone beneath his shirt on the sand. "It's fine. I'll deal with it later. See you in a few?"

I nod a few times, and he hurries to join Gareth at the edge of the beach. I watch them paddle out to sea, working hard to fight the height of the small waves until they're far enough out to avoid being pushed back by the current.

I watch them become smaller in the distance. I hear his phone rumbling against the sand.

Hannah hasn't shown up yet, and I'm a little worried about getting a farmer's tan if I stay like this much longer, so I pull my shirt over my head while Kai and Gareth are far away and stuff it behind me.

God, I feel so vulnerable.

I convince myself I'm not nervous about the water or the surfing or the bikini top, but when the boys return I suddenly feel overwhelmingly embarrassed.

Thankfully, Kai doesn't notice.

He shoves a hand over his wet hair to clear his forehead. Drying his hands on a towel, he rummages under his shirt and finds his cell phone. He swipes a few times, frowning at the screen. "*Seriously?* You've got to be kidding me."

Gareth motions me off the cooler and finds a can of juice. He cracks the lid and gulps it down like he's been traveling across a desert. When he comes up for air, he looks at Kai. "Is dat Hannah? She close?"

"No," Kai says. "It's my dad." He shakes his head irritably. "Give me a second, brah. I have to make a phone call."

When he's about ten yards away he presses the phone to his ear. It's only a few seconds before his voice turns hurried and defensive.

Gareth chugs the rest of his juice and stuffs the empty can in the sand next to his leg. "Water's good today." He motions toward me. "Eh, wea' you learn how fo' sing? You eva take lessons?"

I pretend I can't hear Kai's conversation. I think Gareth's doing the same. "I just picked it up, I guess. Lea and I used to sing together, ever since we were little."

"Who?" he asks.

"My sister." I pause, looking at Gareth like I'm not sure if he's pretending or not. "Didn't Kai tell you?"

"Kai neva said anyt'ing about a sistah. Is she back on da mainland?" he asks innocently.

"She's dead," I say.

Gareth's face looks like someone just pushed him off the edge of a cliff and he's falling so fast he can't comprehend what's happening. "Oh, man. I'm so sorry. I didn't know dat." He shifts his knees, straightens himself, tries to figure out what to do with his hands. He's uncomfortable. It makes *me* uncomfortable.

I try to figure out why Kai wouldn't have told him. It would've made it easier for them, to know something like that so they could ask the right questions or avoid them if they wanted to. But then I wonder if he was trying to do me a favor—maybe he thought it would be easier for me if people didn't know.

Gareth is trying so hard to think of what to say next. He's like Aunty Ani. And suddenly I really appreciate Kai for giving me some time to feel human and whole, even if it was only pretend.

"You don't have to be weird about it," I assure him.

Gareth nods, but he still looks unsure. "I not so good wit' heavy kine stuff li'dat. But if you like talk wit' me about it, you can. I one good listnah." He pauses, then looks up at me with a raised brow and the fat part of his lip sticking out. "You like one hug?"

"I think I'm all right, thanks," I say, finding the nerves of someone who resembles a mountain to be a little amusing.

Gareth enters into a stream of consciousness about the weather. He doesn't stop until Kai returns.

"Sorry about that." Kai shoves his phone back under his pile of clothes.

"What did he want?" Gareth asks, probably relieved to have someone else to talk to again.

"He's pissed I'm here. Says he wanted me fo' help clean out the garage." Kai scratches the back of his arm and clenches his jaw. "Anyway, it doesn't matter. He's already mad, so I'll just talk to him when I get home." He forces a smile and nods to the water. "How about you, hapa? Ready fo' hit the waves?"

Not yet, my mind screams.

"Isn't Hannah going to be here soon? I'll wait for her," I say.

Kai opens his mouth like he's about to argue, so I add an extra lie. "There's something I wanted to talk to her about."

Gareth jumps up and grabs a football out of one of the bags. "Okay, we'll be back." He motions Kai to follow him. I'm pretty sure he asks him about Lea as soon as they're out of earshot.

I don't know how much time passes, but Kai's phone never stops ringing. When Hannah and Jerrod turn up, I'm almost used to the sequence of piccolo notes and chimes muffled beneath Kai's T-shirt.

Jerrod sets off down the beach with his phone, holding it out in front of him like it's a metal detector.

"What is he doing?" I ask.

Hannah snorts. "Taking pictures for his Instagram. He has, like, twenty thousand followers. It's so weird. I can never get any of the guys I like to notice me, and he's got girls in South Korea offering marriage proposals."

I can't imagine how anybody *wouldn't* notice Hannah. She's gorgeous. Maybe guys find her intimidating.

Alice once told me that it's important for girls to laugh a lot, especially if they're shy. Because guys mistake shyness for bitchiness, and that's the last thing a guy wants.

I think Alice gave terrible advice. I don't think girls should have to smile all the time in order to make other people think they're approachable. Maybe girls don't want to be approachable to everybody. And anyway, smiling is basically the same thing as lying. Most of the time when people smile, they're trying to hide what they're really thinking. *I don't trust you. I can't understand you.*

I'm finding this very uncomfortable. Good God, please leave me alone. The world would be so much more honest if people *didn't* smile all the time.

And quite frankly, anybody who would turn down Hannah for not being "approachable" doesn't deserve her.

Twirling her hair at the side of her chin, she purses her lips and makes a noise. "It's so warm today. I hope Italy is this warm."

"You're lucky you get to travel so much," I say. Lea and I used to dream of traveling around the world, singing in all the major cities and launching our careers. I don't think it will happen now. I think Hawaii might forever be the only pin on my map.

It wouldn't be the same without her.

Hannah leans back on her hands. "Yeah, it's pretty cool, I guess. Except the 'having to make new friends all the time' part. Do you miss your friends back home?"

I clear my throat. If Kai didn't tell Gareth about Lea, there's no chance he'd have told Hannah. "I've been too busy to really notice," I lie instead.

She makes a face, the skin around her nose crumpling. "Too busy hanging out with your neighbor?"

I stiffen. "It's not weird. Mr. Watanabe is cool. He doesn't ask questions and he doesn't—"

"Whoa, whoa, whoa," she interrupts me. "Calm down. I'm not talking about Mr. Watanabe." She lets out a harmless laugh. "I meant your *other* neighbor."

I look up and see Kai throw the football through the air like a spear, laughing casually as Gareth lands on his side to catch it.

"Oh," I say.

Hannah smiles without her teeth and shakes her head. "I know a crush when I see one."

"I don't have a crush on Kai," I correct quickly. "It's not like that. We're friends."

She sits up and lowers her chin. "I never said *you* were the one with the crush."

My cheeks darken. I don't say anything. What is there to say?

When the boys come back, they say they want to pick up Hawaiian barbecue for lunch. Gareth offers to drive but insists he isn't going by himself like someone's personal assistant. And when Kai offers to go, Jerrod insists he's not staying on the beach with Hannah and me like a third wheel. Hannah says we'll keep an eye on the surfboards and tells them to order her the pulled pork. I don't know what they have, so I tell them to surprise me.

When it's just the two of us, Hannah alternates between talking about movies, nail polish, music, and college majors like we're old friends hanging out.

When her phone rings, she leans forward excitedly. "Hello? Hey, can you hear me?" She looks at me and holds up a finger to say she'll be right back. "Sorry, Kyle. The service here is crap."

She paces around the sidewalk for a while before she finds a good spot near the parking lot. And suddenly it's just me, sitting on the beach, staring at the water with only my thoughts.

Her phone call seems like it's lasting forever. I'm watching the crash of sea-foam against the almond-colored sand, wondering what it would feel like to be a wave. You wait forever to have your turn on the shore, and in a matter of seconds it's all over. That one wave—that blanket of water—goes back into the sea. It's special for a moment, and then it's just like everything else.

And maybe that's like life. You live for a moment—one single moment. And then you don't matter. Because there are years of the past and years of the future, and we're all simply one tiny blip in time—a surge of water waiting to leave our mark on the sand, only to have it washed away by the waves that come after us.

And Lea, with her brief, tiny wave. She didn't get to make a mark. If she'd had more time, she would have been a hurricane.

I'm so tired—of remembering and hurting and missing and coping. I just want it all to stop. I need a *break*.

I'm not really thinking when I pick up Kai's surfboard and wander out into the water. I'm still wearing my jean shorts—I'm not really thinking at all.

The water washes over my feet, and it feels warm and cold all at once, like it hasn't been mixed through the whole way. It climbs up my knees, then my waist, and then my stomach is pressed to the board and I'm paddling my arms the way I watched the others do, slowly at first and then frantically because I don't have any technique.

And then I'm using my arms to scoop water behind me, and my eyes focus not on the waves in front of me, but the clouds.

I feel so much like a bird, soaring through emptiness, with the entire world in front of me. I don't stop moving my arms, but I don't feel like I'm swimming—I feel like I'm flying.

A memory

"Come on. It's not even that high." Lea tugs at my wrist, her brown eyes pleading the way a puppy does when they want to go out for a walk.

"Never going to happen." My arms are pinned tight across my chest, partly as a display of my stubbornness, but also because it hides part of *me*.

Lea might have Mom's tangled hair, but I have her curves. I hate swimming with Lea, because Lea is petite and adorable and she makes a bikini look the way it does in the online pictures. I look . . . full. And people stare at full.

Voices sound from far away. "Hurry up!"

"Come on!"

"Are you still up there?"

She moves to the edge of the cliff and cups her hands around her mouth. "We're coming, hold on!" She looks at me. "Please, I don't want to go by myself."

I open my eyes wide. "Why, so Mom has to plan two funerals instead of one? No way. I can't even swim."

"That's why Alex has the raft. All you have to do is doggy-paddle to the surface."

"Umm and jump like fifty feet toward my death."

"It's not that high."

"Doesn't matter. I'm still not jumping."

Lea's face goes still. She lowers her chin. "You have to. I'm using my first wish."

"What? No way. Wishes are supposed to be, like, favors, not you making me do something dangerous."

"A wish is a wish. Jump, Rumi."

I groan. My arms flop to my sides. "If I do this, it counts as two wishes."

Lea shakes her head. "Request denied. Want to hold my hand?"

I look at her seriously. "Don't let me drown."

She laughs. "Promise." She grabs my hand.

We step closer to the edge of the cliff, but I don't look down. I look out at the clouds and breathe through my nose.

"On three?" she asks.

I nod. "One."

"Two."

"Three." I take a breath.

We jump, and for a moment we're really flying.

I can feel her. I can feel her out here in the water, where there is nothing else and I'm not supposed to be reminded of her. I can feel her because she can never truly leave me.

I thought I could be free of her for a little while, but I failed. I can't escape her ghost.

It hurts to think about her, and I'm not sure that kind of pain will ever go away. Healing from a broken heart is exhausting.

More exhausting than anyone ever tells you. And yet . . .

If she's really out here in the blue mess of sky and sea, I never want to leave. I want to live in the same world as her. To breathe the same air as her. To fly beside her.

I want my sister back, and if the only way to find her is to swim out into the ocean where the horizon is empty and the clouds take over the sky, then I'll stay here in the water. I'll become a wave or a cloud or a bird if it means I can have my sister back.

My arms start to get tired, my head starts to spin, but I don't take my eyes off the clouds.

Lea.

Are you up there?

Answer me if you're there. If you can hear me. If you're somewhere.

I miss you so much.

The wave hits me hard—not because it's big, but because it's strong and I'm not paying attention. I'm too busy staring at the clouds that may or may not be my dead sister.

The board flips over, and I crash into the water, the salt and sea filling my nose and pulling me under. I kick and flail, reaching my fingertips up to the surface. For a split second, I'm free again, gasping for air and taking in deep breaths while my eyes scan for anything to grab on to.

But there's nothing. The board is gone, and I'm surrounded by the Pacific Ocean, and I feel myself falling back down because I don't know how to stay above the water. I try to focus, to calm down so that I can doggy-paddle to shore, but another wave pounds against my face and I'm far below again, the world turning a cloudy blue-green and the ocean burning through my nostrils as I desperately grasp for the sky.

It hurts until it doesn't, and right before everything goes black, I hear her voice again.

Her last word.

Rumi.

CHAPTER NINETEEN

When the salt water erupts from my lungs, I feel it heave up my throat and out of my mouth. Water is supposed to be a basic source of hydration, but nothing feels natural about almost drowning. It feels violent and foreign and so unbelievably painful.

I roll onto my side, coughing and gasping, and even though I can hear so many people talking at once, I can't make out a single word.

Eventually I take in enough air to process where I am. My hand squeezes a fistful of sand. I can still hear the ocean. And when I look up, I don't see Kai or Gareth or Hannah or Jerrod.

I see Mr. Yamada.

He's on his knees next to me, his thick brows furrowed with concern. The intensity in his eyes makes me feel empty and cold; his irises are like pools of black ink without a drop of color in them.

"Are you okay?" he asks, his voice like iron.

"Yeah." I cough into the sand. "I'm fine."

Kai appears over his dad's shoulder. His eyes are frantic. There's water dripping down his temples. "What happened?"

I shrug. "I don't know. I'm not very good at swimming, I guess."

He looks puzzled. The water on his cheeks drips down onto his dad's clothes, and that's when I realize Mr. Yamada is soaking wet too. They've both been in the ocean. I think they were both trying to save me.

Kai's dad snaps his head around, his jaw like the edge of a knife. "What were you thinking letting her go out into the water when she can't swim? What's wrong with you?"

Kai looks at me like he's staring at a puzzle with pieces that don't fit together. "You can't swim? You said you knew how fo' surf. . . ."

I pinch the bridge of my nose. It feels like it's about to gush blood, or maybe more salt water. "I just . . . I wanted to be out in the water."

"Why would you lie about something like that? You almost drowned." Kai doesn't look angry—he looks hurt.

I close my eyes to block the sun. I feel so dizzy. "I—it doesn't matter. Not anymore."

Mr. Yamada stands up, pulling Kai's arm with him. "I'm taking you home."

Kai yanks his arm away, the electricity in his eyes flashing like a bolt of lightning. "Don't grab me like that. I'm not a child."

Mr. Yamada clenches his jaw. "No more surfing. No more wasting your time here at the beach. You're too reckless—someone could've been killed today."

I squint, focusing on his eyes even though they're glaring down at me like they're steel blades. "It wasn't his fault," I say quickly. "He didn't know I couldn't swim. And even if he did, he's not my keeper."

"Both of you are irresponsible," Mr. Yamada says. "You for trying to get yourself killed and Kai for leaving you by yourself. You know better." He looks at his son. "You know how dangerous it is to go out in the water alone. We have rules in our family. You broke them."

"He didn't leave her by herself," Hannah interrupts, her voice smaller than I've ever heard. "I was here the whole time."

Gareth and Jerrod are standing beside her, their mouths clamped shut like they know better than to get involved.

Not that I need their help. I don't need anybody's help.

"I already said it was my fault," I say, standing. "And anyway, I don't need a babysitter. I can take care of myself."

"You almost died," Mr. Yamada yells, and my chest tightens. "I don't know what they teach you these days to make you think you're all invincible. This is the ocean. It's not a playground." He turns back to Kai. "If you want me to stop treating you like a child, then you need to stop acting like one."

Kai's face is red. He pulls his eyes away from his dad.

"Get in the car," Mr. Yamada says.

Kai pauses, his fists clenched, and then he stalks off toward the blue Mustang in the parking lot.

Mr. Yamada turns back to me, his dark eyes unshaking. "I don't want you hanging around Kai anymore. You're trouble—all of you—but especially you." He shakes his head. "You could've gotten my son killed too. You think it's easy to pull a body out of the water? When I got here he was trying to drag you out. What if I had lost my son today because he was trying to save your life? Use your brain next time."

And then they're gone, and I'm shaking and not talking and eventually Gareth talks me into getting in the car. When I get home, I don't change out of my clothes. I stand in the shower with the water running over me, pinning my eyes to the drain because it's the only thing that doesn't seem to be moving.

The rest of the world is spinning.

CHAPTER TWENTY

It's dark outside when I creep toward the space between my aunt's house and Kai's. It's mostly flat, with a few bushes and patches of grass that the lawn mower couldn't reach. I look up at his window. The blinds are flat against the glass, but there's light shining through.

I cup my hands over my mouth. "Kai," I whisper. When he doesn't answer, I try again. "Kai!"

There's nothing. No movement, no sound, no change at all.

I roll my tongue against my cheek. I need him to listen to me. I need to explain.

My eyes scan the grass beneath my feet. I follow the path to a gravelly bit near the back fence and pick up a few small stones. Parking myself far enough away from his window for the stones to reach, I squeeze them in my hand.

I throw one. It clicks against the window and bounces back off.

I throw another one. It misses, clattering against the window-sill and falling somewhere in the bush.

I take an extra step back and throw another stone.

It sails straight into the window with a loud crash, the glass puncturing like someone just punched a hole in it. Glittery bits of window fall to the ground, the blinds swaying in the space they left behind.

Fuck.

The blinds fly open, and Kai stares at the glass in horror before peering down and seeing me standing below.

"What the *hell*, Rumi?"

"I'm sorry," I hiss. "I was trying to get your attention."

"By throwing a boulder through my window?" he growls.

My face twitches. "How was I supposed to know your window was made of rice paper?" I growl back.

"My dad is going to kill me," Kai groans softly, a wave of realization washing over his face.

My heart quickens. "I'm sorry," I blurt out, like I'm throwing my words at him. "Not just about the window, but about the whole almost-drowning thing too."

Kai covers his face with his hands. "I'm dead. I'm literally dead."

"I can fix this," I say quickly.

His hands fly apart. "How? Are you as good at house repairs as you are at swimming?"

I roll my eyes. "Okay, you're mad at me. I get that."

"*Mad* at you?" Kai tilts his head back like he wants to scream. "You have no idea what you've done. My mom spent the entire night convincing my dad that I should be allowed to hang out with my friends until boot camp. He *barely* agreed. But when he sees this?" He shakes his head. "I'm screwed."

I shrug awkwardly in the grass, not knowing what to say. "I'll talk to him."

"Don't," Kai warns. "I don't want any help from you. You've done enough. Just . . . go home, Rumi." Not "hapa." He lowers the blinds, and just like that he's gone.

I ask Aunty Ani what she thinks I should do. She tells me to leave it alone. She says she'll talk to Mrs. Yamada about paying for the window.

I ask Mr. Watanabe what he thinks I should do. He tells me to be quiet and listen to the music.

So I ask the music what I should do.

It answers in ukulele strums and woodsy hums and soft claps. I feel like that's all the answer I need.

I knock on Kai's front door the next time I see the Mustang in the driveway. I'm not sure if Kai's home, but I don't care. This feels important.

Mr. Yamada pulls the door open and pushes the screen out in one fluid movement so that he's completely visible, the same way I am to him.

"What do you want?" he asks without breaking his stern face.

I lean back on my heels, feeling the weight of his presence trying to push me off the steps. "It wasn't Kai's fault. I'm the irresponsible one, not him. I'm the one who broke the window, just like I'm the one who decided to wander into the ocean by myself. Please don't punish him because of something careless I did."

He blinks.

I hate the silence, so I keep talking. "I don't really know why I even did it. The surfing, I mean. Not the window. I know why I broke the window. I mean, I didn't do it on *purpose*. I was only trying to get Kai's attention. Not by *breaking* the window, just by throwing a pebble at it, like they do in the movies, you know? Have you ever seen—never mind; that's not important. I guess maybe I underestimated the pebble, kind of like how I underestimated my ability to swim. I'm not very good at that, you know. *Thinking*. My head isn't in the right place these days. That's why I wanted to be in the water—to be free of everything clouding my head. But that's not an excuse—I should've been more responsible. I should've *thought*. About the swimming and the window," I pause and breathe. "And about how it could've put Kai in danger. I'm sorry about that part too."

It's quiet for a really long time.

Mr. Yamada's nostrils flare. "There's something wrong with you."

I nod. "I can see why you think that."

He assesses me, and I wait to be assessed. It's as uncomfortable as it sounds.

"I'll pay for it," I insist. "Tell me what the window costs, and I'll come up with the money somehow."

He takes a few moments to speak, and when he does his words are drawn out. "You need to learn how to swim."

I shift my weight to the other leg.

"If you're going to hang out with Kai," he says, "you need to learn. You might not care about your own future, but at least try to care about his. Never put him in danger like that again."

I look into the darkness of his eyes, and I see something I didn't notice earlier. They're like marbles, reflecting the world in an obscure, deformed way. I thought he was the kind of person who saw things in black and white, but maybe I was wrong. Maybe he doesn't see colors—maybe he sees shapes.

And suddenly I understand him more than I did before. Because maybe it's only when you understand mortality that you see things from so many different angles instead of shades.

He cares about Kai. He doesn't want him to get hurt. And maybe that's because he knows what it's like to lose someone. To watch their life end. Maybe he has his own Lea he carries with him all the time.

Or maybe I'm projecting feelings and emotions that are way more complicated than any seventeen-year-old should be dealing with.

Still. I wonder if I'll end up like Mr. Yamada one day. Trying to control things I simply don't have the right to control.

"I won't put Kai in danger. I promise," I say, and I mean it.

He nods. "And pay me back for the window before the summer ends." And then the door closes and I feel like a weight has been lifted off my chest and replaced with a different weight.

CHAPTER TWENTY-ONE

'm not really sure why I did it. At first I wanted to get away from
her. But then I felt her, out there in the water. It's like she was
calling me. I wanted to be near her." I look up from the floor.

Mr. Watanabe grunts from his chair and scratches the space
behind Poi's ears.

I relax back into the floor, the hum of the fan above me and the
scratch of the record player filling the room. "I don't want to die."
I pause. "Does that make me a bad person? Because I feel empty,
but not empty enough to want to die? Would a better sister have
wanted to kill herself?"

"Dat's a silly kine question," he says shortly. "Love no mean
fo' you go join da uddah persons in dea' grave. Mo' bettah you
live your life wit' honor. An' dat's how you goin' go honor da person dat you love—by living. If you go talk dying all da time, you
t'rowing your life away. You t'rowing away all dea' memories too."

"I guess." I take a deep breath. I don't know how to talk about
Lea without talking about death. They kind of go together now.

It's like talking about surfing without ever mentioning the ocean. They're a two-part deal.

"Now, be quiet. I like hear dis song." Mr. Watanabe leans back and closes his eyes. Poi settles her head in his arm, her nose tucked into his side.

I wait until I hear the rumbles of Poi's snoring. I know Mr. Watanabe's isn't far behind, and I don't really like hanging around during their naps. It makes me feel intrusive. And besides, I'm starting to think I've done enough sleeping for the time being.

I go back home and find Aunty Ani on the couch. She sits up straight when she sees me, brushing a long strand of hair away from her face.

With two fingers, she pushes a large package wrapped in white tissue paper across the coffee table.

I don't have to pick it up to recognize Mom's handwriting. *Rumi.* As if a single word is good enough. As if one word is going to make everything better.

Aunty Ani stands up and grabs her purse. "I'm going to the store. You need anything?" She's escaping while there's still time. It's probably a good idea.

"I'm fine," I say, and then it's just me and the package.

My fingers find the edge, and I rip the top off in one motion. Tilting the package to the side, I slide the contents onto my hand to reveal a journal. It's white with a small blue bird in the middle.

Of course it is. Because Mom always took our lyric ideas so literally. To her, "Summer Bird Blue" was *literally* a bluebird.

I wish I had it in me to smile, because I know Lea would've

laughed too. We would have told Mom she was a nerd, but it's one of the reasons we loved her so much. Because she was always, *always* our biggest fan, even when she got it so completely wrong.

She wanted to be a part of *us*. She wanted to be included.

Which is why I don't understand why she doesn't want to be included now, when it's just me and I need her so badly.

I open the cover. The pages are unlined and completely white, except for the first page. Mom left me a message.

> You've always had a beautiful voice.
> Please don't lose it.

It's a lyric journal.

I want to be furious at her for getting me such a nice present. I wait for the rage to build and build until it explodes from my chest like there's lava and fire and millions of orange and red embers all over the room.

But the anger doesn't come. It's been replaced with something else. Something that feels like thick cotton lodged in my throat, which disappears when I pay too much attention to it.

A memory

I open my eyes and see Mom flipping through one of our spiral-bound notebooks. We write all our lyrics in the spare pages between school assignments, but we've gone through so many notebooks now that it's starting to get confusing keeping track of everything. There are a lot of bent pages and folded corners and tape stuck to the edges like bookmarks.

Mom looks down at me and smiles. "You guys look comfy."

I look over at Lea, sleeping next to me in our cocoon of blankets. We took three of the dining room chairs and made a tent in our bedroom with a strip of Christmas lights that didn't make it on the tree this year.

"She didn't want to sleep in her own bed. I don't think she likes fourth grade," I whisper, careful to not wake Lea.

"Probably because it's her first time in school without you," Mom says gently.

"Maybe she could skip ahead to my grade. She's really smart, you know," I say.

Mom's teeth are like two rows of pearls. "I don't think it works like that, honey. Besides, don't you like having your own friends for a change?"

I shrug. "I'd rather have Lea."

She nods and waves the notebook. "You two are running out of space."

"If Babang sends Christmas money, we're going to buy a new one," I say.

Mom sets the notebook on the desk and leans into the tent. She plants a kiss on my forehead and covers me up with the blanket. "You go back to sleep. You've got school in the morning."

My head sinks into the pillow. "Did you just get home?"

She smiles. "I have to go back out. Night shifts are good money. Jenny's downstairs if you need anything, okay?"

"Okay."

"I love you."

"I love you too."

Mom kisses Lea on the cheek and waves her fingers at me one more time before slipping out of the room.

When we wake up in the morning, there's a new notebook waiting for us at the bottom of the stairs. And not a spiral-bound one—a thick moleskin one with a black cover and perfectly blank pages.

Lea's so happy she jumps up and down and squeals like a cartoon character. I want to thank Mom, but she's fast asleep in her bed, still wearing her makeup because she was too tired to wash her face.

I don't look at the blank pages now and think of how much I hate Mom. I think of how much Lea would've loved this gift.

Something cool fills my chest, like rain after a drought. Maybe this is my answer. Maybe Lea isn't out in the sea or in the clouds or somewhere out of reach. Maybe she's here in the blank pages, waiting for me to meet her, waiting for me to find my way back to her.

I try to let the words take over, the way they used to when it was just me and the music. I even find a pen in my room and open the journal to the first empty page.

But the lyrics don't come.

Lea might've loved this gift, but that doesn't mean I have to. Mom is trying to make up for not being here, the way she *always* tried to make up for not being there, and it's not good enough. Not this time.

I spent most of my life looking after my sister. I made excuses for Mom and took care of Lea when she couldn't be around. I was practically her second parent.

Mom's apologies and presents and excuses worked in the past because Lea was a child and because I didn't want Lea to feel abandoned the way I did. She was too young to understand about Dad and too naive to understand about Mom.

But I'm not a child, and Lea doesn't need my protection anymore.

And it should've been my turn to be the kid, not the parent. Not the understanding one, who accepts Mom's excuses and sees the world through rose-tinted glasses.

All those years I spent looking after Lea . . . Who was looking after me?

Who *is* looking after me?

Not fucking Mom, that's for sure.

Without really thinking, I start scribbling words into the journal. Angry, black scratches into the paper. But it's not a song.

It's a letter to Mom.

I tell her how angry I am that she left me.

I tell her how hurt I am that she's more absent with one daughter than she ever was with two.

I tell her she's the reason I can't write any lyrics, because I'm so full of rage that I can't concentrate on anything except for how mad I am.

I tell her that I need her, but I shouldn't have to tell her that—she should just know.

I tell her I resent her for never realizing how badly I needed to be a child now and then, instead of always looking after Lea.

I tell her I'll probably never forgive her for choosing to grieve alone, without me.

I tell her . . .

I tell her . . .

I tell her . . .

I don't stop writing until my wrist is cramped and I can hardly hold the pen, and even then, my brain is full of all the things I still need to say.

And when I look over my words, my heart pounding through my ears and my breath catching after every sentence, I feel a little bit lighter.

It might not be a song, but at least I wrote *something*.

CHAPTER TWENTY-TWO

Aunty Ani asks me how I plan to pay the Yamada family back for breaking their window when I don't have any money. I tell her that's a good question.

After lunch she tells me she's been to see Mrs. Yamada, and that she agreed to let me work part-time at Palekaiko Bay's hotel salon to pay off the "destruction charge." I'm not sure if those were Mrs. Yamada's words or Aunty Ani's, but when I show up at the hotel the next day, nobody acts like I've broken a window at all.

"Howzit?" Mrs. Yamada smiles from behind a woman with foils in her hair. She looks over her shoulder. "Jae-Jae, can you show Rumi around? Show her how everything works?"

"Oh, oh yeah," says a hurried voice. A young woman with a silvery-blond bob and sharp cheekbones appears from the back room. She curls her finger a few times in the air like she's trying to pull me toward her.

Up close, I can see flecks of rainbow-tinted glitter along her bottom eyelashes. Her perfume smells like cotton candy, and she's wearing acid-wash overalls that look like they've been hacked off above the knee with a pair of children's scissors. She also towers over me like she's a supermodel. Or a Christmas tree.

She smiles at me with just her lips. They're painted a matte purple. And not a dark, velvety kind of purple—it's more like a neon lilac.

"I'm Jae-Jae," she says. "Do you know how to use a cash register?"

I shake my head.

"What about a coffee machine?"

I shake my head again.

She pouts. "Okay. How about a broom?"

"That I can do," I say.

She laughs, and I'm sure a little bit of glitter falls out of her hair. "All right. You sweep. I'll teach."

I clean up a mess of black hair from beneath a chair. Each time a customer needs to pay for something, or someone asks for a hot drink while they're waiting for the hair dye to set, Jae-Jae shows me how to operate everything. At some point, we end up in the back room sorting through a box of supplies that needs to be unpacked.

Jae-Jae tells me she's been working at the salon for a year. She got the job because her mom and Mrs. Yamada are good friends. She tells me she auditioned to be in a K-pop group earlier in the year but didn't make it, and now she's not really sure what she wants to do.

"What about you?" she asks. "What are your plans after high school?"

A memory

"We should apply to the same university together. We could be roommates," Alice says, her eyes an alarming blue next to her angled black bob. "How cool would that be?"

I put a fresh piece of gum in my mouth, and the rush of spearmint envelops my tongue. "I don't know if I want to go to college."

She half shakes her head away and half rolls her eyes. She does that a lot, and I always feel like it's more for show than out of habit. Maybe it's the way she always looks around at the end, checking to see if anyone is watching her. "Everyone wants to go to college. It's basically like high school but with less homework and more freedom."

I shrug, eating another French fry and following her gaze around the cafeteria. Caleb is sitting with the captain of the cheerleading squad. Well, not so much sitting with her as practically lying on top of her. Their faces are pretty much just one face at this point.

I don't know when Caleb stopped being annoying and actually became popular, but I do know it happened after Alice broke up with him. If it had happened before, I think she might have stuck it out until the end of the year. Or at least until prom was over, so she would have had a genuine chance at junior prom queen.

Alice is scowling at the two of them. I'm scowling too, but for very different reasons. I scowl at everyone who thinks it's not disgusting to swap spit in the middle of a public cafeteria.

Sighing, she turns back to me, not realizing I still haven't replied to her. "I can't wait to get out of here. I want to meet new people. A fresh crop of boys."

There was a time I thought we'd be best friends forever—and then she kissed Caleb and turned into kind of a snob.

But something else happened too. Lea grew up. She went from being my baby sister, to my little sister, to my younger sister, to just my sister. She evolved into my best friend. And to be honest, if I'm going to go to college with anyone, it's going to be Lea. She's the only person I know besides Mom who doesn't make me want to punch myself in the face. And she gets me—like, really gets me. I don't feel like I have to constantly explain myself, or justify why I feel the things I feel. She doesn't think it's weird I'm not interested in romance or college or anything besides music. And she doesn't hate me even after all the times I've been horrible to her.

"I want to write music. With Lea," I say. "We talked about going to college at the same time, for music. But in the meantime, we want to try to get a record deal together."

Alice brushes hair out of her eyes. "Your sister is

only a freshman. What are you going to do for two years while you're waiting for her to graduate?"

I scrunch my nose. "What's wrong with waiting?"

"It's kind of a waste of time, no?"

"No. Because I'm waiting *for* something."

"That sounds pretty lazy."

"Lea and I have a plan. That's not lazy—that's following our dreams."

Alice looks irritated. Not at me, but because Caleb doesn't even seem to notice she exists anymore. "Well, that's fine, I guess, as long as you don't care that you'll be two years behind everyone else your age."

I eat another French fry, and then another and another, just so I don't have to keep talking to Alice about things she doesn't understand.

Two years behind. What is the rush? Why does everyone think I should be in some big hurry? What am I supposed to be running toward?

I hate it. I hate the rushing, and the expectations, and the pressure.

It makes me feel like I'm behind everyone else. Even behind *Lea*, who is so sure of herself and confident about what she wants that I don't know how I'm ever supposed to catch up.

I just want to make music with my sister for the rest of my life. Is that so much to ask?

It takes me a second to realize Jae-Jae looks weirded out because I'm almost snarling. I try to look like a normal teenager about to become a senior in high school. I imagine it looks something like Hannah—excited about the future, prematurely tired of school when there's still a year left, and anxious to *go*.

But the truth is, I'm not in a hurry to go anywhere. I'm not sure my dreams mean anything anymore because they died with Lea. Maybe all I have left now is the knowledge that we live before we die—everything in between is simply extra effort to keep ourselves from hitting our expiration dates too early.

It's scary trying to decide what I'm supposed to do with all that extra time. I mean, it could be days or months or years. What if I live to be one hundred? What if I only make it until the end of next week? Does everything in the middle become a waste, because there wasn't enough time to finish what I've started? And what about things I don't know the answers to? Like, what if I die before I ever play an instrument again? What if I die without knowing what my favorite hot dog topping is? What if I die before I ever have sex? Or before I figure out if I ever *want* to have sex?

It's a lot of pressure. Maybe it's easier to not make any final decisions ever again. Because Lea and I were so sure we were going to get recording contracts and tour the world. Look how well that turned out.

I look at Jae-Jae with fleeting interest. "My only plan right now is to get the money to pay Mrs. Yamada back. After that . . . I don't know." It's sort of the truth. I have to finish "Summer Bird

Blue" too, but I'm not sure I'm ready to talk about music to anybody yet. I think maybe I need to keep it to myself for a while, until I'm ready to acknowledge what finishing our last song really means.

After "Summer Bird Blue," everything I do will be on my own, without any trace of Lea.

And I find that so much more terrifying than not having a plan for the future.

We spend the rest of the afternoon barely talking, not because Jae-Jae gives up on me, but because I'm not sure I want to make any more friends when I'm going to be leaving soon anyway. I think it's better if I don't get attached. I think it's better if I just pretend I'm a ghost—here one moment and gone the next.

CHAPTER TWENTY-THREE

Poi brushes her whiskers against my cheek, her cold nose making my face recoil. "Stop that," I say, pressing my hand against her body. She jumps over my stomach and settles on the other side of me.

Mr. Watanabe is whistling in the kitchen along with the music. It's piano music today. It sounds like salt and whispers and abandoned lighthouses.

I take a breath through my nose—he's cooking something with fish, but it doesn't smell exactly like fish. It's sweeter, somehow.

"What is that?" I call out.

"Food," he answers.

"Yeah, but what kind?"

"Good food."

"Yeah, but what is it?"

"Fish."

"Yeah, but what kind of fish?"

"You ask too many questions. If you like know what kine food dis is, den you try cook next time."

I roll my eyes and sit up, pulling my knees back so my legs are shaped like a diamond. "Can I use your bathroom?"

He grunts.

I look down the hall at the three doors. "Which one is it?"

"Da one where da toilet stay."

I snort before pushing myself up and making my way to the first door on the left. I peek inside. It's the bathroom. I walk in, turning to close the door, when something in the room across from me catches my eye.

It's large, and black, and has eighty-eight keys.

I swallow.

I didn't know Mr. Watanabe played the piano. Why didn't I know that?

I can't help it—magic runs through my bloodstream when I see a piano.

My skin tingles like someone turned up the amp. My fingers twitch like they've been starved for years. My heart beats like it's begging for a song. And before I know it, I'm standing in the next room, my right hand hovering over the ivory and black keys, and I forget everything but the notes fluttering through my brain like a never-ending song.

I don't remember sitting down, or pressing my foot against the right peddle, or even caressing my fingertips along the keys. But I do remember the first note that leaps through the room like a fish falling back into the sea. It sounds like everything good in the world. And then I lose myself to the instrument, as if my skin and the piano are all connected as one being.

My fingers fly around the keys, playing one of the many songs that never really leave me. Because music is more powerful and familiar than breathing. Playing the piano again feels like my sight and hearing and sense of touch have all returned in one single moment. It feels like living again.

At the end of the song, I barely take a breath. My fingers jump into the next piece in my repertoire, like a playlist from my memory that can't be stopped. It's good to feel something that isn't hate or anger or hurt. It feels like I'm here, living somewhere within the sounds.

Could that be where Lea lives too? Is that why music hurt so much before?

I don't want to be afraid of finding my sister anymore. I don't want to be afraid of the ache in my chest.

I just want her back.

I think I play at least five more songs before I hear the sound of Aunty Ani's car pull up and realize I'm still in Mr. Watanabe's house and not in the most perfect dream I've had in months. I take a breath, step away from the piano with shaky hands, and walk back to the living room like I'm standing on a conveyor belt.

Mr. Watanabe is sitting in his chair with something heavy and cruel in his eyes. The record player is off, and I think something might be burning in the oven.

I've hurt him. Somehow I've hurt him.

The fan above me spins in fast circles, the seamless motion making me feel faint.

A memory

Dad's strawberry-blond curls flop around every time he shakes his head. He's pacing around the room in circles, like the train ride at the carnival. Around and around and around.

"I can't take it anymore," he says.

He doesn't see me watching from the hall. Mom doesn't either—she's too busy crying.

"One kid was hard enough, but two? I didn't want this, Mamo. I didn't want to be a parent this young," he says.

"It doesn't matter what you wanted—this is what you got," Mom sputters.

I squeeze the edge of the doorframe, feeling the wood between my fingers. Watching them.

"I have my whole life ahead of me. I cannot waste any more of it on"—he waves his hand around erratically—"*this*."

"You're their father. You're a part of their lives whether you want to be or not," Mom says. Her shoulders are shaking.

Dad sighs, reaching for her, but she shoves his

hands away like they're covered in something dirty. Something contagious.

"You selfish bastard," Mom growls.

I feel my heart jump. Mom never swears. Mom never yells.

"I'm sorry," he says. "I only get one chance to live my life. I want to really live it."

"If you do this," Mom hisses, "if you leave now, you don't ever come back. It's not a revolving door—I'm not going to let you break our daughters' hearts again and again."

He blinks. There aren't any tears. "Okay. Okay."

Mom breaks down into a horrible sob, bending over and squeezing her stomach like she's going to be sick.

Dad leans down. "I'm so sorry. I tried. But"—he pauses, closing his eyes and twisting his jaw—"it's just too much. You know I never wanted this. I don't have enough of me to spread around between you and two kids. I'm losing myself. I want to be me again. If we didn't have Lea, I could cope better. But two of them . . ."

Mom starts to say something, but I'm already running to the bedroom.

Lea is in her toddler bed, curled up like a puppy, her blanket pushed down to her ankles. I take her hand and sit beside her, watching the door and waiting for footsteps.

If we didn't have Lea. And I don't understand what any of the shouting and the fighting and the horrible words mean, but I know Dad is saying he doesn't want Lea.

I won't let him give her away. I won't let anyone take her from me. I'll protect her. I'll keep her safe. I'll keep her *here*.

I watch the doorway until I'm too tired to keep my eyes open.

Lea is still there in the morning, but Dad never comes home.

I was supposed to protect my sister, but I didn't. Sometimes I *couldn't*.

I hurt people, even when I don't always mean to. I don't want to hurt anyone the way Dad hurt us—the way he hurt Mom. But I can't help it. Maybe I'm too much like him. Because I say things and do things and I never know how to take them back. Sometimes I don't even know I *want* to, until too much time has passed. It's hard to apologize right away. It's even harder to apologize later on, because then you have to relive arguments all over again.

I should've apologized to Lea. I should never have hurt her the way I did.

The way I've somehow hurt Mr. Watanabe now.

Poi lifts her head from the floor, looking between us with her small pink tongue dangling from her mouth. For all her barking and yapping, she's the world's worst guard dog, letting me into Mr. Watanabe's life. She should've done more to protect him, just like I should've done more to protect Lea.

I walk out the front door and close the screen behind me.

CHAPTER TWENTY-FOUR

I go with Aunty Ani to the mall because I can't go back to Mr. Watanabe's, and I'm still not sure if I'm allowed to hang out with Kai or not. Or, more accurately, I'm not sure he *wants* to hang out with me.

The mall looks like the ones back home in Washington, two stories and split down the middle, but there's no roof and there are trees everywhere. We have chicken long rice for lunch, which isn't rice at all—it's more of a stew made up of clear mung bean noodles, ginger, onions, and lots of chicken.

Aunty Ani is being so careful not to set me off that she doesn't ask me a single question—she never stops talking, like she's worried the silence will give me an opportunity to yell at her for something.

"Shave ice at the mall is junk, but the one at the hotel is ono. We can drive by later. I thought maybe we could see one movie first, because I know you like da kine animated films, and there's a new—"

"I don't," I interject. She stops, her mouth frozen midword. "Lea was the one who liked cartoons."

Aunty Ani looks frazzled, like she knows she's a pile of confetti that's about to be thrown in the air and end up all over the floor, but she's powerless to stop it.

I try to relax my face. I didn't bring my weapons today. "I like superhero movies. I think they have a new Marvel one playing, if you want to see that instead."

She nods so many times. I think she's trying not to burst into tears. "Oh, oh, okay. We can do that. I'll get us one of those big snack boxes, you know, with the nachos and popcorn? Or I could get two, if you want your own." She pauses, still nodding.

"I'm full. But thanks." I force a smile, but I'm pretty sure it still comes out like a grimace.

Aunty Ani almost explodes into an exasperated sigh. "You're welcome, Rumi."

I try to tell myself it feels nice to not be hurting someone for a change, but there's a miserable itch in my chest that makes me want to shout and thrash and snarl at everyone and everything around me. But I tell that urge to shut up. I tell it to quiet down, because Lea would be horrified if she saw how I was treating Aunty Ani. They always got along, the two of them, even though they hardly saw each other. I think it's because Lea was so easy to get along with. She was like a baby animal. You'd have to have a truly wicked heart to look at her and not feel some sliver of joy.

After the movie we take the long route along North Shore. I

tell her I don't want any shave ice, but I wouldn't mind looking at the water.

Because I still think she's out there, somewhere beyond the waves. Lea, with her goodness and giggles and heart made of pink cotton candy. Sometimes it feels like she's waiting for me, but I don't really know what for.

Aunty Ani notices the way I'm watching the ocean—like I wish it would tell me what to do next. "If you like try surfing lessons, I could set that up fo' you. It might be a nice way to spend the rest of the summer, having something fo' do every week."

I dangle my fingers out of the window to feel the wind push against them. I imagine I'm a bird, fighting against the breeze. Birds are lucky—they can fly away whenever they feel like it. They can disappear, start over, exist somewhere else. I'm not a bird—I can't just spread my wings and go.

I clear my throat. "I'm not really interested in surfing, to be honest."

She's quiet for a while. "Then why did you do it?"

She means why did I go out into the water and almost get myself killed.

"I wanted to do something that didn't have anything to do with Lea. I guess I thought it might help." And when she doesn't reply, I add, "It didn't."

It feels like a small victory, to answer one of Aunty Ani's questions without snapping at her. I wonder if finding Lea again has anything to do with it.

I can practically feel her pinching me behind the arm, telling me to be nice. My mouth twitches. It's almost a smile.

Aunty Ani hums like she understands, but I'm not sure she really does. I don't think she knows the right way to take care of a grieving teenager. She still thinks popcorn and shave ice is going to fix me.

"I do want to learn how to swim, though," I say suddenly. It surprises me, since I didn't know it was something I even wanted. Maybe it's not about trying to escape my sister's memory—maybe I just need to feel free again. *Alive* again.

I don't know anything more alive and free than the water.

She turns her head toward me slightly. "Yeah? You like me find you one teacher?"

I shake my head. "No. I have someone I can ask." At least I think I do. Even if Kai won't talk to me ever again, there's still Hannah. Or maybe even Jae-Jae—it would be weird for someone to live in Hawaii and not know how to swim, right?

"I'm not sure Uncle George—Mr. Watanabe—has da kine patience fo' swimming lessons," Aunty Ani says, and it takes me a second to realize she's joking.

I almost laugh, but the weight lodged between my throat and my chest keeps it from coming out. "No, probably not. I think he'd leave me out there for the sharks if he thought it would get rid of me."

"Why do you say that?" She frowns. "I thought you two were friends."

I pull my hands into my lap, clasping my fingers together. "I don't know what we are. I think I upset him." Kai's face flashes in my mind, along with all the broken bits of glass still hidden in the yard. "I think I've upset all your neighbors, now that I think about it."

"The Yamadas? No. I already talked to them about the window. They know it was one accident," she replies with a shrug. "Sun and I are old friends. We went to school together—she knew your mom, too."

My heartbeat quickens. "She was friends with Mom?"

Aunty Ani nods. "Sun is the same age as me, but your mom and I used to be really close—the three of us were always together." There's a memory behind her eyes. I wonder if I look that way when I remember moments with Lea.

"What happened?" I ask.

She looks surprised. "What do you mean?"

"You said you used to be close, but you don't seem close now. I mean, before Lea's funeral I can't even remember the last time you were up visiting." I don't mean to sound like I'm scolding her, but I think my voice somehow defaults to that setting.

Aunty Ani presses her lips together, thinking. "We grew apart, I guess. When your mom met your dad, she found out she was pregnant pretty quick. He wasn't right fo' her, but she never like listen to me or your babang. She moved to the mainland with him, to try to make it work.

"I was angry with her. It felt like she was leaving me, too. And I said a lot of things I probably shouldn't have. And after Lea was born and your dad left—well, she didn't come back home. Maybe she was waiting fo' me to ask, maybe I was waiting fo' her to ask—

but we just never really found each other again. We talked on the phone sometimes, but it wasn't like how it was when we were younger." She offers me a small smile. "It was my fault, though. I shouldn't have been so hard on her. Not when she was trying fo' do the right thing."

"You're just saying that because you don't want me to be hard on her," I say without missing a beat.

She nods. "Maybe. But that doesn't make it any less true."

"She deserves it. Everything I'm feeling."

"I know."

"Then why do you keep making excuses for her?"

"Because I've watched her try fo' do the right thing her whole life. It doesn't mean she doesn't make mistakes. She loves with her whole heart, and sometimes that muddles things up, but she always tries."

"She didn't leave you the way she left me. It's not the same."

"That's true. But she loves you more, too."

I chew the inside of my mouth. *I don't know about that,* I want to say, but I know Aunty Ani wouldn't understand. She wasn't around enough to see how Lea was Mom's favorite.

I wonder if Lea and I would've grown apart the way Mom and Aunty Ani did—and as soon as I think it, I know it would've never happened.

We would've always been close. We would've always found our way back to each other.

Which is why I need to find my way back to Lea now.

I need her—life without her doesn't make any sense.

I pause. "It really was an accident, you know—breaking that window."

Aunty Ani laughs. "It's okay. It's only a window." Her face stills, and suddenly she looks so much like Mom. They have such different smiles—Mom's is wild and excitable, and Aunty Ani's is warm but reserved. But when they're lost in their own thoughts, their mouths rest in the same uneven line, and their eyelids fall like they're tired. In these moments, they are unmistakably sisters. "Sometimes you have to break things. Sometimes you need to smash a window or two before you start to feel better."

I lean my head back, wondering if I'll keep any parts of Lea's face the older I get. We had so few similarities to begin with besides our love of music. She was thoughtful and sweet and would get excited over a new toothbrush. Mom always said I was a tough critic, but Lea would give praise to a dalmatian for having spots. And Lea's eyes always had that little bit of green in them, like seaweed left on a stretch of golden sand. Mine are plain brown, like chocolate ice cream without any toppings. And our expressions were always different—with Lea, everything went up, up, up to the sky like her face was a balloon that was always trying to float away. Mine droops and sinks like I just can't be bothered, and maybe that's how our personalities were too.

But we had the same nose and maybe the same hands, because if we ever took a photograph of our fingers playing an instrument, we could hardly ever tell whose hands were whose.

I look at my hands. Lea's hands. The hands that want to tear down the world.

And I know Aunty Ani's wrong. There aren't enough windows in the world I could break to make me feel better.

But I'll try not to break them if it means protecting my hands.

Because from now on, every single day I age is another day Lea won't have—another day her hands won't change. When I look at my hands, I'll be able to see what hers would've looked like too.

I need that to mean something, just like I need the ocean to mean something, because I'm running out of things that mean anything at all.

CHAPTER TWENTY-FIVE

I bring Kai a peace offering: an incredibly awkward smile and all the money I've earned so far from working at the salon.

He's wearing a black T-shirt with the outline of a gecko on it and a pair of pink and gray flowered board shorts. When he realizes what I'm holding, he snorts. "Is that a bribe?"

"No. A debt." I pause. "Didn't your dad tell you?"

He sighs, pulling his lean, muscular arms across his chest. "Of course he did." He narrows his eyes. "You didn't have to do that, you know. Talk to him. He would've ended up letting me surf anyway. He talks big, but the truth is he hasn't been around long enough to have a real say in what I do." He shrugs. "Sometimes my mom lets him think he does, that's all."

I wave the money in front of him. "Just take it. My arm is getting tired."

He does, folding the cash between his palm. "So, you coming back to the beach, or what?"

"Am I allowed?"

"My dad doesn't own the beach."

"I didn't mean your dad."

"What did you mean?"

I shuffle my feet. God, why does he have to make everything so painful? "Well, I didn't know if you wanted us to hang out anymore."

"As long as you stop throwing rocks at me." A grin appears on the left side of his face.

I feel my body stiffen, and it's the first moment I realize how nervous I've been about coming here to see him.

Kai releases his arms and shakes his head. "You look like one puffer fish holding all the air in—whatever you want to say, just say it."

"Can you teach me how to swim?" The words rush out of me like a wave.

He blinks.

"I thought maybe, you know, the basics would be good. For safety purposes. And also because your dad said I can only hang out with you if I learn how to swim."

He blinks again, chewing his thoughts, and eventually shrugs. "Okay. Tomorrow morning?"

I nod, and a twisted knot forms in my throat. I wish it wasn't so hard to be grateful for a change, but my God it's so hard with Kai. He smiles too much, like he's constantly ready to laugh himself out of an argument. Besides, I'm not good at thanking anybody right now. It makes me feel like I have things worth being thankful over, when really I feel like I've been dealt the crappiest hand in the world.

So I press my mouth together and give him a thumbs-up. He laughs for all the seconds it takes me to get back inside the house.

The next day, when we are in the water, Kai makes me lean against a boogie board. I feel like a child.

"There's nobody even here," he growls. "Stop worrying about whatchu look like."

"I mean, I might as well wear those inflatable tubes around my arms if I'm just going to be announcing to the world I can't swim," I say dryly, spitting the seawater back out of my mouth.

"You're impossible."

"I think there's a shark in the water."

"There's no shark."

"I saw something move."

"Where?"

"There. To your left."

"That's my leg."

"Why is it moving that way?"

"Because that's how you swim." Kai lets out an exasperated sigh. "You goin' try fo' take this seriously or what?"

"I am taking this seriously," I growl back. "I'm holding on to this giant piece of Styrofoam, aren't I?"

Kai tells me about moving my arms and legs and the rhythm to use to keep my head above the water. At first I find him really annoying, maybe because I don't like being told what to do, but after a while I get used to the way he's trying to teach me.

By lunchtime I can doggy-paddle around the boogie board without sinking, which is kind of what I could already do before, but I don't tell Kai that because he seems to think I'm learning quickly. And who am I to turn down a compliment?

We take a walk to a nearby McDonald's. I order saimin—yes, they have *saimin*—and French fries. We eat, talk about why I never learned to swim—wasn't interested—and why Kai took up surfing—because Gareth was doing it—and why I keep hanging out with Mr. Watanabe even though he's really old.

"I don't know," I say. "We have a weird understanding. We can be in the same room and not speak, and that feels good sometimes."

It's also the only place where music doesn't hurt me. If it weren't for Mr. Watanabe and his records, I'd probably still be hiding from Lea's ghost—hiding from the promise I made her.

I know I haven't been able to find the strength to finish our song, but going to Mr. Watanabe's house is helping me heal. Being around his music—it puts a little bit of life back into my soul.

I don't think Kai would understand. I don't think *anyone* would understand.

"He always has the most annoying dogs," Kai says, taking a drink. "Before Poi he had one Shiba Inu called Marnie. She would jump the fence and chase me and Gareth out of the neighborhood. It was terrifying."

"Has it always been just him and a dog? He was never married?" I ask.

"Not that I know of. You guys never talk about whether he was married or not?"

"I told you, we don't really talk," I say tersely. I think of Mr. Watanabe's face after he heard me play the piano. I think of how much pain was in his eyes. "I think he lost someone. Someone that might've been a bigger deal than a dog."

"You might be underestimating how much people love their pets," Kai says.

"I'm not saying people don't love their pets, but they usually don't feel haunted by them once they're gone. Mr. Watanabe has a ghost in his eyes."

"You have that too." His eyes soften, like he's lowered the electricity to a hum. Like he thinks a hum can't do any damage.

He has a freckle near the corner of his eye, right above his left cheekbone. A softness in his lips. Ears that stick out too far, which he hides beneath all his messy black hair.

Hums are dangerous.

I pull my eyes away from him and focus on the remaining French fries.

We finish our food, walk back to the beach, and spend another hour and a half swimming in the ocean. Kai tries to get me to put my head under the water without pinching my nose, but salt and sea keeps rushing through my nostrils and down my throat, and at some point I tell him I've had enough for the day.

Still, we spend more time laughing than being frustrated, and by the time he drives me home, I actually feel like I might have had a little bit of fun.

CHAPTER TWENTY-SIX

When Mr. Watanabe opens the screen door, he considers me the way someone considers a piece of fruit at the grocery store, unsure whether I'm worthy of being let into his home. He shifts his jaw around like he's eating food, but I'm pretty sure the only thing he's chewing on are his thoughts.

"Wea' you been? You no like fo' visit me no moa?" he asks.

I shrug. "I thought you were mad about the piano."

He grunts like I've never been more wrong. "I make too much shoyu chicken an' nobody stay here fo' eat it. Now have too much leftover." He pushes his chin out so his entire face becomes a frown.

I look down at Poi. She's standing near his feet, wagging her tail from behind the screen, a soft whimper rising from her throat. I think she actually missed me. Maybe Mr. Watanabe did too.

"I didn't know about the chicken," I mumble awkwardly.

He pushes the door open and I follow him inside, leaving my flip-flops on the mat behind me. For a while we don't talk, and I find a place on the floor and let Poi snuggle into my lap. She snuffles a little while she tries to get comfy, and after a few minutes she nestles her head over my thigh and lets out a tired sigh.

Mr. Watanabe disappears into another room, and when he comes back he's holding a square-shaped wicker basket filled with stacks of folders and paper.

"What's that for?" I ask when he sets it in front of me and parks himself on the edge of the couch.

He grunts and points.

I peer into the basket and see notes and bars and treble clefs and bass clefs and words written in Italian. Pages and pages of sheet music, most of them covered in light pencil markings, and all of them worn around the edges and yellowed with time.

I turn them back and forth in my hands, looking through the basket like it's pirate treasure and every single page is of value. I hear the music in my head, read the way the melody rises and falls, and my mind is racing with so many notes and sounds that I don't even realize how deathly quiet the room is until I put all the sheet music back in their tomb.

Mr. Watanabe is watching me, and even though his eyes are perfectly still, there's something wild and racing inside them that makes me feel like I'm in a hurry.

"Why are you showing me this?" I ask him.

"So you can practice," he says stiffly. "Even dat Mozart guy wen' practice."

"How long have you been playing?"

He waves his hand, dismissing my question. "I no can play piano."

"Why do you have a piano, then?"

His eyes find mine, and it doesn't matter that they're small—they're so full of the world and life that I think they might swallow me up. "Dis my wife's one."

And because death feels more like family than a stranger, I forget what it means to be sensitive about something so dark. "What happened to her?"

Mr. Watanabe doesn't stop looking at me. He twists his mouth and moves his cheeks around like a rabbit waking up from a long nap. "She died long time ago. Cancer."

"That sucks," I say.

"Yeah," he says.

And then I pick up the basket of music, take a place at the piano stool, and practice until the sun goes down. I don't write any of "Summer Bird Blue," but I'm still playing an instrument. I'm still making music.

It feels like a step in the right direction.

Eventually Mr. Watanabe calls me to come eat some of the leftover shoyu chicken.

I don't tell him that my eyes wandered around the room. I don't tell him that I saw the picture frames on the wall. I don't tell him that I saw him and his wife and a little boy.

And I certainly don't ask him what happened to the boy and why he has a son who never comes to visit.

Because there are no photographs of a teenager or a young man. Just pictures of a little boy, frozen in time much too young. A child who will never grow up.

Just like Lea.

CHAPTER TWENTY-SEVEN

Jae-Jae pushes the cash register closed and taps her glittery black nail along the table. She's wearing high-waisted white shorts and a pink T-shirt with the face of a cat on it. Her hair is slicked back against her head, and her makeup is just as perfect and glittery as every other time I've seen her.

"You should let me cut your hair," she says suddenly, her eyes dazzling like genuine topaz.

"Why? What's wrong with it?" I ask defensively.

I haven't cut my hair in years, and I blame Lea for that. I've threatened to chop it off so many times. I wasn't blessed with her and Mom's carefree curls—my hair is bland and boring.

But Lea liked practicing on mine. She said it was easier to braid than hers. So I let it grow longer and longer until it slowed somewhere in the middle of my back. And I got used to Lea playing with my hair all the time. It was nice—like she wasn't the little sister I was still taking care of. Instead, she was the one taking care of me. And I guess that felt nice, to not be the second parent. To be her equal.

I can feel her fingers sometimes, scraping against my scalp and weaving through the black strands that don't understand the meaning of the word "volume." I don't know how I feel about cutting my hair now—the hair that Lea loved. Once it's gone, it will be gone forever. I'll never have hair again that Lea played with and giggled behind and envied at times. I'll have hair that Lea's never seen.

Jae-Jae shrugs. "Nothing is *wrong* with it. I mean, you do kind of have that Wednesday Addams thing going on."

"Who?" I repeat.

"*The Addams Family*? Tim Burton? Nineties classic?" Jae-Jae looks horrified.

I shake my head.

She sighs, and it's almost a purr. "You don't know the joy you're missing. Everything good came from the nineties, but for some reason it's the most underrated decade of all time."

The door opens and Kai walks in. The light shines behind him, and he almost looks like a shadow with his dark complexion and his sturdy frame. When he sees me, he throws his hand up in a shaka sign.

"Howzit?" he asks, leaning over the counter. His hair has sharp, angled lines; he looks like he could be one of the hair models plastered all over the room. Even Jae-Jae is staring at him almost giddily.

Hannah was wrong about Kai being pretty. He's bordering on unrealistic, even if he does have big ears and a weird freckle. I wonder if anyone else has noticed it before? I kind of hope they haven't. I kind of want to be the only one who knows there's a freckle in the corner of his eye, that there's the tiniest hint of red in his hair when the sun shines on it, that one of his eyes is half a millimeter smaller than the other, that sometimes he smells like burnt sugar and firewood, and that sometimes when he catches me smiling, he looks like someone who made it through an entire piano piece without making a single mistake. Like making me smile is a triumph.

I also kind of want Jae-Jae to stop looking at him the way she is.

I swivel my chair back and forth like I'm bored. Mrs. Yamada is rinsing someone's hair at the back of the salon, and Jae-Jae is waiting for her next nail appointment to turn up. There are two other girls who normally work here too, but one called in sick and the other is on her lunch break. It's a slow day.

"Is that Kai?" Mrs. Yamada calls from the back. "Did you pick up lunch?"

"It's here," Kai replies, lifting a semi-transparent white bag onto the counter. "They didn't have Spam musubi, so I got you the beef curry."

"Did you get some for the girls?" she asks, appearing at the top of several steps. A woman with a towel wrapped around her head follows her to one of the chairs.

Kai nods. "Beef curry fo' everybody."

Jae-Jae reaches into the bag and takes one of the boxes. "Thanks, Aunty Sun."

"You're welcome, my dear," Mrs. Yamada replies in a singsong voice right before the hair dryer drowns out the noise.

Kai holds up his hands and jokingly scoffs in Jae-Jae's direction. "What about me? You think the food walked in here by itself?"

Jae-Jae taps him on the nose once. "Thank you, Kai. You're a real sweetheart."

I stop swiveling the chair back and forth and feel the coil of something green crawling through me.

He lets his arms drop and smiles proudly. He pulls two more boxes out and pushes one toward me before flipping his own carton open and digging in with a plastic fork.

I mumble a "Thank you," and the three of us eat near the cash register, our eyes following the passing hotel guests outside the window for potential customers, but nobody comes in.

I'm focused on my food, feeling a weird sense of agitation building up inside me before I realize it's because I'm trying not to look at Kai. What is wrong with me? Since when did being around Kai make me so self-conscious?

I try to distract myself in the mess of beef curry instead.

"You seem quiet today," he says, taking another bite of sticky white rice.

"This is how I always am." I stab a piece of beef with my fork, frowning.

He shakes his head in disagreement, the stray pieces of black hair moving back and forth against his forehead.

Jae-Jae nods toward me but looks at Kai. "I'm trying to convince her to let me do something with her hair. I think she's worried she can't trust me."

He blinks up at her silvery-blond bob. "I don't blame her."

She rolls her eyes. "I'm not going to make her look like me. You can't replicate perfection like this."

Kai laughs. "Whatchu think, Rumi? You interested in turning into one fairy-cyborg?"

I drop my fork into the empty to-go box and straighten my back. "I don't want a haircut. I made a promise."

"You promised someone you wouldn't cut your hair?" Jac-Jac asks, resting her chin in her hand so her glitter-infused nails frame her jawline.

"Yeah. We were going to get ours cut at the same time," I say.

"Well, tell them to come too. I'll do you both," Jac Jac offers.

"I can't," I say, and Kai's eyes dip down because he already knows I can't make it through a single conversation without talking about Lea. "I promised my sister."

The two of them go awkwardly quiet, and a few seconds later the door opens. Jae-Jae looks like she's going to explode with relief as she greets her next client and leads her to the nail area.

Kai scrunches his face and peers at me with accusing eyes. "I can't believe you did that."

"Did what?"

"You used the dead sistah card to get out of a haircut."

My eyes widen. "I did not!"

"You absolutely did." He shakes his head. "You weren't even trying to hide it."

"There's no such thing as a 'dead sister card,'" I say. "You're an ass for even saying that."

He laughs lightly. "I never said I was sensitive. But I am honest."

I roll my eyes, but I'm smiling too.

Smiling.

At Kai.

Who is so obnoxious I want to push his face into the beef curry.

And then he says he has to leave, but would I want to go to the Coconut Shack with him later tonight because it's open-mic night and he knows I like music, and I say yes because, well, I don't know what is going on with me but I don't have the energy to stop it.

What is happening to me and why don't I hate it?

CHAPTER TWENTY-EIGHT

We're sitting in the Coconut Shack watching a parade of amateur singers take their turn on the stage, and to my relief, the music doesn't make me want to run away. It steadies me somehow, the way it does at Mr. Watanabe's house.

Two women are singing a duet, their voices like a pair of songbirds perched in an apricot tree. Happy, delicate, and bright. And when I close my eyes, I can feel Lea's spirit drifting through my thoughts, reminding me what it was like to be up on a stage with my best friend and a piano.

I might not be ready to perform—I might not be ready to sing—but that doesn't mean I don't miss it.

When the song ends, Kai claps his hands beside me. His eyebrows are raised, and one side of his mouth is curled up in a smile. "Was pretty good, eh?"

I nod but pull my eyes away from him. I know we're friends, but does he have to smile at me the way he does? With his mischievous eyes and baby-smooth skin and the way his face dimples like he's always on the edge of a punchline?

He's too . . . happy. I'm worried it's contagious.

Lea was always the romantic one, not me. Mom says I might be a late bloomer, but I'm not so sure. Late implies there's something that's still going to happen—something I don't fully understand yet.

But I do understand it. I can see why some people like falling in love, over and over again, because it's addictive and it feels good. It's like opening presents on Christmas—that immense wave of excitement, followed by blissful happiness. I assume love must be *something* like that; otherwise why would people keep doing it?

But people fall out of love too, the same way people want different presents the next time Christmas rolls around. Because their tastes change, or they need something different, or they want something new.

I mean, it's a lot of pressure to be expected to love someone *so much* forever. Someone who isn't a family member or a pet. Someone who isn't guaranteed to love you forever back.

It's also a lot of pressure to know exactly who you're looking for. It's not like saying, "I'd like a coloring book for Christmas," and being happy no matter what kind of coloring book shows up. Because not everyone is compatible with each other. Love is specific. And if you don't know exactly what you're looking for, you risk wasting months or years getting to know someone who is ultimately not "the one." What's the point of wasting all that time?

That's the part I don't understand. Time isn't replaceable, and you never know how much of it you have left. Why waste so much of it on *dating*?

It doesn't make me a late bloomer—it makes me practical.

I don't know what I'm looking for in love. I don't even think I'm looking for love at all. I don't see people and feel that rush of excitement Lea always described when she had a crush—the kind of excitement that leads to touching and kissing and whatever else. I just see people that might make good friends, and I've always been okay with that.

Which is why Kai's ridiculous jawline is bugging the crap out of me.

I don't know what it means.

Kai turns and says something to Gareth, who's sitting beside him with a can of soda in his hand. Hannah is here too, without her brother. She leans toward me, and I catch the scent of the strawberry body butter she's always putting on her hands and arms. It makes her smell like dessert.

"You should go up there," she urges, motioning toward the small stage where a young man is sitting on a stool with his guitar. "You'd totally kill it." She's wearing big silver earrings and her hair is in two braids. They kind of remind me of Lea—she wore her hair in two braids all the time as a kid because she wanted to be Dorothy from *The Wizard of Oz*.

"Last time I tried to sing in front of people it didn't go so well," I say sheepishly.

Hannah waves her hand like what happened the other day

wasn't a big deal at all. "Everyone gets nervous. But you can *sing*. You belong up there."

I don't know how to explain that I wasn't nervous—I felt my dead sister's ghost nearby and I panicked. Because singing makes me feel close to her, and being close to her reminds me of all the things I never said to her and should have. All the things I can't undo.

"Maybe another time," I say instead.

But after another few songs, being on that stage is all I can think about. Music is what makes my heart beat. The thrill of performing is something that's impossible to replicate.

First the room would empty, and then my chest would empty, and then suddenly my heart would dissolve into pieces all around me, swirling like a tornado of everything I feel inside. When I'm performing on a stage I'm connected to everything and everyone, yet somehow it is still just Lea and me in front of the world. And the moment before the first note—the moment before the first piano chord or guitar strum or word—is like closing your eyes during a snowstorm, and the next time you open them you're surrounded by grass and flowers and the warmth of spring.

It was like waking up and realizing you've landed in Oz.

I miss the stage. I miss my music. I said I'd never miss anything as much as I miss Lea, and I won't for as long as I live, but maybe I can miss something in a different way. Maybe hearts have layers, and the layer that misses Lea is simply different from the layer that misses creating songs.

I look up at Hannah and Gareth and Kai. Am I a bad person for making friends? For wanting to be on that stage, even if it's by myself? For having fun on the beach and smiling with Kai and maybe wanting to cut my hair?

Does it make me a bad person for wanting to move on?

I don't know what that means about me as a person. I don't want to move on from Lea—I never could—but moving on from my grief? From the pain? From feeling the overwhelming ache of her loss?

I guess I want it to stop. I want to go somewhere else—be someone else—and fly away from it all, like a bird.

I want to be free of my own sadness.

And maybe I am a bad person for wanting these things when Lea can't want *anything* ever again, but I'm not sure what I'm supposed to be doing anymore. If I *ever* knew what I was doing. I don't know what the rules are for grieving.

And more important, *when can I stop?*

Mom should be the one helping me with this. She should be here, right now, telling me what I should be feeling. But she left me in an ocean of pain and didn't bother to make sure I knew how to swim.

A guy strumming a guitar starts to sing. It's a sad song—like broken marionette puppets and rain pouring down on an abandoned fun fair. But it fills my soul with something powerful—something necessary.

The music fills me with *life.*

I take in a breath of air like I'm coming up from the sea, and the music transports me to a foreign shore. Somewhere high up in the clouds where my thoughts are crisp and sharp and I feel like I'm floating above the entire world.

I can't swim, but I've taken flight.

And I know I should never feel guilty about loving music. Not when it means feeling closer to my sister. Closer to myself.

I *need* to be myself again, before the person I was vanishes forever. I hope Lea can forgive me for that. For missing the normalcy of being confused, indifferent, cynical old me. The version of me who didn't know what it was like to lose a sister—the version of me that always existed through music.

Kai brings back sodas for everyone and a plate of nachos for us to share. At some point we're sitting so close together our arms graze—twice—and neither of us says anything, but we both look at each other when it happens.

I don't know what I feel when I look at Kai. I think he's attractive, and smug, and really confident, and maybe even a little cool. But I don't know if that's an equation for anything at all. Because when I look at Hannah I think she's attractive, and *not* smug, and really confident, and *very* cool. I don't understand what the difference is supposed to be. Lea always talked about a spark—the thrill of magic or lightning or fireworks.

But those are the feelings I get from music. Can I just be in love with music?

Because music is a carnival at night, lit up by a thousand stars and bursting with luminescent colors and magical illusions.

Music is magic *and* lightning *and* fireworks.

Music is going to help me live.

I just need to find my way back to it.

CHAPTER TWENTY-NINE

The next time we're all at the beach, I finally get to meet Gareth's sister, Izzy.

She's built like a gymnast and probably has more muscles than Kai, Gareth, and Jerrod combined. When she shakes my hand, she squeezes hard. It makes me squeeze hard back, and when I do she flashes her teeth.

"I like a girl wit' a strong handshake," she says.

"Izzy is da one I was telling you about—da one in da band," Gareth says. He looks proud of her, like he looks up to her. It's how Lea used to look at me.

We sit in the middle of the sand—me, Kai, Hannah, Jerrod, Gareth, and Izzy—and nobody has a surfboard with them today. Instead, they have a red and white cooler filled with ice and drinks and a beach bag filled with food ready to barbecue.

While Hannah and Gareth set the coals and hover over the growing fire, Kai and Jerrod throw a football back and forth a few yards from the incoming waves. Izzy sits across from me, her guitar slung around her neck, and she strums effortlessly while she's watching their game. She doesn't have to think twice about what chords she's playing—her hands just remember what they should be doing.

She catches me looking at her a few times, and eventually she says, "Gareth told me you have a really good voice."

"It's okay, I guess."

She pulls the guitar strap from her neck. "I know dat look. I know a fellow musician when I see one. You looking at my guitar da way one surfer looks at da water—you like jump in." She holds the instrument toward me. "Go try play."

I want to object, but I can't. Not after watching the stage at the Coconut Shack and hearing the music call out to me. My hand is shaking as I take the guitar from her. I tuck it against me, my thumb hanging above the top string and my other hand forming a chord.

Breathe. Just breathe.

The notes rush back to me as easily as they did on the piano, except I'm not hiding in Mr. Watanabe's spare room. I'm out in the open, surrounded by the entire world, with the ocean and the sky and land all around me. There's nothing to hide my voice or my notes. I'm exposed.

I sing the lyrics to Lorde's "Liability," change chords, strum a melody, and I'm so lost in the lyrics and the emotion in the song that I close my eyes and Izzy isn't there anymore—it's just me and Lea.

She's here. She's *right here.*

My chest tightens. I feel like I'm trying to keep my heart from splitting in half. Maybe it will always hurt to think about her—to *see* her. But I don't care. I want her here with me.

I don't want to be alone anymore.

She's wearing a pair of jeans with holes all over them—a staple in her closet—and an *Amélie* T-shirt we always fought over. It's so worn and faded that you can hardly recognize the film cover at all. We loved it—we loved the soundtrack, and the movie, and how the T-shirt was one of so many things we just loved *the same*.

Lea smiles at me. Her hair is swept to the side, her waves and tangles framing the left side of her face like a pillow. Her cheeks dimple because she had that cuteness about her that doesn't exist with me, and God I miss her so much I want to throw myself at her and hold her and hold her until time takes her away from me again.

But I keep playing. Because Lea is here, right now, for the music. She's listening—I know she's listening.

A memory

Lea's face is so small. She's still missing her front teeth, so when she smiles at me from the side of the piano, I can't help but laugh.

"That one was really good," she says with the kind of enthusiasm that happens only when someone is too young to know what real talent sounds like.

I nod, because I don't know what real talent sounds

like yet either. "It's a pirate battle. I'm going to mail it to the people who make the *Pirates of the Caribbean* movies and see if they'll use it."

"They will. You're going to be famous probably," Lea says, starry-eyed.

I nod. "Probably. Hey, do you want me to teach you how to play it?"

She's sitting next to me before I finish my sentence.

I show her the notes, again and again. She makes a lot of mistakes, but she's so determined to learn them that I don't give up on her.

After a while she sighs. "I wish we had two pianos. Then we could play together."

I make a face. "I've never seen anyone on TV with two pianos before."

Her face falls, disappointed.

I pause. "You could learn the guitar, though. Pianos and guitars go together."

Lea's smile stretches so wide I can see all the teeth she still has left. "That would be amazing. We could write songs together."

I nod. "Yeah, until you get really good and then you won't want to listen to me play anymore."

Lea shakes her head, her eyes so full of happiness. "No way. I'll listen to you play even when you're ninety and old like Babang."

"Babang isn't ninety."

"Well, I'll still listen to you when you're older than Babang, then."

"Promise?" I ask.

"I promise," she answers.

Lea never broke her promises, even when I broke so many to her. Because she was the best sister in the entire world. So much better than me.

Guilt crawls up my throat. I don't deserve to be here when Lea isn't.

I swallow hard, fighting the queasiness building in my stomach.

I have to focus on the music—I have to focus on what Lea would've wanted; otherwise I'll never finish our song. I'll never be able to make amends for what I did.

And maybe holding on to "Summer Bird Blue" is how I can hold on to *her*.

When the song ends, I open my eyes and find everyone staring at me. Hannah looks impressed. Jerrod and Gareth look like they're trying to comprehend something. Kai looks like he's seen something wonderful, his brown eyes full of childlike joy. I don't know why he looks at me that way—like I'm one of the great wonders of the world.

Izzy motions her hands at me. "One moa, one moa."

And just like that, I'm playing the guitar again, singing along to the echo of the waves and the flutter of coconut trees behind me, searching for Lea in the poem of every broken chord and lyric, wishing for her to be real again.

I've finally found her. The music is where she exists now. Not in the ocean, or the stars, or my dreams.

My sister lives in the songs.

And that's when I know I have to keep playing. I have to keep writing.

Because it turns out music isn't just keeping *me* alive—it's keeping Lea alive too.

CHAPTER THIRTY

Mr. Watanabe stands in the doorway with two mugs of green tea. When I come to the end of my song, I take one of them from him, sipping carefully. He doesn't move from his spot, but he doesn't come inside the room, either. Maybe it's too painful to be around the piano, or the photographs, or the music.

He motions to the piano. "I neva hear dat one before."

"It's nothing. It's just something I made up a long time ago," I admit. "Something I wrote with my sister. You know—before." Before she died. Before the music left me. Before I forgot how to write.

So much has happened *before* that sometimes I worry about what's going to happen *after*.

I wonder if some people spend their whole lives being scared of what's to come. It's the not knowing that's always terrified me. I'm forever worried I'm going to make a mistake that's going to set my life on a course I can't change. And I spent so much time worrying about myself and whether I'd turn out like Dad that I never stopped to think about how Lea's life might change.

I never expected her to just *die*.

She was on a path. The right path. A good path.

I don't know who makes the rules, but Lea definitely didn't deserve to die. If it had to be one of us, it should've been me. Because Lea would've made the world better—I look at the world like I don't want anything to do with it.

I think it makes me ungrateful, but I don't know how to change it.

My sister fit in the world so perfectly. Whereas I'm the random, extra piece that you find inside a box after you've put everything else together. Everyone knows it probably belonged *somewhere*, but everything runs perfectly fine without it, so it gets tossed in the trash.

That's me—dispensable. Without a purpose.

I feel my hands start to shake, so I tuck them beneath my legs and stare at the piano keys.

Mr. Watanabe pretends he doesn't notice, but he's been quiet for so long that I know he must be noticing something. "Mmm," he says eventually. It sounds like a grunt. "You pretty good, eh? Sound like one professional."

"Thanks," I say, scratching my shoulder awkwardly. "It's not really supposed to be for the piano, but I'm not ready to touch my sister's guitar yet. It . . . it wouldn't feel right, you know?"

He thinks for a moment and then disappears. When he comes back, he's holding a ukulele instead of his tea. "You can go borrow dis one."

"That's not a guitar," I say, even though my heart starts to beat faster.

"Dis mo' bettah," he says. "Guitar take too much space."

I take it from him, feeling the strings beneath my fingers. And holding the instrument close to my chest, I strum to hear the pitch of the notes. It's so different from a guitar—more of a wooden, gentle sound. Guitars sound metallic and firm, like the instrument has a sharpness, waiting to fight if it needs to.

This ukulele doesn't want to fight. It wants to lie on the beach and feel the sand in its fingers. It wants to float on a raft in the ocean, drifting off to sleep with the rise and fall of every wave. It wants to come alive at the warmest part of the day, when the sky is the most perfect blue and the sun makes the world feel like home.

"Sound good, eh?" he says.

I brush my fingers against the smooth wood. "Why do you keep all these instruments?" I look up at him like he's holding a secret that I'm desperate for. "If you don't play—if they were your wife's—why do you keep them around? Don't they haunt you?"

Mr. Watanabe twists his mouth around, chewing a word or two before he speaks. "Ghosts no stay here." He waves at the ukulele, then at the piano. "Dey stay *here*." He presses a finger to his heart.

I blink. "Do they ever leave?"

He doesn't hide the fact that his eyes fall to the old photographs of his wife and son. "Dey neva eva leave." When his gaze finds mine again, he grunts. "But dat no mean you need fo' give up living. You too much young fo' be sad all da time."

"When I think about Lea, I don't know how to *not* be sad," I admit.

"I's li'dat fo' long time, yeah. Maybe even fo'eva. But bumbai going start to hurt less."

"I don't want to be sad anymore. I don't want to feel guilty forever." I pin my lips together. I shouldn't be saying all of this out loud. It makes it sound like I don't care about my sister as much as I should.

Mr. Watanabe nods like he understands, and maybe he does. "You know, my son, he used to love his music. He would sit on da stool next to his muddah. Den he would start fo' play—all da wrong notes, da same time she stay playing all da right ones. An' den, after when he pass away, all we know how fo' do was fo' feel sad. Wen' take a real long time, but afterward, my wife, she said she like bring back da music to da house. But I tol' her 'No, I no like.' Cuz our son, fo' me, he still stay living inside da music, yeah? An' it wen' hurt me—every time when I hear her play. So den she neva eva play da piano again.

"An' den one day she got real sick too. When she wen' pass away, I feel like I wen' lose da two of dem both all ovah again. Dat's because da music went die wit' her, yeah? An' da memories—da ones of our son, da ones of her—dey gone. Jus' li'dat. An' I regret dat. I regret neva letting her remembah our boy wit' his music. I wish I wen' spend less time being haunted and mo' time facing my pain, so dat way—me an' her—we could have been living wit' his memories instead of hiding from dem."

My heart beats against the back of the ukulele. The quietest drum in the world.

"No feel bad about living, eh? You never know how much time you have left."

I sit with the ukulele, learning its personality and toying with the familiar notes, and pretty soon Mr. Watanabe disappears again, but this time he doesn't come back. He leaves me to hum along to the music erupting from my fingers, and I don't know if I'm teaching the ukulele or the ukulele is teaching me, but it feels wonderful.

And then I hear her voice, here in Hawaii.

I hear *Mom*.

CHAPTER THIRTY-ONE

I leave the ukulele at Mr. Watanabe's and rush next door.

Mom is standing in the middle of the living room. I don't know where Aunty Ani is—all I see is *her*, holding her hands up like she's ready to grab hold of something if she falls over.

She looks weak.

She *is* weak.

The volcanic rage inside my chest is practically ready to blow the whole house away. If I wanted to, Mom wouldn't stand a chance.

But I don't need her to fall over. I need her to not be here at all.

"Why are you here? Nobody wants you here. You left me. *You left me.*" I'm screaming the words over and over again. Aunty Ani appears from behind the corner, her hands raised to calm me down, but everything is starting to go so starry and muddled that I can't figure out who is saying what.

"Don't shout, Rumi."

"You're not being fair."

"Just let me explain."

"Stop."

"Slow down."

"You need to hear this."

"Please talk to me."

"Please listen."

"Rumi."

"Rumi!"

"Rumi!"

I don't care what they have to say—either of them. I don't want to see Mom, and Aunty Ani is Judas, as far as I'm concerned, for letting her into this house without warning me first.

Mom raises her hands up to her mouth like she's trying to pull her words out or stuff them back in. I can't really decide. Her dark wavy hair is lifeless and flat, and I'm not sure if it's mascara mixed with tears all over her eyes or if dark circles can actually get that dark, but she looks like a mess. She doesn't look like Mom—the Mom I remember—and good, because all my good memories are with that mother. The woman in front of me is just a ghost.

A memory

"Happy birthday, baby!" Mom taps her finger against her phone. "Oh, wait. That one came out blurry—let me take another one. Okay, okay, happy birthday, baby!"

I roll my eyes. "You don't have to say 'happy birthday' twice, Mom. Just take the picture."

"You know what, this lighting is really bad. Could you stand on the other side of the table? No, not there—just—okay, that's good, but I want to get the cake in there too." Mom's staring at her screen again.

Lea giggles infectiously from the counter. I throw her a look, but it only makes her laugh harder.

"Mom, seriously. Nobody is ever going to see this photo. Who cares what the lighting looks like?" It's not really a question. I just want her to see my point.

"You might want to put it on Instagram. Or the other one. The Snapgram," Mom says innocently.

Lea snorts. "It's Snapchat, Mom."

"Okay, that one too," Mom says.

"There is zero chance I'm putting this picture on Snap-anything. Are we done yet?" I say, my fingers fidgeting near my sides.

Mom looks at Lea and raises her eyebrows. "What's wrong with her?"

Lea shrugs like she's clueless. She's not. Even if I hadn't told Lea what was wrong, she wouldn't have ratted me out to Mom. We have an arrangement. It's called the Circle of Silence, and only me and Lea are allowed to be a part of it.

I pull off the pointy birthday hat Mom made me

wear for the picture and toss it onto the table. "I'm fine, okay? I just don't like birthdays."

Mom steps toward me and puts her phone on the kitchen table. She smells like shea butter lotion and coconut shampoo. When she reaches her arm up to rub my shoulder, I catch sight of her engagement ring hanging from a silver chain around her neck.

After Dad left, things were hard for a while. But Mom is one of the hardest workers I know. She managed. She made sure we were okay, even if it didn't always feel like it at the time. Even when almost everything we owned was sold in favor of food and school clothes.

That's how she found out her engagement ring was fake. She was going to sell a diamond ring without a second thought, but a cubic zirconia? She couldn't part with it. She wanted a reminder of the lie.

Now Mom never takes it off. She says it reminds her how grateful she is that she never got married and how her relationship with me and Lea is more sacred and forever than a man with a diamond—fake or otherwise.

Mom is one of those people who say a loving family makes them richer than any billionaire. And she believes it too.

Sometimes I worry Mom thinks I'm too much like Dad—distant and cold. A ghost. I might not kiss Mom on the cheek and wrap my arms around her like we're best friends, but that doesn't mean I don't love her just as much as Lea does.

But I don't know how to explain that to her. I don't know if it's too late—if she already decided Lea is her favorite because I'm too much like the man who abandoned her.

"Rumi." I feel Mom's fingernails trail along my sleeve. "Talk to me, honey. What's bothering you?"

I bite my lip. The sandwich method. "The cake looks great. Birthdays make me feel like the world is moving too fast and I'm running out of time. The balloons are nice."

Mom's quiet for a while. "You don't have to be scared about getting older. Everyone gets older—it's the rules."

I look at Lea. She knows my fears—about vanishing the way Dad did. Here one moment and gone the next because I couldn't figure out how to anchor myself. Because I couldn't figure out how to be worthy of existing the way Lea and Mom do. They're better than me. I need more time to figure it out.

Otherwise I'll become Dad. Everything will just be too much, and I'll feel pressured and suffocated. I'll disappear one day, exactly like he did.

I don't want to disappear.

I want time to slow down. I want everything to slow down.

"I'm not ready to grow up yet. And I don't mean in

a Peter Pan way. I mean I'm literally not ready. I don't know the things other people know at my age. I haven't made the choices other people have made. I'm . . . not ready." I think of Dad, not ready to be a father. Not ready to give up his life.

I'm too scared to start mine, in case I make a mistake and change my mind and end up like him.

Mom nods slowly and pulls me close so that her mouth is next to my ear. "It's okay to not be ready. It's okay to take your time. You don't have to decide right this second who you are or what you want. There's so much time for that, you know? I just want you to be happy. And, you know, I'll always be here for you. For every decision you ever make, for as long as you need me, I'll be here. Because I love you, and that's what real parents do." She cups her hand around my cheek and kisses the side of my head. "I'm here for you, always."

I wipe a tear away with my knuckle and suck my breath in.

"But," she says after a while, "we're still singing 'Happy Birthday.' You don't get out of 'Happy Birthday.'"

Mom lights the candles and she and Lea sing as loud as they can, cheering at the end like there's twenty of us in the room instead of three.

I close my eyes, wish for more time, and take a breath.

"You promised," I say, my heart pounding wildly at the same time the memories of Mom shatter like a thousand broken mirrors. "You said you'd always be there for me. You said that's what real parents do. But you're as bad as Dad—worse even, because at least he admitted he couldn't take care of his kids. You kept pretending until you couldn't take it anymore."

Someone reaches for me—Mom or Aunty Ani—but I'm turning away so fast I don't know who it is.

"Don't touch me," I shout angrily. "Stay away from me. I don't want anything to do with you."

I retreat from the house and wander through the hills of the neighborhood until my feet blister. I'm practically near the water before I decide to turn back around, and thank God I was way too angry to walk in anything other than a straight line because I have no idea where I am. I just wanted to put distance between us, because I can't be close to Mom right now. I'm not ready to forgive her, or hug her, or talk to her about Lea and what happened. She's here to apologize. She's had time to work things out in her head, and now she's ready for things to go back to normal.

It's bullshit. It doesn't get to be that easy. It's not that easy—not for me. Not when thinking of Lea buried in the ground surrounded by worms and beetles and a coffin she would have hated—dark wood with pink trimmings like she was some weird Victorian lady who collected haunted dolls—still makes no sense to me.

When I get back to the house, the car is gone and nobody's home. I sit in my room, staring out the window and waiting for the headlights to flicker through the glass.

Aunty Ani is the only person who gets out of the car.

CHAPTER THIRTY-TWO

Mr. Watanabe is outside pruning his collection of orchids behind the house. I think he knows I'm about two seconds away from setting something on fire, because he tells me I can go inside but, if I feel the need to break something, to leave the piano alone.

I tell him I'd never break an instrument. That's like taking your anger out on a puppy.

I flip through the basket of music he left me. I try to play a little bit of everything, hoping to find something that could unburden the heaviness in my chest. I want something angry. Something untamed. Something alive, like the orange blaze of an explosion, with glass shattering and wood splintering in every direction. I want a song that makes me feel like I've conquered the world through hate and fury.

Mr. Watanabe must've heard me playing the keys too hard, because his voice interrupts me. "You play dat one too fast. You sound like you ready fo' war."

"I'm *in* a war," I correct, pulling my hands back all the same.

He nods to me. "I can see dat. But I no care about your war—I like you stop butchering Tchaikovsky."

I rub the skin behind my ear. "It's called venting. Therapists encourage it."

He grunts, then steps into the room, staring absentmindedly at the sheet music. "You know, war not only t'rowing grenades and shooting da bullets all ovah whereva you feel like it. Dea's an order to it. Dea' rules." He shrugs. "If you no like Tchaikovsky's rules, den you go try make your own."

"What, like write my own song? I've been trying that. It's not working."

"Try mo' hard den."

"It's not that easy. The next song I write will be the first one I've written without Lea. It's like saying good-bye to her. It's like I'm accepting she's never coming back." I blink at him. "It . . . it scares me."

"You no can help going trew life wit'out being scared sometimes. But if you face your fears, you no need fo' be scared anymore," he offers. And then he heads for the doorway. Without turning back around, he adds, "Whateva you do, try play sumt'ing dat no sound like one exorcism. If you keep upsetting da plants, dey not goin' bloom anymoa."

I think of my song with Lea. I think of being here in the summer without her. I think about birds flying away to the place she exists—somewhere out of my reach. The place I'm still trying to escape to. And I think of the blue . . . water? Sky? Heart?

It's too literal. It doesn't mean anything.

And then I think of a summer with the world on fire, birds like chunks of lava flying through the air, and blue turning violet turning red. A world that's determined to swallow me up, because the fire keeps building and building and it's impossible for me to get away from it—to fight the mountain of rage that's finally ready to explode.

It's a volcano. I want to write a song that sounds like a volcano. So I do.

I know it's not the song I owe my sister, and I know I'm still letting her down by not keeping my promise.

But right now I don't care. *I need the volcano.*

And it feels fucking good.

CHAPTER THIRTY-THREE

Aunty Ani tries to bring up Mom every single day. She says
I've put if off for long enough. She says I need to forgive her.
She says she deserves to be forgiven. She says it's time. She says
Mom isn't going anywhere, no matter how much I want to run
away from her.

Thinking of her nearby, staying in a hotel, waiting for me—it
should be comforting, but it's not.

"I'm not interested in talking," I say. "It's too late to fix this."

"It's never too late," Aunty Ani says.

I spend a lot of time at the beach writing lyrics. I get so used
to the feel of the hot sand beneath my legs that I actually start to
feel cold when I'm not there.

"Summer Bird Blue" is taking up so many pages of my notebook that I'm starting to wonder if I'll ever get it right.

It's either too personal or not personal enough, too depressing or too cryptic. It's never right, no matter how many times I
rewrite the words.

The sky is so blue
like the summer I left you.

Wrong.

The summer is so cold
and the birds are getting old.

What even.

I watch you fly away
like the birds in May.

Oh my God, these lyrics are the worst.

They're weak, and volcanoes shouldn't be weak.

I need Lea. Writing isn't the same without her. Living isn't the same without her.

But I have to finish this song. I owe her.

I look across from me. Anyone else would see the base of a coconut tree and a scabby patch of grass mixed with sand. But I see Lea, wearing white cutoff shorts and the blue and yellow flannel shirt that—like the *Amélie* one—we always fought over.

It was a good shirt. It made us look like we came out of an Urban Outfitters catalog, and I really can't explain why. We both were always different sizes, but it hugged all the right places and draped in the most flattering way possible.

Lea's hair is in a side braid, and it always looks great like that because her hair is thick and wavy. She's smiling at me.

"I'm trying," I say.

I know, she mouths.

Trying to write, trying to keep her close, trying to not be so violently sad all the time.

I feel a spray of water land on the back of my neck, and I pull my notebook toward my chest to protect it from water damage.

"Dude," I say instinctively.

Kai's head is hidden under a towel. He pulls it off, his spiky hair pointing in every direction. "Huh? Oh, sorry." He laughs and drops the towel near his surfboard.

"You're like a golden retriever," I say, wiping the water spots away.

He rubs his hand through his hair and more water flies toward me.

"Stop," I say, but I'm smirking too and shaking my head. I'll admit it—Kai is growing on me.

He sits beside me and leans all the way back until his head hits the sand and his knees are bent. Pulling his hands behind his head, he sighs. "Ahh, I'm so tired."

I look at him for a second. God, his arms are big. He doesn't look big, but I've never seen that amount of arm muscle on anyone in my life. They're like Marvel comic muscles.

He nods to my notebook. "You almost finished? Does this mean I'll finally get to hear you play the guitar?"

"It's not my guitar to play," I say. "It's Lea's."

He raises a brow.

I shoot him a look. "This is not me pulling the dead sister card."

"I never said anything."

"You did that thing with your eyebrow. Yeah, *that* one. I know what it means."

"*I* don't even know what it means."

"You do it when you're thinking of the most annoying thing possible."

"Harsh."

"Accurate."

"You really think I'm annoying?" He pushes himself up on his elbows.

I stiffen. And blink. And find myself poking holes in the sand. I try to think of something to say with the sandwich method, but then I realize I don't have an insult to say to Kai. Only three compliments.

You have nice arm muscles. I like your eye freckle. It's nice when you smile at me like you actually care what I think.

And that's not a sandwich—that's just three pieces of bread. An overload of carbs. Nobody needs that many compliments.

"I know it's your thing and everything, but you don't have to be so mean all the time." Kai flicks at the ends of his hair like he's swatting a fly away. "I mean, we are friends."

I stop thinking about bread and Kai's freckle. "You think I'm mean?"

"Are you kidding? You're *so* mean." He dusts sand off his forearms and looks out into the water. Not smiling. Silent.

I frown. "Oh." I look across at imaginary Lea. She's rolling her eyes, shaking her head, and *tutt*ing at me like I'm the last one to figure all of this out.

I get it, I want to tell her. *I've messed up. I've hurt Kai's feelings.*

I swallow, my hands clasped together in my lap. "I'm sorry. I'm not trying to be mean."

"Holy shit." Kai sits all the way up. "Did you just apologize to me?"

"Okay, for the record, this is what I meant about annoying."

He laughs. It sounds like a wave, loud, then soft, like it's rolling to a stop. His mouth falls flat, and when he looks at me his eyes are scrunched. "If you ever like talk about her, you can. I won't keep making jokes about it. I only make jokes to try to cheer you up, you know? But I can be serious if you need someone fo' listen."

I try to look in his eyes, but honestly, his pectoral muscles are *so* distracting. Instead, I look across the beach and push my toes farther into the sand. "Honestly, why do you never have clothes on?"

He pulls his chin back, but his jaw is so defined it doesn't disappear. "I'm wearing shorts. It's not like I'm in my Bibbidees." He grins, then straightens. "Wait. Are you checking me out?"

"No." I roll my eyes, picturing Lea's giggle. She used to tell me she liked watching me talk to boys because it was like watching a house of cards collapse or a wedding cake fall over. One giant disaster.

"It's okay if you are. I don't mind." Kai pauses, tapping his thumbs against his knees. "I check you out sometimes too."

"What? That is such a weird thing to say." My cheeks burn.

Kai covers his eyes with the back of his hand and lets out a tired laugh. "Okay, I take it back, then."

"It's too late. I can't unknow what you've just told me. Now it's awkward."

"How do I make it not awkward?"

"I don't know."

"Do you want to smell my arm?"

"What? Why would I want to smell your arm? What is wrong with you?"

He laughs and holds his arm in front of me. "Come on, I like know whatchu think."

"You are making this worse. You know that, right?"

He doesn't pull his arm away. I sigh.

"Fine." I groan, taking a quick smell of his forearm. He smells like vanilla and sugar and maybe some chocolate, too.

"Why do you smell like a bakery?" I ask.

He laughs, pulling his arm back. "Body butter. With SPF."

"You're *so weird*."

"Do you like it? The body butter, I mean."

"I guess."

"That's good."

"Why is that good?"

"Jerrod read something about how girls are more likely to go out witchu if they like the way you smell. Something about biology and being able to smell if someone's a good genetic match."

"That sounds like complete nonsense."

"It's science."

"Even if it is, you used body butter that smells like chocolate chip cookies. That's cheating."

He shrugs. "You like go fo' dinner with me? Tonight?"

My skin goes tingly. "Are you asking me on a date?"

Kai nods. "Yeah. Want to meet me outside at six o'clock?"

I look across from me. Lea's watching, urging me to answer.

My heart beats and beats and beats. Are these nerves? Is this what butterflies feel like? Or is this something else?

"Okay," I say finally, and I honestly don't know if I said it because I want to or because it's what Lea would have wanted me to do.

Kai smiles. "Okay." He waits a few seconds, looking way too proud of himself. And finally, he says, "Well, I should probably get you home. I have to get ready—I have a date with one girl tonight."

CHAPTER THIRTY-FOUR

Kai's waiting by the gate at exactly six o'clock. He's wearing a blue T-shirt, black shorts, and flip-flops. When I get close to him, he doesn't smell like a bakery anymore—he smells like soap and mouthwash and maybe chewing gum, too. It's like he's sterilized himself clean with every variation of mint known to man.

He grins when he sees me. "You look great."

"Don't be ridiculous. I look exactly the same as I did earlier," I say, because it's true. I thought about changing, but I wasn't sure how much "getting ready" was normal. Just a shower? A shower and fresh clothes? A shower, fresh clothes, and full makeup?

It started to feel too confusing. It started to feel serious.

So I sat in my room writing lyrics and waiting until I saw Kai's bedroom light go out and knew it was about time to go.

Kai drives to a Japanese restaurant called Takara. When we arrive, the parking lot is so full we have to park across the street and walk.

I can hear live music coming from somewhere—probably one of the hotels nearby. There seem to be hotels everywhere. People spill out onto the sidewalks in groups of three or more, and I actually have a hard time finding anyone who isn't wearing flip-flops and clothing that shows off their legs.

In Washington everyone is always wearing jeans. Is it weird that these are the kinds of things I notice on a date?

Takara is shaped like a giant square with dark beams and windows. Inside, everything is wood and cushions, and all the lights hang low to the tables like they're meant to be intimate.

It's kind of fancy. Oh God, I think this is an actual real date. Not like a, "Hey, let's go to the movies and see if we like each other" kind of date. This is the kind of date you go on with somebody you already *know* you like.

I suddenly feel like there's a lot less air in the room.

The waiter asks us if we want to sit at a table or the sushi bar, and Kai says the bar. There are a bunch of people sitting in the booths, but only a few sitting along the sushi counter. We take two of the empty seats, and Kai picks up one of the menus and passes it to me.

"Do you like sashimi?" he asks.

"I've never had it," I say.

"I always get the Samurai Platter. It comes with two of these, one of these, and miso soup." He pauses. "You like crab?"

"I'm not sure." I look at the menu. "I'll get whatever you're having. Except not the eel—I don't think I can do eel."

"Okay. No eel. Got it." Kai nods, and when the sushi chef

leans over to ask what we want, he asks for two Samurai Platters and green tea for both of us.

"Does your dad know you're hanging out with me?" I ask.

Kai's laugh is so relaxed, like he's never worried about anything. "He knows I've been teaching you how fo' swim. But, I mean, we don't really talk that much. It's not like he asks who I go on dates with."

"Do you go on a lot of dates?" I ask.

"Not really. I had the same girlfriend fo' a long time in high school, so I went on dates with her."

"When did you guys break up?"

Kai makes a face at me, his eyes smiling. "You interrogating me? Let's see, we dated fo' two years, decided we were better as friends, broke up three months ago, and if you're wondering, no—I don't still have feelings fo' her."

I feel my cheeks turn pink. "Sorry."

"It's okay, hapa. You got any exes you like talk about while we're on the subject?"

I think about Caleb. I think about the last time I saw him. "No," I say firmly.

Kai taps his finger on the table and tilts his head like he's juggling a question. "How come you never learned how fo' swim?"

"We live in Washington. I think Mom was so used to having a beach on her doorstep in Hawaii that it never occurred to her to take us to a public pool."

"Doesn't Washington have plenty kine beaches?"

"Yeah, but have you ever been swimming in the ocean up there? It's freezing." I remember cliff jumping with Lea and how when we'd hit the water it felt like jumping into a pool of ice cubes. I'd hated every second of it—the flying, the falling, and the swimming. Well, the doggy-paddling, anyway.

"Why did your mom leave Hawaii?"

"My dad was in the navy," I say. "Mom followed him when he got stationed in Oak Harbor."

Kai's eyes go wide. "You're a navy brat too and you never said anything?"

I crack my knuckles uncomfortably in my lap. "Well, I'm *not* a navy brat," I say stiffly. "My dad was only in for a little while, and he left us when he got discharged. So it doesn't count."

Kai's quiet. "Do you stay in touch with him?"

"No." I don't say anything else about it, and Kai doesn't ask.

The waiter brings us two cups and a pot of hot tea. Kai pours it out for both of us, and I wrap my fingers around the cup to feel the warmth.

"I hope I can get orders here in Hawaii. Or California. Somewhere where I'm not going to freeze my okole off." He sips at his drink.

"I don't understand why you're even joining. I mean, you don't even want to join. What if you end up somewhere cold? What if you end up on a submarine?"

He shrugs. "It would be hard fo' surf on one submarine. But it's only four years. And then I can go to school back here and maybe help my mom with Palekaiko Bay."

"Seems like a waste of four years," I say quietly. "Because you'll be stuck there—on your submarine or whatever. You'll be stuck somewhere where you can't surf and you don't even really want to be, all because your dad wants you to. You can't change your mind and quit. Doesn't that scare you?" Making big decisions terrifies me. It always has, but it's even worse now that Lea is gone. Because every decision I make—or don't make—it's one more decision Lea doesn't get to have. Her life ended—her choices were taken away from her.

I feel like I owe her more than I'm able to give her. I feel like I'm living the life she should have had—the life she deserved so much more than me.

Kai doesn't realize how lucky he is. He doesn't realize what he's giving up.

"No, not really," Kai says. "Like I said, it's only four years. I'll have money fo' go school, and my dad will stop breathing down my neck. It's not like I have some big dream."

I don't understand it. I don't understand willingly throwing away *four entire years* of your life just because you don't want to fight with your dad about it. Or because you can't think of anything better to do.

I don't know how to make decisions because I'm terrified of making the wrong choice, but to make a choice I don't even want? Or to make a choice that requires years of commitment I can't take back? It's ridiculous. Kai is walking into a prison sentence and he isn't even flinching.

How can someone be so unafraid of a life they don't even want, when I'm petrified of starting the one where so many doors are still open?

And I don't know why I'm suddenly so angry, but I am. Angry that Kai is going to waste his life. Angry that I don't have anything to waste mine on. Angry that Lea didn't get a chance to waste hers at all.

It's not fair.

"Why does it bother you so much?" he asks.

"Because you only have one life, and you're throwing it away like it doesn't matter."

"I'm not throwing it away. I'm trading four years fo' a lifetime of peace."

"But what if you don't get a lifetime?" My voice sounds sharp and jagged. "What if you spend four years in the navy and then die in some freak accident? What if those four years were literally all you had left?"

"Well, then, that would suck." He stops, studies the edge of the counter for a moment, and then looks at me. "You talk about her a lot."

"She's my sister. She's dead. I talk about her. What do you expect me to do?"

"No." He shifts, leaning forward so I can smell a rush of mint. "I didn't mean it like that. I didn't mean it in a bad way." He pauses. "I'm sorry, okay? I'm really sorry she's gone. And I'm sorry if that scares you when you think about the future."

I wait. "Is there a 'but'?"

He shakes his head. "No. I'm just sorry."

His eyes look brighter under the fluorescent lights. Rich and brown with the signature spark of Kai's energy. Electricity shouldn't be comforting, but it is. It's the kind of warmth that reminds me of home.

The sushi chef places two bowls of miso soup in front of us. I think Kai doesn't know how to recover from "dead sister," so we start talking about the food and the chairs and the shape of the teapot instead.

The sushi arrives in a wide box tray. Kai points out the California roll, the rainbow roll, and the spicy tuna tempura roll.

I try the California roll first. As soon as I start chewing, something sharp and cold slices up my nostrils and my eyes flood with tears. I set my chopsticks down and squeeze the bridge of my nose, trying to fight the pain.

"Oh my God, what is happening?" I manage to say.

Kai is laughing next to me. "The wasabi."

"It burns," I say, breathing out.

"Too much? Here, try scrape some off. It's the green stuff."

I paw at my tears and sniff. "You realize that's like eating spreadable tear gas, right?"

"You get used to it."

"I won't. I will always regret the wasabi."

I try one of the pieces of the rainbow roll next, and it's so hard to chew through the raw salmon without gagging that I end up swallowing the entire thing and shuddering at the end.

Kai is eating beside me like someone watching a painfully awkward comedy sketch. "You regret the sashimi too?"

"I'm still processing the sashimi." I look at the spicy tuna tempura roll and sigh.

The piece is so big I can only bite into half of it. It's crunchy and . . . really, really good.

"Whatchu think?" Kai asks.

"I like this one a lot," I say.

I put the rest of it in my mouth, chewing and chewing until suddenly the heat kicks in. It's not just hot—it's like acid against my tongue. My eyes start watering, and my mouth is open and I'm taking big breaths of air in to cool my tongue, and then I'm trying to drink green tea to wash it away but it's way too hot, and I put the cup back down and flail my arms around like a fish who just leaped out of its aquarium and landed on the floor.

"That is *so spicy*," I say.

Kai is leaning backward and laughing hysterically, the back of his hand covering his mouth, which is still full of food. "Seriously, what's wrong witchu? You act like you've never tasted food before," he manages to say through his fingers and chopsticks.

"No. I've never eaten raw fish and the spices they use for chemical warfare before."

When his mouth is clear, he plucks all the sashimi off the top of the rainbow roll. "Here," he says. "It's just the crab and avocado left inside."

"Thanks," I say. I finish the roll, get used to the California roll and the wasabi—with heavy gulps of tea in between—and let Kai finish the rest of the spicy tuna tempura roll from my plate.

When we're finished eating, Kai asks for the bill. I try to pay for half of it, but Kai shakes his head.

"I ate most of your food. You can get the ice cream, if you really like pay fo' something," he says.

"Ice cream?"

"Yeah, we're going fo' ice cream. Because there's no way I'm taking you home after the most disastrous date in history."

"I didn't think it was a disaster."

Kai looks at me with a wrinkled forehead.

I roll my eyes. "Okay, the food part maybe, because I have baby taste buds. But, like, the date part wasn't a disaster." He's silent for at least three seconds before I start twitching impatiently. "Was it really that bad?"

He pulls his lips in and smiles mostly on the left side of his face. "That depends. Do you feel like you want to kiss me?"

"What? No—what?" I pull my face back in total confusion.

He pulls his shoulders up innocently. "If you wanted to kiss me, then that means the date isn't going too bad. But if you like kiss me as much as you like eat more wasabi—well, you get the idea."

"A kiss doesn't mean anything," I say, mostly because I just feel like arguing with him.

"Rumi," he says seriously, "a kiss means *everything*."

I roll my eyes and snort. "Come on. I want ice cream."

Kai laughs like I'm the funniest person he knows. Even though it doesn't make any sense, and even though I feel guilty about having fun when I still haven't kept my promise to Lea, it feels good.

It feels like I'm human again.

CHAPTER THIRTY-FIVE

We walk to a Baskin-Robbins and I buy each of us two scoops of ice cream. I pick pralines and cream, and Kai gets vanilla.

We follow the sidewalk parallel to a row of bushes covered in big white flowers. Before I can stop myself, I measure the distance between us while we walk.

Four inches. Maybe five. Just a hand apart.

I clear my throat. "I can't believe you picked vanilla. Who picks vanilla?"

Kai's nostrils flare like he's half snarling. "It's universally loved. And I don't like ruining my ice cream with a bunch of weird flavors that shouldn't go together. Pecans and caramel, are you kidding me? You're eating squirrel food."

"Even the squirrels know it's superior. Vanilla is the most boring flavor in existence. It's like getting a cheese pizza."

Kai doesn't say anything.

My eyes go big. "Oh my God, you like cheese pizza."

His laugh is like two short bursts. "I'm not answering that."

Now I'm laughing. "Do you eat plain oatmeal too? Or spaghetti without the red sauce?"

"Okay, now you're being ridiculous. Nobody eats spaghetti like that," he says, and shakes his head. "I can't believe you're giving me a hard time about food when you almost passed out trying sushi fo' the first time."

"That is . . . fair," I say, and Kai smiles with his whole entire face like it's the most effortless thing in the world.

Our ice creams are gone by the time we find a bench, but we sit anyway because I guess neither of us is ready to go home yet. I can hear drums beating in the distance—probably one of those dinner shows with the fire and dancing that all the hotels seem to put on. It makes the darkness feel alive, even though the breeze has stilled and the warm, sticky air is making me want to take a really long nap.

I feel like I've been tired for months. I wonder if I'll ever stop being tired and if feeling awake is somehow tied to Lea. Maybe this is the best it will ever get—smiling with the last bit of energy you have because the rest of you feels depleted.

"You should sing your song at one of the open-mic nights at the Coconut Shack. I think you'd really like it," Kai says. He doesn't smell like mint anymore—he smells like himself. Like the ocean and the sand has been rubbed permanently under his skin.

"It's not finished," I say. "I'm not really sure if I know how to write anymore. It used to be easier with Lea. I didn't have writer's block with her."

He waits like he wants me to keep talking, and I think maybe it's good that I do.

Because it's been a long time since I've been able to talk about Lea and not feel the world dissolve all around me, or talk about music without feeling the rage that wants to erupt from my soul. It's been a long time since I've been able to be myself, without being controlled entirely by my own grief.

It feels like a step forward, so I keep talking.

"We had this game," I continue. "We used to say a random word and then say the next two things we thought of as fast as we could. And then we'd write a song about it." I laugh softly to myself. "They didn't have to be good or anything. Some of them didn't even make sense. But it kept the creativity alive. It helped us think faster. And sometimes we came up with really good lines. Sometimes we found a really good song."

"You like me play the game witchu?" he asks, and I know he's trying to be kind.

"No," I say. It wasn't a game for anyone else. It was just for Lea and me. "I already have the last three words Lea and I picked. Now I just need the right lyrics."

He nods. "Well, if you ever like play it fo' someone—you know, fo' a fresh set of ears or something—I'm here. I mean, we don't even have to leave our houses. You could open your window and I can listen from across the yard."

I don't thank him. I watch the way his eyes soften—the way his mouth dimples in the corner and his bottom lip juts out ever so slightly. It's a gentle smile. Hopeful. And something else, too. His head is tilted, and his shoulders are slightly raised. I think he's actually a little nervous. Maybe it's because we're sitting so close.

His knee bounces up and down like he's cold, even though he can't possibly be. And then he swallows, and I notice the way his throat moves and the delicate space below his jaw and above his Adam's apple. It's soft and brown and curved, like I could settle my head below his chin and fit perfectly into him.

Lea used to tell me that's what love felt like—like two puzzle pieces fitting together. She thought she was in love a lot. Every few months, really, and sometimes it was with fictional characters from her favorite TV shows.

I don't know much about love, but I do know what it's like to feel like you fit perfectly with someone else. I felt it with Lea and Mom. And I don't know if love can ever be more real than that.

"I like your hair," Kai says suddenly, his fingers flicking a loose strand like he's brushing dust off me.

"Why?" I ask stiffly. He's so close. Less than a hand away, definitely. We're practically touching.

"I don't know. Because it's attached to your head," he says.

I laugh. "You're so weird."

"So are you," he says, grinning.

I open my mouth to say something back, something probably rude but hopefully sort of clever, but I don't get the chance because Kai pushes his mouth against mine and I forget all my words.

His lips are really soft—way softer than Caleb's—and when he kisses he breathes in instead of out, like he's trying to breathe in the moment. And I kiss him back because that's what I'm supposed to do.

Right?

A memory

"It was awful," I say, rubbing my hand against my nose. It's wet, but I'm not sure how much of it is snot and how much is tears. "It was so embarrassing."

Lea settles in the space next to me on the bed. "I don't understand. I thought you liked him."

"I—I don't know. I thought I did too. I mean, I do. I think. I don't know." My sob erupts out of my throat like a cough. "How am I supposed to show up to school tomorrow? It's humiliating."

"It couldn't have been that bad. I mean, it was just a kiss, right?" Lea asks.

I smear my tears away with my palms and see the mascara on my hands. "Oh, great."

Lea laughs softly and passes me a tissue.

I wipe the space under my eyes and try to tell her the whole story. About being at Alice's sixteenth birthday party. How Caleb and I went up to the roof on our own. How we had been talking for months at school, and Caleb said he couldn't stop thinking about kissing me. And how I let him, because I thought I wanted him to. I thought I was *supposed* to want him to. And as soon as our mouths touched I felt like my stomach was spinning and turning and coiling like it was meat loaf being squeezed. And then he held my neck with one hand and my thigh with the other, and my heart started to pound, but not in a good way—in a squeamish, racing, painful kind of way. And then he pushed his tongue into my mouth and I couldn't take it anymore, so I shoved him away and ran back inside.

Except I didn't stop inside. I ran all the way home.

"What if he tells everyone there's something wrong with me?" I ask, the tissue crumpled in my fist.

Lea's brown eyes don't leave me. She's too good. She's too kind, thoughtful, and gentle. I don't deserve it.

"There is nothing wrong with you, Rumi." She shrugs. "You don't have to like kissing Caleb. You don't have to like kissing boys. And you know what? Maybe you don't even have to like kissing, *period.* It doesn't matter—you're still just as normal as everyone else."

"You're only saying that because you're my sister."

"I'm saying it because it's what I believe." She settles her head against mine. The perfect fit.

I bite my lip. "But what if he tells everyone anyway? What if he tells everyone that I led him on for months and then ditched him on the roof? What if he tells everyone I'm an awful kisser, too?" I don't care what people at school think about me as a person, but I do care about the fact that they might have an opinion on my sexuality before I do. It feels . . . invasive. It feels like I'm being rushed.

"You didn't lead him on—you thought you liked him. Sometimes people change their minds." I can tell she's rolling her eyes—I can feel it in the way her head moves against mine. "Maybe *Caleb* is the bad kisser."

"I don't think I changed my mind," I say. "I think I never really wanted to kiss him. I don't think I want to kiss anyone." I try to find my words and dust them off so that they mean what I want them to. "I know what asexuality is. But there's also demisexual and gray asexual and then romantic orientation, too—and I don't know where I fit in. I'm not comfortable with the labels, because labels feel so final. Like I have to make up my mind right this second. Like I have to be as sure of myself as everyone else seems to be. And honestly, I don't really *know* what I like or don't like. I didn't like kissing Caleb, but does that mean I'll never like kissing anyone? I don't know the answer to that. I don't know whether I'll ever meet someone and want to kiss them, or date them, or have sex with them. I just know that I'm not attracted to people the way you are."

"The way I am?" she asks.

"You know—like when you look at guys and think they're 'hot' or whatever. That word makes me so uncomfortable. It feels so . . . *sexual*, I guess." Lea snort-laughs. I blink back at her.

"Sorry," she says with a grin. "Keep going."

I roll my eyes. "I don't really know how to explain

it. I don't have the vocabulary for it, which is why labels scare me. But I know I don't look at people *that* way. And labels make me feel so much pressure to know things about me that I just haven't figured out yet."

"Your sexuality—and how you identify—is nobody else's business. You can change your mind, or not change your mind. Those labels exist for you, and not so that everyone else can try to force you into a box. Especially if that box is their close-minded idea of fucking normal."

I groan. "*Please* don't let Mom hear you swearing. She's going to blame me for that."

Lea giggles. "Mom already does blame you. She says you swear like a sailor."

I think that's code for "You swear like Dad," but I don't really care. Sometimes swearing feels good.

I sigh. "You're lucky. You're never confused about anything—you just know yourself, and other people know you. I wish it were that simple for me." *I wish I were more like you,* I want to add, but I don't. Some things are better left as secrets in the dark.

"I think you're less confused than you think you are. You just need to learn how to trust yourself," she replies.

"Maybe," I say, and I try to believe it.

I feel sick. My skin doesn't feel like it belongs to me—it feels foreign and itchy and like I want to peel it all off. There's something heavy turning in my gut, and I realize suddenly that it isn't nerves or butterflies—it's my stomach rejecting these feelings. It's my body rejecting Kai.

I pull away from him and close my fists because it's the only thing I can do to stop shaking.

He looks alarmed. "What's wrong?" He's lifting his hands, wondering if he was leaning against me the wrong way. "Did I hurt you?"

"No," I say, and my jaw trembles. "I—I don't want to do this."

Kai straightens his shoulders, and it makes him look taller. "I'm so sorry, Rumi. I think I misread—" He shakes his head back and forth like he's on the verge of panicking.

"It's not you," I say, and I can barely hear myself. "I'm just not ready for this. It doesn't feel right."

Kai runs his hands over his knees and bounces his toes. Now we're both shaking. "Did I do something wrong?" he asks quietly.

I pull my arms across my chest, pressing my fingers into my ribs. I want to tell him it's not his fault—it's mine. Because all the conversations I started with Lea about who I like and don't like—they were never finished. All those difficult questions, all those *confusing* questions—I was working through them with Lea. And now . . .

Now I can barely make sense of what day it is, let alone what my sexual or romantic orientation is.

I want to tell him that it's not that I don't want to kiss him—

it's that I might not want to kiss anybody. Not right now. And maybe not ever.

But I don't know how to form the words.

"Can you take me home?" I ask instead.

Kai doesn't ask any more questions—he just nods.

CHAPTER THIRTY-SIX

Mr. Watanabe is holding a spray bottle in one hand and the hose in the other so he can water the orchids and bushes simultaneously. I'm sitting on one of the outside steps with the spare watering can, watching him work but mostly hoping for someone to give me the perfect answers to all my questions.

Poi is nearby, chewing on one of those red Kong balls and occasionally perking her ears up when she hears a car drive past. When she realizes I'm looking at her, she picks up the toy and drops it near my feet. I close my fingers around it, feeling the dog slobber she so graciously left, and chuck it somewhere beyond the mock orange bush. She scurries after it like a rabbit on the loose.

"So?" I ask, spinning the watering can at my feet out of boredom. I just finished telling him about my date with Kai and how horribly it all went. I even told him about the kiss, though by that point he was spitting like a cat and waving at the air like he desperately wanted me to stop. So I stopped talking about the kissing and told him I don't know what it means to be a seventeen-year-old who doesn't want to date. I told him I don't know what it means to want to be around someone all the time but never want to be intimate. I told him I don't know what it means to want a best friend that won't date anyone else.

And then I waited in silence while Mr. Watanabe continued to ignore me.

"*So?*" I repeat.

"So—so what? You see me doing all da work. You like talk, go water da plants," Mr. Watanabe barks.

Rolling my eyes, I stand up and tip some water onto the pink orchid closest to me. "Come on, I really want to know what you think."

"What, because you t'ink I'm old I have some kine wisdom fo' share witchu?"

"Well, yeah." When he looks over his shoulder at me, I hold the watering can up in defense. "Do not get me wet. These are the only clean clothes I have."

He snorts and turns back to his plants. "Try fo' do your laundry and go talk to your aunty."

"I don't want to talk to her," I argue.

"Okay. Your muddah den."

I let my arm drop. "I don't want to talk to her, either. I'm still angry at her times infinity. And I can't talk to my sister because she's dead. You're like Obi-Wan Kenobi—you're my only hope."

There's a brief pause, and just when I think he's ignoring me, he starts to speak. "No sound like you like dis boy," Mr. Watanabe muses, his eyes never leaving the trail of water, even when he's spritzing the flowers to his left.

Poi appears again at my feet with the red ball. I throw it again, and she races after it. "But how do I know that for sure? Because I thought I liked him. I mean, I went on a date with him, right? And we were getting along fine. Is kissing supposed to make you feel sick? Does it just take a while before you start to enjoy it?"

"I t'ink dis a discussion fo' you and your muddah," he repeats.

"No," I practically bark.

"Why not?" he barks back.

"*Because*," I say, "I don't need her help. If she didn't want to be around when my sister died, she doesn't get to be around when I have questions about boys. Those are the rules."

"Bah!" He huffs. "Silly kine rules."

But they're not silly—not to me. I'm still not sure if I want to forgive Mom, and I don't think I should have to feel guilty about that. *She* left *me*.

I feel bad about a million things I've done wrong over the years, but not forgiving Mom is definitely not one of them.

When I keep staring at him with iron eyes, he sighs. "I t'ink if you like dis boy da same way he like you, you would like kissing him, too."

I feel my heart sink. "But I don't think I like kissing anyone. I mean, it's possible to like someone and *not* kiss, right? Or maybe it's like practicing an instrument, and it gets easier over time?"

When he looks over his shoulder, he's frowning. "What fo'

you need to be kissing anyways? Mo' bettah you focus on your studies. No need fo' you waste time wit' lolo boys."

I watch the drip-drip of water fall from the orchid petals. It's almost like it's crying. "I just want to know if I'm feeling what I'm supposed to be feeling. And . . . if I'm not . . . then what's wrong with me? Why does everyone else seem to know themselves so much better than I do?"

Mr. Watanabe turns the water off, drops the hose where he's standing, and moves closer to the orchids. He twists and turns their pots, spraying them all over until they're buried in a cloud of mist. "Da only t'ing stay wrong witchu is you don't know how fo' water plants."

My laugh is weak but audible. I spray another orchid, this one white with purple in the centers. Poi comes back—without the ball—and sniffs around at the recently turned off hose, licking up the puddle of water it left behind. "What was it like when you met your wife? How did you two meet?"

Mr. Watanabe freezes, his hand resting on one of the flower-pots. Eventually he wipes his brow with a finger and sighs. "Michiko wen' to da same school as me, but she was two years older. I was friends wit' her bruddah, so we all wen' go walk to school together. She tol' me I was too young fo' her, so every year on my birt'day, I would go her house fo' ask her out on a date.

"An' even aftah I wen' college, I still wen' stop by her house every year, even though she was engaged to some uddah guy. Finally, one day she ask me, 'Why you keep knocking on my door when you know I getting married to someone else?' So den

I tell her, 'I know you no like marry dat uddah guy—you like marry me, as soon as I get old enough.' So she ask me why I would t'ink li'dat, and so I go tell her, 'Because aftah all dis years I was asking you out, you neva did once tell me no.'"

I'm watching him carefully. "So, did she break off her engagement?"

His laugh is short and deep. "No. She said I was lolo and said fo' leave her alone—dat now she was finally telling me no." He shrugs. "So I left. I wen' go do some traveling, wen' try fo' date uddah girls—but dey wasn't Michiko. I wen' move to da mainland fo' look fo' work, t'inking dat Michiko was happily married.

"And den one year on my birt'day I was sitting in my apartment watching TV, and den she suddenly show up at my door. And she jus' said, 'What about now?'" He shrugs. "So I quit my job, move back to Hawaii, and den we got married."

"Holy shit," I say. "That's really romantic."

He makes a rumbling noise in the back of his throat. "Huh, watch your language, eh, you?"

I hold up my hands. "Sorry." Chewing my lip, I shake my head. "I don't think you can help me, actually. You can't have a love story that epic and be able to understand what it feels like to not be interested in falling in love or kissing people you go on dates with."

Mr. Watanabe clicks his tongue against the roof of his mouth, and even though he's partially facing away from me, I *swear* he rolls his eyes. "I tol' you dat already. You don' know how fo' listen."

"Yeah, yeah, yeah." I sigh, trailing my fingertips along the orchid petals.

"Hey." He grunts with his chin dipped low. "Go talk to your muddah. No good stay angry fo'eva. She your family, you know."

I don't say anything. I water the rest of the flowers in silence.

CHAPTER THIRTY-SEVEN

It's been three days since I've seen or talked to Kai. I don't think he's avoiding me—it's more like he's waiting for me to tell him it's okay for us to still be friends. But I haven't finished processing my feelings. I'm still trying to understand what they mean.

Lea's guitar is next to me on the bed. There's a hungry itch in my fingertips, begging me to pluck just one of the strings. And I want to—I really do—but I'm too scared to hear the sound of her guitar.

When I'm writing lyrics or singing music and I see her across from me, I feel like a part of her still exists. It feels like I'm not alone anymore—like she's with me. A part of me.

But I'm afraid if I play her guitar, she might disappear for good. I don't know what it will mean if her guitar becomes mine—if her *sound* becomes mine.

I'm worried it will mean she doesn't exist anymore. Not even in my head, where the music keeps her alive.

And I'm not sure if I'd be able to bring her back after that. I'm not sure if I'm ready for her ghost to leave me.

I'm not ready to face the world without Lea. I'm not ready to go back to how it felt when I first came to Hawaii—so full of rage and pain.

I'm not ready to say good-bye to my sister.

There's a knock at the door, and Aunty Ani appears with white flags in her eyes. "Can we talk?"

I nod and move the guitar to the floor to make space for her.

She sits next to me, folding her hands together in her lap. "Mrs. Yamada says she hasn't seen you in a few days."

I tuck my legs behind me. "Tell her I'll go in tomorrow. I just needed a few days to clear my head."

Aunty Ani nods, not wanting to pressure me, but not wanting me to get out of too much. "Okay. But remember, you're not working fo' her as a favor—you owe her family fo' the window."

"I know that," I say in a flat tone.

Her eyes flit around the room, to my notebook and Lea's guitar and the pile of laundry in the corner. "Is there anything you want to talk about? Anything you want to ask me?"

"About Mom? No."

"About anything," Aunty Ani clarifies. "About why you've been hiding out in here fo' three days and avoiding the neighbor."

"I hang out with Mr. Watanabe all the time."

She narrows her eyes. "No get smart. You know who I mean."

I pick the edge of my thumb because I don't know what to do with my hands. "We went out on a date. It went . . . badly."

Aunty Ani raises her eyebrows, and her forehead wrinkles. "I didn't know you liked him like that."

I let out a breath of air. "I don't. That's the problem."

"That's dating—you can't like everyone. Sometimes you have to have a bad date to figure that part out," she offers.

"I think," I start, "that all dates will end up being bad dates for me. I'm not sure I even *like* dating."

"Nobody likes dating." Aunty Ani laughs. "It's the worst."

"No," I say gruffly, twisting my body toward her. "I mean I don't have any interest in dating. Like, maybe at all."

She looks at me curiously. "Why does that bother you so much?"

"Because I hate that I have to know the answers to these things. And not just when it comes to dating. I feel like I'm supposed to know everything, right now, and never change my mind for as long as I live." My heartbeat picks up, and I dig my fingers into my rib cage.

Dad learned the answers to his questions too late in life, and because of it, he disappointed people. He disappointed his family.

I don't want to spend my life breaking promises to everyone, but I also don't want to feel pressured to make them at all. Not right now, when I don't know what I want.

And I'm worried I'm a drifter, like Dad. I'm worried I'll spend the rest of my life not really knowing what to do, and hurting other people by jumping in and out of their lives.

I don't *want* to be like Dad, but maybe I can't help it. Maybe I just am.

And maybe that's why Mom always preferred Lea.

"It's okay to change your mind." Aunty Ani looks at me seriously. "You're seventeen years old. Nobody expects you to have the answers fo' everything, even if you think you do sometimes. You're still a teenager—you have all the time in the world."

I drop my eyes. *All the time in the world.* It's what Lea should've had—not that she needed any extra time to figure out who she was and what she wanted. She already knew.

Most of the time I feel like I don't know anything, and sometimes it makes me feel like I don't deserve to be here. It feels like I took Lea's place, when she was so much more worthy of life than I ever will be.

Just like she's always been more worthy of Mom.

Mom coming back into my life doesn't change the fact that she left. It doesn't change the fact that she *wouldn't* have left if Lea had been the one to survive.

I look back at Aunty Ani, who's still waiting for me to talk. "Lea had all the answers. I only know how to make things worse." My throat feels scratchy and achy, like something is lodged far in the back of it. "I should've been the one to die. Lea wouldn't have made a giant mess of her life the way I will. The way I am right now. She would never have disappointed anyone."

"Don't say that." Aunty Ani looks horrified.

My nostrils go wide, and I take in too much painful oxygen. "It's true. Lea knew who she was and what she wanted out of life. She had plans. She fit in this world better than me. I'm wasting this life. I know I am. And I don't know how to stop it—I don't know how to *not* waste it, because I don't know what the fuck I'm supposed to be doing."

Her eyes dart back and forth, and then she's hugging me, her hair tickling my nose. "You don't have fo' do anything. Just live, one day at a time."

I close my eyes. I know time is supposed to heal a broken heart, but maybe some hearts are broken worse than others. Maybe some hearts need a lot more time.

"I know it's not your fault," I say finally. "You didn't ask for any of this, and I know I haven't been nice to you. And I'm sorry for that. It's just hard to keep track of who I'm angry at sometimes."

"You don't have to apologize to me. I'm sorry I'm not better at dis kine stuff," Aunty Ani says gently. "I'm sorry I'm not what you needed most. *Who* you needed most."

"I know you want me to talk to Mom, but I'm not ready. I will be, maybe, but not today. Not right now," I say.

I feel her nod against my skull. "Okay. Just tell me when you're ready."

CHAPTER THIRTY-EIGHT

I wake up to shouting outside the house. I roll over, looking at the early-morning sun starting to bleed through the window, and part the blinds so I can see out onto the street.

Mr. Yamada is face-to-face with Kai, his arms moving from the car to the house and back again. He's yelling something I can't hear. Something I know I probably shouldn't hear.

Kai is shaking his head, holding up his hands like he's refusing to do something.

And because it's early and they should be inside if they care about eavesdropping, I pull the window open slightly so I can hear what they're saying.

"Do you know how embarrassing this is for me? These are people I work with," Mr. Yamada shouts.

Kai's face is dark red and he's staring at the ground with his fists tight.

"Get in the car, Kai. Now."

"No. I'm not going."

"Get in the car!"

Kai lifts his face. "I said no! I'll call the recruiter myself when I'm ready."

"You are not staying home for a year just to screw around on the beach."

"Lots of people take a year off between high school and college. I want time to decide what I want to do. I don't want to jump into anything."

Mr. Yamada looks at his cell phone. "We're going to be late. Get in the car. You're not missing this appointment—not after I've already had to reschedule twice."

Kai's shoulders shake. "I said no, Dad. Stop pushing me."

And then Mr. Yamada starts shouting louder and Kai's shouting over him, and it's too difficult to catch all the words because suddenly Mrs. Yamada is there too, yelling at them both to be quiet.

It happens really quickly—Mr. Yamada grabs a fistful of shirt from the back of Kai's neck and tries to shove him toward the car door, but Kai swings his arm up to get his father to let go. I think it's an accident—I'm not sure—but Kai's hand clips the bottom of Mr. Yamada's chin, and then all hell breaks loose.

Mr. Yamada pushes Kai back with force. Mrs. Yamada screams at them to stop and then jumps in between the two of them. Kai is shouting from behind her. Mr. Yamada is raging in front of her.

"Get in the car!"

"Don't fucking touch me!"

"Get in the fucking car!"

"Stop!"

"Stop!"

"Stop!"

And then Kai walks up to the blue Mustang and smashes his fist through the glass.

"Oh my God." It's my voice, sharp and quick and sucked back inside me like I'm taking in a gasp of air. There's glass everywhere, and Kai's knuckles are bleeding, and his mom is reaching for his hand. And crying. And shaking. Even Mr. Yamada is leaning forward with concern.

And then, "Get in the car. You need stitches."

The three of them climb inside Mrs. Yamada's car, leaving the windowless Mustang in the driveway. When they're gone, I stare at the shattered bits of bloodied glass and feel my heart pound and pound.

A memory

I can hear sirens. My heartbeat. Someone's heartbeat? Oh God, whose heartbeat is that? Why is it going so fast?

I can't feel my legs. I can't feel my arms either, and oh God, am I paralyzed? I can't move.

A sound escapes me, but it sounds like something shriveled and weak. There's broken glass against my face. It must be pressed into my skin, but I can't feel it—I just see it reflecting off the road like crushed ice.

Lea? Mom?

I'm trying to call their names, but my voice isn't working. I'm not sure if anything is working.

There's footsteps. Ringing. Voices.

A woman's face appears in front of me.

"Can you hear me? You're going to be okay. I'm going to get you out of there. You're going to be okay."

I'm going to be okay. What about everyone else?

Mom?

Lea?

Can you hear me?

Why can't I say the words?

Why can't I hear them?

Why am I all alone?

The panic attack hits me hard. I feel a burst of something heavy rise up my stomach and fill my chest and throat. My heart is beating like a snare drum—over and over and over again like I'm bracing for the end of something. I clutch my shirt, pulling the material away from me like I'm pulling my skin off, and before I know it I'm sitting on the floor with my head between my knees, my sharp breaths making the back of my throat feel like it's full of coarse sand.

I try to focus on something—a thought or a memory that isn't broken glass and lost voices. A melody that isn't screeching tires and my sister calling my name for the very last time. A song that feels more like home than a volcano.

I think of Mom.

Mom who should be here, Mom who should be telling me what to do, Mom who should be making me feel like everything is going to be okay.

"I don't know how to do this on my own," I whisper before it's even a real thought.

It's a strange feeling, to be okay and not okay all at the same time. I'm okay in the sense that I haven't cried. That I haven't completely lost it. And I'm *not* okay in the sense that I haven't cried. That I haven't completely lost it.

I've bottled up my emotions and hidden them somewhere that was supposed to be safe. I thought it was to protect myself, but maybe it's because I haven't been ready. Maybe I didn't want to feel everything all on my own.

I lift my head and see Mr. Watanabe's ukulele across the room from me—the one he told me I could borrow to help finish my song. My heart is still racing and my breathing is rapid, but I crawl across the floor and pick it up anyway.

I close my eyes and Lea is already there. I let out a slow breath, and suddenly Mom is there too.

There are fuzzy stars behind my eyelids, and my head is spinning with the horrible memory of the crash.

But I focus on my family instead. I focus on home.

I make my way to the edge of the bed and strum the chords to my mother's favorite song. I sing the words to "Dream a Little Dream of Me." I feel the warmth of my mother and sister next to me—the two ghosts I need to feel whole.

I don't write any new lyrics. I'm too busy remembering the ones that used to make me happy. The ones that used to make me feel something.

I don't notice the panic attack subsiding. I only notice the tingle in my nose and the moment when I almost cry, but don't.

I miss Lea, but I miss Mom, too.

I don't leave the bed until I see Mrs. Yamada's car roll back up the driveway. I rush outside and down the steps, and I reach the gate as Kai's closing the car door.

His hand is bandaged in gauze and tape, like he's wearing some kind of pretend boxing glove. Mr. Yamada doesn't get out of the car because he's not here at all. I wonder if he went to work straight after the hospital.

Mrs. Yamada sees me first. She gives me a tired smile and nods at Kai. "I'll see you inside." She tilts her head to me, in case he hasn't noticed I'm there.

And he hadn't, because when his eyes click to mine, he pulls his face back in surprise. "Hey," he says, like he forgot I live next door.

I push the gate open and walk toward him. "Dude, back off—breaking windows is *my* thing."

He looks worn out and in desperate need of a nap, but he still manages to grin. "Well, the good news is my dad has probably forgotten about the money you owe him. He's too busy planning my life sentence."

"That's too bad. I kind of like working at your mom's place," I say.

He shrugs. "I might have to work there too, if I don't get shipped off fo' basic training first. Unless you still don't want to be around me." He pauses. "In which case, I'll ask my mom to fire you so I can take your place."

A laugh escapes me, and my eyes quickly drift away from him. I pause, hoping my words will come out the way I intend. "I've been thinking a lot, about what happened."

Kai opens his mouth, but I lift both my hands like I'm trying to stop him.

"No. This is important." I clear my throat. Sandwich method. "I really like hanging out with you. More important, I like *you*— but not the same way you like me. And I'm sorry if this sounds selfish and unfair, but I want us to keep hanging out, as friends. Because I'm really fucking lonely, and you are the literal sunshine in my life right now, and I look forward to seeing you—even if I don't want to date you—and I need you to not hate me. Because it's not you. I just don't want to date anyone. Maybe not ever, but definitely not right now. And I need you to act the same with me and be my friend—because you're a really good friend—and I don't want to lose you, because if you're not in my life I think the world is going to go dark again and I'm not sure I have the strength for another war. So please don't quit me. I kind of need you."

Okay, so less of a sandwich and more of a really messy, falling-to-pieces, twelve-inch sub.

To my surprise, he laughs. It sounds like a thousand cherry blossoms floating through the air in spring. Bringing his unwrapped hand to his forehead, he pushes his hair back. "I don't hate you, hapa. I like you. In fact, I like you enough that it doesn't matter if you don't like me. And even though I'm really tired and in all honesty probably didn't catch everything you said in your breakup speech"—I make a face at him, which only makes him laugh harder—"friends is fine." He shrugs. Smiles. "I can do friends."

"Okay." I look at the broken glass still scattered around the pavement. "How many stitches did you get?"

"A few."

"Does it hurt?"

"A little. The doctor said it's a miracle I didn't break my hand. I'm more angry that I can't surf like this."

"I'm sorry."

"It's not your fault."

"It's not my fault you changed your mind about the military?"

Kai cradles his hand against his chest. "You heard that, huh?"

I motion toward my bedroom window. "Sorry for eavesdropping, but there's something about a good old-fashioned public meltdown I just can't say no to."

He laughs. "Well, don't feel bad. It wasn't only because of what you said to me. I haven't been sure about joining the military for a while. I guess I'm trying to figure out what to do."

I roll my weight to the back of my heels. "I think it's good that you told him how you feel."

Kai tilts his head back and takes a huge breath. It releases from him slowly. "I think the problem is I'm not sure how *I* feel. Maybe I'll still join, and maybe I won't. Just . . . be my friend too, okay?

Support me no matter what I decide. No more judging my life choices and waving your dead sister card around to make me feel guilty."

I bite my lip. "I do that?"

"A little." His eyes soften.

"Okay," I say finally. He looks grateful, but tired, too, as if the electricity is fizzling out behind his dark stare. I decide to give the sandwich method a chance to redeem itself. "I'm proud of you. You look like a dementor is draining the life out of you before my eyes. I kind of missed you."

First he looks surprised. Then happy. And then hesitant, like he's remembered something that's stopping his grin from turning into a full smile.

"I missed you too, hapa," he says at last. He turns back for his front door, and when he gets to the top step, he looks over his shoulder and waves before disappearing inside.

CHAPTER THIRTY-NINE

Jae-Jae finishes styling a woman's hair, flipping the ends like she's getting her ready for a magazine photo shoot. With a glorious smile, she pulls the apron from the woman and asks, "What do you think?"

"Perfect." She turns left and right, eyeing herself in the mirror. "Thanks, Jae-Jae."

The woman makes her way to the cash register, where I'm sitting with a pen still wedged between my fingers. After I pass her a receipt, she waves to Jae-Jae and slips through the door to make her new debut on the sidewalk.

I pull my notebook out from under the counter and try to finish my lyrics.

I'll remember you in summer,
when the bluest sky turns black,
and the stars form words across the sky,
saying you aren't coming back.

I feel Jae-Jae's fingers run through my hair. "I could make this beautiful."

I let my head drop back so I'm staring up at her. "Can you make this beautiful too?" I tap my pen against the page of unfinished lyrics.

Jae-Jae scoots around me and leans against the counter so she can read my messy handwriting. "You're missing the sparkle."

"The sparkle?" I repeat.

She nods. "The magic. What's your inspiration?"

I shrink. "Three words my sister and I chose right before she died. Does that count?"

Jae-Jae makes a face like she's smelling bad food. "That could be your problem. You're writing a eulogy, when you're supposed to be writing a song."

I lean back in the chair and swivel from side to side. "I've lost it. I can't write anything anymore. I used to be good at this."

"Don't you have any other emotions to pull from?"

"You mean other than my dead sister?"

She fidgets. "Well, you *can* use that. But you *aren't* using that." She flips through my notebook. "It kind of reads like you're trying to write the song your sister would have wanted instead of writing the song *you* want." She waves at her own hair and outfit. "It's like if I tried to style myself like someone famous. It's mimicry. It isn't a Jae-Jae original." She looks serious. "You don't want someone's hand-me-downs. You want a custom Marchesa gown that's made just for you."

"Custom Marchesa gown. Got it." I pause. "What is that exactly?"

Jae-Jae laughs. "I'm just saying maybe you need a reboot. I could always start with your hair." She bites her lip and widens her magenta-lined eyes hopefully.

"I see what you did there," I say, laughing. "But I'm not ready for hair. When I am, I promise you'll be the first to know."

The phone rings, and Jae-Jae winks at me before picking it up. "Hyung-Lee's Salon at the Palekaiko Bay Resort, how can I help you?"

I write the lyrics over and over again, in so many different ways. I practice melodies on Mr. Watanabe's piano. I hear guitar chords in my head. I sing until my throat hurts.

But I can't put the words together. It's like there's a giant roadblock in my brain, and trying to dig to the other side is like trying to claw my way through a mountain.

I'm torn between writing the song that sounds like fire and writing the one that sounds like home.

I feel like I'm stuck in between something, only I don't know exactly what the *something* is.

When I came to Hawaii I was someplace dark and cold. I felt trapped, but instead of coming up for a breath of air, I flung myself into the galaxy because I wasn't ready to face what the world became without Lea and Mom. Now my time in space is up, and I'm falling back to earth with no idea what's waiting for me.

My lyrics don't feel right because *I* don't feel right.

Kai invites me to another barbecue at the beach—as friends—

and Izzy shows up with her guitar and her girlfriend, Camille, who happens to also be the drummer in their band.

"Izzy says you can really sing," Camille tells me when everyone is sitting in a circle eating fish burgers and beef skewers.

"I tried to get her fo' go to open-mic night, but she no like come," Gareth offers through a mouthful of burger.

"I've never really played in front of strangers before. Not on my own, I mean." I realize I'm already alluding to Lea, and the thought makes my heart jump. Not because of how much I miss Lea, but because I'm already picturing Kai rolling his eyes at me.

But he's not listening. He twists his can of guava juice into the sand to make sure it doesn't tip over. His hand is still wrapped in bandages, and he hasn't said much since we all sat down together. He still seems tired—maybe yelling at his dad really took it out of him.

Camille flashes a smile. "You should come this Thursday. It's good fun."

Hannah nods in agreement beside me. She's sitting with her knees up and an arm draped over her legs. "Yeah, we're all going. These two will be playing." She raises her chin toward Izzy and Camille.

"My song isn't really ready," I admit, looking at Kai for any sign of interest.

He gives me a weak smile, but that's all.

I wonder if things are really bad with his dad, and then I feel like a terrible friend for not asking before we got here.

"Let's hear whatchu got," Izzy offers, shoving the last piece of her burger into her mouth and clapping the crumbs from her hands. She reaches for the guitar neck and passes it to me with a strong arm.

"Seriously?" I ask, and she nods. I pull the guitar close to me and flatten my palm over the strings. "Okay, well . . . maybe the melody. I'm not ready to share the lyrics."

I brush my thumb over the strings a few times. It's strange going back to a guitar after using Mr. Watanabe's ukulele for weeks. The fret board feels enormous, and the strings feel so thick in comparison. But still, it's familiar.

I run through the chords for my work in progress a little more carefully than normal because I hate making mistakes in front of people. Lea was different—she'd mess up and laugh and laugh like it was the funniest thing in the world. I, on the other hand, internalize humiliation very well.

After I move through each chord and find a rhythm, I repeat the song a little faster. My heartbeat picks up, and I feel the rush of Lea's ghost blur through my thoughts.

I'm starting to need her. Knowing I can reach her with music leaves me with a hunger. An ache. I wonder if it's possible to keep a ghost with you forever.

Maybe I don't have to say good-bye.

Maybe I don't have to be alone.

Izzy bobs her head up and down, while Camille rests sweetly against her shoulder. Hannah is whispering to Kai—something that makes him tuck his chin lower and grin—but I start to lose myself in the music and my eyes drift away.

A memory

Alice leans into Caleb's neck, whispering something that makes both of them laugh.

I hate that I feel jealous of them. Not because of what they have together, but because of what I'm not a part of anymore. It was either me and Caleb or me and Alice—not Alice and Caleb. It was never supposed to be the two of them and me on the outside.

I lost both my friends as soon as they started dating.

I take my eyes away from them and lean back against the brick wall right outside the bus stop. Lea is standing beside me, her guitar wrapped around her shoulder, watching the last school bus pull away.

She tilts her head toward me and raises a brow. "Why do you still wait for her?"

"We always walk to first period together," I reply irritably.

Lea crunches a mint between her teeth because impatience is one of the few things we share besides our love of music and the world's busiest mother. "She can walk with Caleb—I'll walk with you."

I raise my fingers to my temples. "Oh my God, what is happening? You're supposed to be the freshman who doesn't have any friends, and I should be the cool big sister who walks you to class so you don't feel embarrassed."

"Honestly, Rumi, you were never that cool," she replies.

I choke out a laugh and place a hand on my heart like she's hurt me. "Brutal honesty. We really have traded places."

She laughs easily. "I'm kidding." And then she's looking at me with her big, round eyes that remind me of Mom. "I like walking with you. I'm kind of glad you're not as close to Alice and Caleb. It made room for me."

I open my mouth to say something snarky and dismissive but realize I don't want to. Because it's the truth. Losing my two best friends made more room for Lea. And maybe it's better that way. Maybe I like it better that way.

Lea lifts her guitar strap over her neck and passes the instrument to me. "Come on, let's practice our new song."

"Uh, there are people *everywhere*. No way," I hiss.

She thrusts the guitar into my stomach. "Trust me. We're doing this."

"I'm not playing in front of the whole school, Lea. It's embarrassing," I say. "Besides, it's your guitar. If you want to make a scene, you can do it on your own."

She curls her hair behind her ears and purses her lips. "You have to play. I'm using my second wish."

I feel my heart pound.

She holds her hand out like she's waiting for her intro.

I sigh. "You don't get a do-over. Wishes are nonrefundable. You'll only have one left for the history of ever. Are you sure you don't want to reconsider?"

"*A wish is a wish.* Play the song, Rumi."

I strum the melody of "Boy Wink Music," and before I know it, I'm losing myself in the song, our voices harmonizing together like fire and oxygen. Every note makes our confidence grow, and midway through the song I realize there's a crowd surrounding us. They're as hypnotized by the music as we are.

When the song ends, our schoolyard audience breaks into enthusiastic applause. My face burns fiercely and my chest is thumping rapidly, but I'm smiling wider than I have in weeks. Lea grabs my hand and forces me to take a goofy bow alongside her. I'm dizzy with adrenaline, and by the sound of her infectious giggling, she is too.

She nudges me with her shoulder. "See? Wasn't that fun?"

My ears are ringing from the excitement of performing. Some people are still clapping and urging us to sing another song. I'm not going to lie—I'm ready to sing another ten.

But I roll my eyes anyway because Lea wouldn't recognize me if I didn't. "I still can't believe you wasted a wish on that."

"It wasn't a waste," she whispers. "Look how happy you are."

I can't fight my smile. It's stretched so far across my face that my cheeks hurt.

Because I love the crowd. I love the energy of people who like my music—our music. It's encouraging and inspiring and it fills my soul with motivation to keep writing. To keep creating.

And Lea knows what the crowd does to me, the same way she always knew as a child how much I needed her to listen to me practice scales on a piano or strum clumsily along to songs on the radio.

I like sharing music with the world. It's one of the very few things I know I'll never change my mind about.

My sister used one of her wishes to give me a moment of happiness.

I don't think I'll ever deserve her for as long as I live.

Even when she's gone, she's still leading me back to music—back to what brings me the most joy. She's selfless even in death, and I don't know what to make of that.

I miss her so much, and I'd grant her a thousand more wishes if it meant I could have her back.

But I have her ghost. I have her in the music.

I need that to mean something.

When the song ends, I flatten my palm against the strings and look up at the faces across from me.

Life buzzes over every inch of my skin.

Izzy raises a fist in the air and lets out a melodic howl. "Eh, not bad, sistah. Not bad at all."

Camille smiles. "You definitely need to come to the Coconut Shack on Thursday."

When I look at Kai, he's smiling too.

"Maybe I will," I say to him more than anyone else.

Izzy reaches behind Camille and finds the football. Spinning it in her hands, she asks, "Who like toss da ball around wit' me?"

Gareth and Jerrod are the first to leap up. Kai starts to, and then remembers his hand and gives a sheepish wave to send them off.

Hannah giggles, shaking her head at him. "That's what you get for trying to act like the Hulk."

Kai buries his eyes in the crook of his arm and muffles his groan. "Don't pick on me. I'm suffering enough."

Hannah keeps making fun of him, egging on his stifled laughter, but I'm suddenly tuning them out. There's a guitar in my hands—I'm not interested in anything else but the hope of music.

I strum a few more chords, slowly at first, and then I fall into a gentle rhythm that mimics the sound of the water, the dull laughter across the sand, and the football sailing through the air.

I think of my words—the ones I'm having such a hard time finding. I think of what Jae-Jae told me—about missing the sparkle. And I look across at Kai, and even though his voice is drowned out by the music in my head, I frame my lyrics around his dark hair, his electric eyes, and the hope that maybe—just maybe—Lea lured me to him with the song on the radio.

Not because she wanted me to kiss him, but because she knew how much I needed a friend.

I think of the words I want to write down.

And when I get home, I scribble everything into my notebook so I'll never forget them.

CHAPTER FORTY

For the next two days, I don't stop writing. I write and rewrite and do it all again. I write late into the evening, strumming against the borrowed ukulele like it's the very cure for everything I'm feeling.

By Thursday afternoon, I not only have a song I like, but I have a song I want to perform. And feeling ready to perform feels so incredible and powerful that I don't stop smiling all day.

"What's wrong?" Aunty Ani asks when she sees me at the table.

"Nothing. I'm just in a good mood," I say.

"That's exactly why I'm confused," she replies.

I shrug, but I'm still smiling.

When Kai drives me to the Coconut Shack, even he notices something is different.

"Are you okay?" he asks, his eyes filled with concern.

I shake my head, cradling Mr. Watanabe's ukulele in my lap. "I'm great, actually. I'm excited, and I haven't been excited in . . . well, a while."

And then he smiles too, and I feel like I'm doing the right thing for the first time in months.

Izzy, Camille, and the rest of their band perform first. They're really good, and it doesn't even make me nervous. I'm not sure if that's strange.

Jae-Jae turns up when I'm still waiting to go onstage.

"Aunty Sun told me you were performing tonight. I didn't want to miss it," she says, giving me a huge hug.

I bounce with giddiness. *Giddiness*. I don't know what's happening to me.

More and more people go up to perform. Some of them are amateurs, some of them are seasoned pros, but all of them are up there because they're passionate about music.

I love every second of it.

Kai, Hannah, Gareth, and Jae-Jae all sit around the same table drinking soda and picking at a nacho platter when I go backstage. There's a problem with the list, so I wait off to the side while the manager squeezes in a couple extra singers.

That's when the nerves hit me.

I'm jittery and jumpy and I feel like there's lightning shooting through my fingertips. I squeeze the neck of the ukulele in one hand and tap the side of my leg again and again and again with the other, like I'm playing "The Flight of the Bumblebee."

And then I'm sitting in the middle of the stage with the lights shining down on me and a microphone at my lips.

I don't see the audience. I don't see the room. I close my eyes and I don't see anything at all.

"Hey, guys. My name is Rumi." Someone shouts and claps—maybe Kai, but maybe Izzy. I clear my throat. "This song is kind of a work in progress. It's called 'In Time.'"

It was late at night,
I was sitting in the dark,
You found me on a driveway
with a broken heart.
You were looking at a ghost,
but I don't think you knew,
All you saw was a girl
that you somehow saw through.
And I think you should know,
you can't erase the pain,
but that doesn't mean,
I'm not ready to live again.
I feel restless, hopeless,
Useless, powerless,
I feel as still as a photograph,
I don't know how to go back
in time.
And I'm not fearless, painless,
Selfless or harmless,
But whenever you're near me,
I find myself falling
in time.

My fingers shift across the fret board in time with the verses and bridge, and when I strum the final chord, I open my eyes and see the fluttering picture of cheers and applause rolling through the crowd.

Onstage with my heart and ukulele, I'm beaming like the sun after an eclipse. The bright overhead lights make me flinch. I'm quickly trying to look for our table—for Kai—but I don't see him. Just his empty chair and a half-empty glass of Pepsi.

"Thanks," I mumble into the microphone, hopping off the stool and making my way to the side of the small stage.

People clap their hands on my shoulders as I walk past them, congratulating me on the song and telling me how much they enjoyed it. I keep muttering "Thank you" over and over again, my eyes forever scanning the busy room.

For a moment my heart sinks. I don't see Kai anywhere. Did he miss the song?

God, I hope not. I needed him to hear it. I needed him to get it—not just the words, but what it means to have finished a song at all. To have written something that was *Rumi* without *Lea* and not have it destroy me completely. I need him to know he's been helping with that, just by being my friend.

But I don't see him anywhere.

I look out toward the table one more time, and I see Gareth and Jerrod demolishing the rest of the nachos. Izzy and Camille are talking to themselves, their eyes skipping around the crowd now and then like they're waiting for someone—probably me.

I bite the edge of my lip and take a step toward them. I don't know where Kai is, but I don't want to be alone right now. I want to talk about what happened onstage. I want to talk about the music and how it made me feel, and—

I feel his fingers brush my arm before his voice reaches my ears. "Hapa."

I turn around and see Kai, his irises glinting like tigereye stones—brown and gold and warm. I clutch the ukulele closer to my chest.

"You like walk with me?" he asks, and I'm nodding before he's even finished the question.

We go downstairs, weaving through tables and groups of people waiting at the bar, and make our way across the parking lot toward the sandy beach. The sky is a deep plum, and if it weren't for the scattering of stars above, I'd find it hard to see where the sky ends and the ocean begins.

The scent of burning coals on a barbecue from the restaurant across the road makes my mouth water. I haven't eaten anything since breakfast because I was too worried I'd vomit onstage.

But now my stomach is rumbling, and Kai's silence and indiscernible expression in the darkness are making me nervous.

"So," I say, because the silence is heavier than a beluga whale.

"So," he says back, and I'm relieved to hear the grin in his voice. "You wrote a song about me."

"I did," I say. "But not in an Adele kind of way."

"What's that exactly?"

"The I-wrote-a-song-about-you-because-I-feel-emotionally-

attached-and-maybe-still-have-romantic-feelings-for-you-but-
I'm-too-scared-to-tell-you-in-person kind of way."

His laugh sounds like wild raindrops covering the entire
earth. I take a breath and inhale the sea.

Kai shrugs. "You don't have to say anything. I get it."

"You do?"

I can see the movement of his nod—the shift of shadow and
moonlight. I know he's beautiful, but just because something is
beautiful doesn't mean I want to kiss it. Someone can be beautiful
and I don't want to have a romantic relationship with them.

There are other kinds of relationships I find more important.
Family. Friendships. Music.

What I have with Kai—it's helping me to heal. I didn't realize
it at first, but that's because I was too stubborn and confused and
angry at the world. I used to think I could be happy alone, but
that's when I still had Lea and Mom.

With them gone . . .

I don't want to be alone.

I shouldn't be alone.

Being friends with Kai makes me feel connected to the world
again. It makes me feel grounded.

I don't know how he could possibly understand all of that
without me explaining it to him.

Kai crosses his arms. Uncrosses them. Scratches the side of
his head. "You're not a ghost, you know."

I swallow a lump in my throat I didn't even realize was there.

"I know you think you are, but you aren't. I'm not saying you don't feel broken or lost or incomplete without your sistah, but you're whole. You're a whole person. Your family might not look the same as it used to, but *you're* whole. And you don't have to worry that I'm going to stop being your friend." He stops walking, and I look up at the whites of his eyes, which glint in the darkness. "It's okay that you don't like me like that. You need a friend, and I care about you. So I can be that friend. I know that's all it's ever going to be, and that's okay. And . . . you don't need to worry I'm going to stop being your friend. Or that I'll leave you and you'll be alone again. Because I think maybe that's why you wrote that song."

I frown. "What do you mean?"

"I know what a big deal it is that you finished writing a whole song and that you were able to perform it onstage. But I think you wrote it fo' me because you're worried we're going to stop being friends or something."

"That's not true," I say.

He lifts his shoulders. "You didn't go along with kissing me because you were afraid of telling me sooner that you didn't like me that way?"

"No—I—that's not," I start, but I can't untangle my words. Because the truth is, I hadn't really thought about it. The truth is, maybe he's right.

"I think you know yourself more than you realize," Kai says. "You don't have to be afraid of who you are. Especially not around me. I'm not going anywhere, okay?"

I feel like I should argue with him and tell him he's wrong. I feel like I should say a hundred different reasons why I kissed him and why I wrote a song for him. I want to insist that I'm not afraid of anything, and I don't care if he wants to be in or out of my life, because I don't need anybody and I'm fine by myself.

But I can't lie to Kai. I don't want to.

"Thank you," I say instead.

Kai is so stoic and serious. I feel like we're supposed to hug, or cry, or . . . something emotional. And I'm halfway through deciding whether I should lift my arm and wrap it around his shoulder when he raises his hand and *boop*s me on the nose.

Seriously. He's *so weird*.

I blink. "Did you just *boop* my nose?"

Kai laughs at the same time a wave crashes into the sand, which makes me feel like the entire beach is laughing at me. "I'm sorry. It was getting awkward."

"And you thought that would make it *less* awkward?"

He shrugs. "You're smiling."

"I am not. You can't even see anything. It's way too dark."

"I can see your teeth. They're glowing under the streetlights, like one bigfin reef squid."

"What are you even talking about?"

"Bioluminescence."

I try to keep a straight face, but there's no point—the laughter pours out of me until my eyes are watering, and then I'm telling Kai he's the one who's lolo, and he's telling me he loved my song.

We're friends, walking along the beach at night, and it feels like maybe the world is steadier than I realized.

CHAPTER FORTY-ONE

I don't expect to see Aunty Ani when I get home because it's almost midnight, but she's sitting at the dining room table with her hands cradling a mug of tea. She must've taken a shower recently because her dark brown hair is heavy and damp, and she's wearing her purple bathrobe.

I set the ukulele on the couch and stop in the middle of the room, like I'm standing at a crossroads between Aunty Ani and bed.

"Were you waiting up for me?" I ask.

She pulls her fingers away from the mug and lets them fall to the table. "Of course I am. You're seventeen. You're my responsibility."

I scratch the back of my arm. "You don't have to worry about me."

"But I do." She motions to the chair across from her. "You like keep me company fo' a few minutes? Tell me how your night went?"

I let myself fall in the chair because I'm too tired to argue. And also, it feels like I've been avoiding Aunty Ani for a long time. Maybe too long.

It's not her fault Lea died. It's not her fault Mom left. I need to stop punishing her for events she had no control over.

I let out a sigh, and I don't think I'm tired from walking around the beach with Kai and spending the night singing karaoke with my friends—I think I've been tired for a while.

"Come on, I'm not that bad, eh?" Aunty Ani makes a face.

I smile and shake my head. "It wasn't meant for you. It's just been a long"—I pause—"few months."

She reaches toward me and places her hand over mine like she doesn't want me to fly away too quickly. "I'm always here, you know. If you ever need anything. Even if you don't need anything—even if you just like know somebody is here."

I think about Kai and Hannah and Gareth and Jerrod and Aunty Ani and Mr. Watanabe and even Poi. They're all *here*.

Losing Lea and Mom was sudden. It felt like the world threw me overboard and I was swimming in darkness. And maybe I've been terrified all change would be like that—scary and lonely and confusing. But maybe some change is gradual. It creeps up on you so slowly you don't even realize what's happening, until suddenly the world feels stable again.

I don't feel like I'm floating anymore. I don't feel like a ghost.

"She wants to see you. She's desperate." Aunty Ani's eyes don't leave mine. "Maybe you could just give her a few minutes? See what she has to say?"

I withdraw my hand slowly and push it into my lap. Aunty Ani flexes her fingers before doing the same.

"I'm not angry at you for asking," I say, staring at the table.

309

"But I'm angry at her for thinking it's okay to talk now, after she left me for weeks to deal with all of this on my own. Because what kind of mother does that? My sister died, and I needed my mom. She's my parent—my only parent—so she's the one who should be teaching me things about real life. Like how to grieve, or how to stop missing Lea so much, or how to stop feeling like my sister deserved to live so much more than I do."

"Oh, honey," Aunty Ani says with a timid voice. "You *both* deserved to live. What happened was just a horrible accident."

"I know it was an accident, but you don't understand—Mom would never have left Lea. She would've cared more, because it was so easy to care about Lea. And Lea would've known how to comfort Mom back—they both would have been *better* together." I'm shaking my head like I don't understand, even though I sound like I do. Because I know everything I'm saying to Aunty Ani is true, but I also don't know how it can be—how Mom could treat Lea and me so differently when we were both her daughters.

It's not that I think she didn't love us both, because I know she did. But Mom never remembered to care about me the way she cared about Lea. Because Lea was her baby, and I was her helper— the one who took care of Lea when Mom couldn't be around.

And maybe it's my fault too, for being sharp around the edges and not huggy-feely enough. I mean, people don't love porcupines the way they love puppies.

Or maybe Mom resents me for surviving when Lea was the better daughter.

I cross my arms and dig my fingernails into my skin.

"I know I'm not always the easiest person to be around, but I never thought Mom would actively need to get *away* from me. I never thought she'd find more comfort in being alone than being with me. And I always thought Lea might've been her favorite, but I never had confirmation. I never knew for sure. And now I do." I clamp my mouth shut and focus on my breathing.

Aunty Ani drags her thumb along the edge of her ceramic mug like she's trying to find the courage to speak her mind. "Your mom didn't leave you. Not the way you think she did. She didn't send you here because she didn't want you anymore, or didn't care enough. She cared *so* much. That's why—" Aunty Ani chews the inside of her mouth like she's chewing on a secret. When she brings her eyes back up, they're glistening with a sadness she's been fighting to hold together. "Your mom checked into a clinic. A psychiatric hospital."

I blink. "What?"

Aunty Ani pushes on. "She wasn't doing too good, Rumi. She felt responsible fo' the crash—fo' killing one of her daughters and fo' taking away your best friend. And she knew she couldn't be a mother to you until she got help. Because sometimes that's important—asking fo' help. There's no shame in saying, 'I can't do this alone.' There's no shame in saying, 'I'm not okay.' And your mom knew she couldn't be any good to you if she was broken a thousand different ways. So she checked into the hospital to take care of her mental health, so that she'd be able to take care of you."

I shake my head, my hair swaying back and forth furiously.

"That's not an excuse. She should've told me. She should've tried harder. Because *I'm not okay* either. *I can't do this alone.* Or at least I didn't want to, but there was no other option for me. Because Mom never gave me one."

Aunty Ani nods solemnly. "I know. And I'm not saying your mom did the right thing by not talking with you, but I know she was trying to do the best thing *for* you. Grief is a monster—not everyone gets out alive, and those who do might only survive in pieces. But it's a monster that can be conquered, with time. And your mom just needed some time."

"She still should've told me," I say.

"I know," she says.

I take a deep breath. "I don't know what I'm supposed to say. I don't know how to forgive her."

Aunty Ani tilts her head and lifts her brows. "Maybe you just need time, too."

CHAPTER FORTY-TWO

It's too hard to write lyrics when I'm thinking about what Aunty Ani told me. For the first time in a long time, I feel like I need to talk about her—about Mom. But not with Aunty Ani, because she's too . . . involved.

So I tell Mr. Watanabe everything instead, and he doesn't tell me to be quiet. He just listens, with Poi in his lap and his head tilted back against his armchair. The piano record—the one that sounds like magic—spins beside him.

"You no can be mad at your muddah fo' dat. You feel sick, you go see one doctor. Dat's da rules," Mr. Watanabe says finally.

I frown. "Mom's not sick."

He grunts. "Her mind feel sick, eh? Same same."

"Well, you don't get to check out as a parent just because you're sick. *Those* are the rules. I needed her, and she didn't pick me," I say grimly.

Mr. Watanabe watches me carefully, unmoving. "Who you t'ink she pick, den?"

I swallow. Blink. Ball my fists together. "She picked Lea. She always picks Lea."

"How's dat?" he asks.

"Grieving Lea was more important to her than making sure I was okay." I feel my heartbeat in my chest, and it hurts.

I expect Mr. Watanabe to feel sorry for me, or to agree with me, or to tell me my feelings are making him uncomfortable. I don't expect him to say what he actually does.

"You no stay mad at your muddah. You mad cuz you like her all fo' yourself. You act like one kid at da playground—you no like share."

"That's not true. Mom isn't an object; she's a person," I say defensively.

"So you bettah start treating her like one. You not da only one dat feeling hurt—try t'ink about how she must feel to lose a child." His eyes burn with memories. "Not so easy, you know, trying fo' talk story wit' everybody and trying fo' act normal when nothing feels like normal—never mind trying fo' take care of anuddah person. Sometimes it's real hard jus' fo' get out of bed."

"I'm not just any person. I'm her daughter," I say, my face getting hot.

But he doesn't flinch. He's not worried about my ghosts being hurled at him because he already has his own. "Exactly. Dat's why—why don't you give her a break? Go at least talk to her. Because losing one kid hard enough—no need make her have fo' lose two."

"Jesus, Mr. Watanabe. I don't know why I even bother coming over here," I say, and I move to the back room and play the piano until lunchtime.

A memory

Mom and Lea are dancing around the room to "Bennie and the Jets" with wooden spoons in place of microphones. Mom can actually hold a tune, even though she always insists Lea and I are the musicians of the family.

They're up on the couch, bouncing and waving their arms in the air, and I know I'm an asshole for not smiling and joining in, but I stay firmly planted on the armchair.

"Come on," Mom sings, holding her hand out to me, with Lea giggling beside her.

"No," I say flatly, turning back to my notebook. Lea and I are in the middle of a song—"Otter Northern Lights Twinkle." She already wants to give up because the words are too hard, but I don't want to quit on our song. I don't want to quit on us.

"Come on," Mom repeats. "We're celebrating."

"*You're* celebrating. I'm going to have to make new friends at a new school halfway through junior year in a new city I don't know anything about."

"Ouch," Mom says, clutching her heart.

Lea throws a pillow at me, and it hits my thigh. "Seriously, cheer up. This new job is going to be amazing. Mom will be home every night. You might even get a car for your birthday."

"Okay, that's maybe a little bit of a stretch," Mom says with a laugh.

I'm scowling. "I don't want a car. I don't want to move."

Lea rolls her eyes. "God, stop being so selfish. It's not like Mom doesn't deserve this—she's worked two jobs since we were babies. Have some empathy."

"I'm not selfish," I shout, throwing the pillow back— it hits her in the face.

"Hey!" Lea yelps, her face twisting into a frown.

"*Rumi,*" Mom starts.

"Oh my God, stop picking on me. I'm allowed to not be happy about moving," I shout, and then I'm on my feet and marching to the bedroom Lea and I have shared all our lives.

It takes Mom only about ten seconds to follow me.

She stops in the doorway, her hands clasped together and hanging in front of her like she's ready to plead with me. My back is pressed against the wall and I've already pulled my pillow into my lap so I can have something to squeeze under my fists.

"Seattle isn't that far away. You can still visit all your friends," Mom says. She's wearing her Target uniform and the same dark, sunken bags below her eyes that seem as much a part of her as this bedroom is a part of me.

She needs this job. I know she does. I'm not trying to be selfish—I just don't like change. I look beyond Mom and at the posters and photos all over Lea's wall. Her favorite bands, the pictures of the two of us, and one really good one of her and Mom.

The truth is, I never really felt like one of Mom's kids. I felt like her helper—I felt like a second parent for Lea.

And if Mom's around more, everything is going to change. Lea will have her real mother back, and Mom will get to be a parent to Lea, who's still young enough to need one.

I don't know where I'll fit in our family.

"It's going to be different," I say.

Mom nods. "Of course it will. It will be different for all of us, but we'll get used to it."

"I don't want to get used to it," I say with focus. "I want us to stay the same."

Mom watches me like I'm a peculiar kind of flower she hasn't quite decided is poisonous or not. I don't like the way it makes me feel.

"I'm not going to steal Lea away from you," she says finally.

Salt starts to form in my eyes. I breathe through my nose to keep them from flooding over.

"You two are best friends. You'll always be close, even if I am home more often," Mom says softly.

"I know you think that makes me a jerk"—I burst into tears—"but Lea is all I have. When you weren't here, and Dad wasn't here, I just had her. And I know she's your favorite, but—"

"What?" Mom interrupts, her eyes wide and brown. "Rumi, I love you both equally."

"You don't have to lie to me. I know Dad loved me better and you loved Lea better. Everyone has a favorite."

"That's not true. That's not even a little true." She takes big steps across the room and sits so she's facing me. "Your . . . *father*," she says like it tastes bitter in her mouth, "liked himself best. And I liked both of you more than him, and that's the way it's always been."

I wipe a tear from my cheek.

When she speaks again, her voice is careful. "What makes you think I like Lea more?"

"You guys are always having fun together. She's just . . . more lovable than me, and I know that and it's fine, but still." I shrug. "It sucks sometimes, seeing someone spend their whole life being coddled by the only parent they share."

Mom's laugh takes over the room like a firework, and then she's holding my face in her hands and kissing me on the forehead. "You goof." Mom shakes her head at me. "I always coddled Lea because *you* always coddled

Lea. I thought that was our thing—taking care of Lea."

"I took care of her because I had to. You were never around," I say thinly, and when I see the hurt in Mom's eyes, I wish I could take it back. I don't mean to blame her—it's just how things have always been.

"That's why this job is so important. I'm missing out on too much. Maybe you're missing out on things too," she says.

I feel the tears pooling in the corners of my eyes and clench my jaw to force them away.

My voice is less than a whisper, and it clips when I speak like I'm so afraid of the truth I want to chop it up into tiny pieces. "I love Lea. But that doesn't mean I can't be jealous of her too. She's better than me—a better singer, a better friend, a better teenager, a better daughter. I'll always be in her shadow, and if she doesn't need me to look after her anymore, what if she decides she doesn't need me at all?"

"Oh, honey," Mom says, taking my hands. "You're too hard on yourself. And that's my fault—for not being here to let you feel like you got a childhood too. I'm sorry if that meant you didn't get time to be the baby. You're one of my babies too, you know." She kisses the side of my head. "And Lea will always want you around, because you're sisters and you both love each other. Please don't be jealous of her. You have no idea how much I love you two—I wouldn't change a single thing about either of you."

I swallow. "Even if I'm too much like Dad?"

She sighs and leans her forehead against mine. "You're not like him at all. And if you ever want proof, all you have to do is look at Lea. The way you feel about her—he never felt it. He was incapable of feeling it. With anyone."

I try to pick the best words, even though they feel muddied and incomplete. "What if Lea's the only person I can ever love? Lea and you? What if I'm like Dad the rest of the time?"

Mom smiles. "Then we're the luckiest two people who ever walked this earth."

I wander back into the living room and find Mr. Watanabe in his chair.

"You're right. I don't like sharing Mom." My voice cracks. "But that's because I hardly ever had her when Lea was alive. She worked all the time. And she spent more time with Lea than she did with me, because Lea was like sunshine and golden retriever puppies and the perfect blend of sweet tea. And when Lea died, Mom should've been mine."

I take a breath and the oxygen feels colder somehow. Even my nose tingles like it's full of winter air.

"I'm mad Mom didn't realize that. I'm mad she didn't pick me on her own. And I want to be mad at Lea, too, for being so unrealistically perfect that I can't be Mom's first choice even when I'm the only daughter still alive." I press my lips together tightly and wait.

Mr. Watanabe's face falls into a frown, but he nods despite it. "I's okay fo' be mad. But i's okay fo' you stop being mad too."

I raise my shoulders an inch. "When will that be? When did *you* stop being mad?"

He grunts. "When I found myself all alone—aftah my son died and my wife died and when I wen' push everybody away." He points his finger at me seriously. "You don't wait dat long. You no let your anger drive you into solitude. Dat's because one day you goin' wake up and find your anger has been replaced wit' loneliness, and i's mo' easy fo' stop being mad dan it is fo' stop being lonely. You understan'?"

"But is it too soon to be happy again? Because I feel like it is."

"I's neva too early to start fo' live again. You jus' make sure you talk wit' your muddah. You have to make sure dat you both speak your peace. Because if you no can, all da hurt—i's still goin' stay inside, yeah? You have fo' let it out." He holds up his hands. "Grief is only a visitor, but it goin' stay mo' longer when it sees you hiding from it."

I retreat to the piano room and play until my fingers blur and I can't see the black and white of the keys—I only see movement.

CHAPTER FORTY-THREE

I go back to work at the salon because Mrs. Yamada says the window is almost paid off, and I don't see any point in dragging it out.

At the end of my shift, when I'm finished sweeping hair off the floor and bringing coffee to one of the women getting her nails done with Mrs. Yamada, I find Jae-Jae at the counter.

"I want you to cut my hair," I say almost sternly.

She raises a glittery brow. "I can do it now if you want."

I nod. "Yeah, okay. But . . . I want something else done. Something . . . specific."

Jae-Jae flattens her lavender lips. "I like the sound of this."

I knock on Kai's front door, but Mr. Yamada is the one who answers. When he sees me—or rather, my new hair—he scrunches his face and shakes his head.

"For God's sake, what is it with you kids always trying to get attention?" he barks before turning back toward the living room. "Kai! Door!"

Kai appears in the doorway and laughs with all the brilliance of the sun. "Wow, hapa." He pauses. "Wait, wait. Summer, bird . . . blue?"

I grin—he gets it. Of course he does. I run my fingers self-consciously over the freshly chopped pixie cut that's as blue as the sky. "I needed a change."

He reaches out and pulls at one of the shortest pieces. "I like it. You look good."

I stuff my hands in my pockets and lift my shoulders. "I feel like I need to stop hiding, or worrying, or whatever it is I'm doing most of the time. And, I don't know, I thought cutting my hair was a good place to start."

"Did you get rid of some of your emotional baggage, too?" he asks in bewilderment.

I scoff. "*Emotional baggage?* I—"

"Lost a sistah, I know, I know." He rolls his eyes, laughing.

I shake my head slowly. "I seriously have no idea why we're friends."

"This is exactly why we're friends. Because we don't hold back with each other." He shrugs.

I sigh. "Well, in any case, I wanted you to be the first one to see it. I thought you'd get it more than anyone else would."

Kai grins, his eyes going back to my short blue hair. "This is going to take some getting used to."

*　*　*

I go to Mr. Watanabe's house next. When he opens the door he shouts, "Aye, lolo, whatchu do to your hair? You look like one ice cream cone." And then he laughs and laughs and doesn't stop until he's sitting back in his chair with his eyes closed.

CHAPTER FORTY-FOUR

Mr. Watanabe sets a bowl of lightly salted edamame on the coffee table, and we eat them while we listen to one of his records.

"What's a good word that rhymes with 'breakable'?" I ask, tapping my pen against the lined page.

"Unbreakable," Mr. Watanabe replies.

"No—that—what?" I make a face.

He laughs through his teeth and it comes out like a whistle. Poi looks up from the floor, her ears perked up like she's listening for a secret language.

"Dis song take long time, eh? When you goin' be all pau?" he muses from his chair.

"You can't rush creativity. It's like the rain. You wait and wait and wait, and when it finally comes, it soaks the earth and revives all the plants," I say.

"Whatchu talkin' about? I wait fo' how many weeks fo' you

to learn how fo' water da plants. Dey all goin' stay dead if I wait fo' da rain," he grumbles.

I laugh, my pen still constantly tapping. When the vinyl crackles to a stop. I stand up to flip the record, but Mr. Watanabe waves me off.

"I get 'em. I get 'em. Finish your sistah's song," he says.

Finish the song. That's all she wanted to do, and I wouldn't let her. The memory feels like a sucker punch when it comes back to me, and I close my arms around myself like I'm bracing for impact.

A memory

"Stop it!" Lea shouts at me. Her guitar, half covered in stickers, is wedged in her lap.

She strums a few chords again, singing the lyrics of one of her favorite songs, and I start playing my own completely different song on the piano at the bottom of my bed.

"Seriously, stop!" Lea yells. "Just let me finish this song."

"You're not the only one who wants to practice," I snap.

"Put on headphones."

"Go to a different room."

"I was playing first."

"You're just playing—I'm trying to write something important."

Back and forth and back and forth we go like Ping-Pong balls, neither of us wanting to give in. Eventually we're both standing, fighting with each other like two siblings who've been living in the same room for far too long.

I know I should've let her finish the song. She was here first, *playing* first, and now I'm trying to drown her out so she'll be forced to stop practicing.

I could say it's because she's been playing for hours and it's my turn. I could say it's because I need to write a song before it leaves my head, which is more important than what she's doing. I could even blame it on wanting control, because I'm older and because there should be perks to being a backup sort-of parent.

But they'd all be lies.

I started playing the piano because Lea is starting to sound really, really good.

And I want her to be good, but maybe not *that* good. Not better than me.

It's not fair—music was always my thing. And I didn't mind sharing it for a while, when Lea was still learning and she needed to come to me every time she wanted to learn a new chord or get help with a new melody. But I can hear the way she strums like it's second nature, like her guitar is merely an extension of her hands. Her soul.

She doesn't need me to teach her anything anymore. And pretty soon she's going to realize it, and she won't look up to me anymore either.

Music is my identity. If it becomes hers, will it stop being mine?

It's confusing. I feel so many ugly, crawling emotions inside me—I don't like it at all.

But instead of fighting the feelings, I'm fighting with Lea.

She marches across the room and swipes my sheet music off the stand. I rip one of her posters off the wall. She cries and tells me she hates me. I'm screaming that I wish I had my own room.

Mom isn't home to separate us or intervene or defuse the situation. It's just the two of us, like it is most days. And it's unfortunate, because the fight goes on.

And on.

And on.

"I wasn't always nice to her," I say quietly. It's an admission I didn't realize I was ready to make.

Mr. Watanabe looks up, a record between his hands.

"I know it seems like I'm a good sister for being so upset she's gone and for trying to finish this song, but I wasn't always a good sister. Sometimes I was a horrible sister." I don't know why I'm telling Mr. Watanabe this, but I can't stop. I've opened the floodgates and now there's nothing to do but let the words escape. "I never let her win. I was always trying to be in charge. I never told her how much I appreciated her, even though she was always there for me, even though I've said some of the most horrible things to her. She forgave me when she shouldn't have, when I spent my whole life being jealous of her. Isn't that weird? That I could love someone so much and still be so impossibly jealous of them? I don't know how to make sense of that. I think it just makes me a shitty person. And I want you to know that—that I'm not that nice a person."

Mr. Watanabe places the record in the player but doesn't start it. He twists his mouth and thinks. "I t'ink maybe when we lose somebody we love, we remember da best and da worst. An' we fo'get all da in between—and dea's a lot of in between—dat make up for da extremes. An' you know what, you no can be all dat bad, uddahwise you wouldn't be here fo' keep me company all da time."

I frown. "But . . . I didn't start coming here to keep you company. I started coming here because of the music. Because of the escape. And because—I don't know—maybe I didn't have anywhere else to go. I think that makes me kind of selfish."

He shrugs. "You came ovah here cuz Poi got outta da house and you knew she mean somet'ing to me."

I don't know why I keep arguing with him, but I do. Maybe because I need him to know I'm not good. Or, maybe I want him to convince me I am. "I went after her because it's what Lea would have done."

"Eh, if you like do, do. If you no like do, no do." He shrugs. "You talk too much and you look like one Smurf wen' cut your hair, but you a much bettah person dan you t'ink."

I spend a long time hearing his words on a loop in my head. Long enough to decide maybe it's worth considering. "Thanks," I say after a while.

He nods. "Now stop talking—I like dis song."

CHAPTER FORTY-FIVE

Kai invites me on a camping trip over the weekend. Aunty Ani seems thrilled with the idea. She doesn't stop talking about it all week. She lets me borrow her old sleeping bag and makes enough Spam musubi for our whole group. I think she's mostly excited I'm starting to act like a normal, well-adjusted teenager again. I think it makes her feel like she's doing something right.

I take Mr. Watanabe's ukulele with me, because guitars and ukuleles are practically a campfire requirement.

When we reach the Malaekahana Beach Campground, Gareth, Hannah, and Jerrod are already waiting for us. They're sitting around a small fire crackling within a metal enclosure, and three blue tents are set up behind them.

Hannah sees me and flashes a smile, her hand raised to block the sun from her eyes. "Hey, Rumi. Want a s'more?" She holds up a stick with a dripping, gooey, near-black marshmallow on the end.

I sit next to her and smile. "Yeah. Okay."

She smashes the melting white and brown bubble into a sandwich of chocolate and graham crackers and hands it to me. "Jerrod keeps setting his on fire, and Gareth can't seem to stop dropping his, so I'm the designated marshmallow roaster."

Kai sits down next to her and presses his hands together. "You like make me one too?"

She rolls her eyes. "Seriously, you guys are useless."

"Oh God," I say, "who set up that tent?" Everyone turns to look at the uneven row of tents behind them. The one in the center is large, but half of it has already collapsed like it's slowly deflating. The carcass of an air mattress is hanging out of the front.

"Jerrod," Hannah and Gareth say in unison.

Jerrod looks up from his phone and holds a hand up in retaliation. "Seriously? Why was I left all on my own to do that? I don't know how to set up a tent."

"You could've googled it," Hannah says.

"No cell service," Jerrod snaps back.

"Den whatchu been doing fo' da last half an hour?" Gareth stares.

"I'm taking pictures. Stop interrogating me," Jerrod says, shuffling away from them with a scoff.

I finish my s'more, play some ukulele, and watch Kai and Hannah try to put the last tent together while Gareth keeps an eye on the fire and Jerrod wanders off to take pictures of the beach.

"I's good you and Kai are still friends. You mo' bettah dan one iPod," Gareth says, nodding toward the ukulele against my chest.

I grin. "Glad to be of service."

His laugh comes out in short bursts, and he scratches the back of his neck. The width of his arm is practically the entire width of his head.

I look over my shoulder at Kai and Hannah, strumming absentmindedly. They're laughing at each other while trying to get the air mattress to inflate.

"I t'ought you were into girls, to be honest," he offers out of nowhere. "Until Kai said he doesn't t'ink you're interested in romantic relationships at all."

I freeze, my fingers forgetting to change chords for a moment. "Kai said that?"

He nods like it's not a big deal, and I guess maybe it's not. Maybe it doesn't have to be.

"Wait, but why did you think I was into girls?"

He shrugs. "Because you weren't into Kai. I mean, Kai is kind of beautiful."

"Well, I don't like girls like that." I pause. "I don't think I like boys like that either. Is that weird?"

He doesn't hesitate. "No, not at all. Lots of people identify da same way as you."

"But I don't know how I identify, exactly. I know about the labels, and I guess if I was basing it off what the Internet says, I'd identify as asexual. And maybe somewhere on the aromantic spectrum, too. But I feel like I don't fully relate to any of the labels that exist. Some of them are mostly right, but not exactly right. And the asexual and aromantic labels—they're about *attraction*.

They don't explain why I'm not sure if I like kissing, or how I'm not interested in sex right now. It's so confusing to me."

"Izzy's taught me a lot about understanding how everybody is different. I guess—and not to get weird—but sexuality is fluid fo' a lot of people. I's different fo' everybody, and dea's not really a right or wrong way to be. We fall into different places on a spectrum, I guess, like different colors in a rainbow."

"But, like, how are people supposed to know what they like for sure? And what if they change their mind?"

"Den dey change dea' mind. I don't t'ink you have fo' know right dis second. Whatchu, sixteen? Seventeen? I'm eighteen, and I no have all da answers fo' everything. But dat's da fun part—figuring everyt'ing out. I don't want all da answers right now. I like try living instead."

"Yes!" I practically shout. "That's what I want. But I feel like I'm supposed to know everything right now. Everyone else always seems so put together."

"Dat's because some people are liars." Gareth laughs. "Dey as clueless as us; dey only bettah at pretending."

I grip the ukulele and tilt my head back like I'm groaning. "I knew it."

"An' you know what I t'ink? I's okay fo' be confused, an' i's okay fo' not be confused. One isn't mo' bettah dan da uddah, yeah? Dey both normal. Dey both okay."

I smile. It's okay to be confused. It's normal.

I'm normal.

And part of me knew it all along. Because feeling the way I

feel always felt normal to me, until I realized it wasn't what other people were doing—when I realized how sure everybody else seemed to be about their likes and dislikes.

But maybe it really is okay to be unsure, and to change my mind, or to never change my mind.

Maybe it's okay to be exactly the way I am.

Gareth pulls a marshmallow out of the bag and wedges it onto the end of a stick. "Okay, eighth time's da charm."

We talk about Izzy's band and Gareth's plans for college and his tabby cat named Mele Kalikimaka, which means "Merry Christmas" in Hawaiian. Three more marshmallows fall into the fire.

I take the stick from him. "I can't watch this anymore. It's too sad. Pass me a marshmallow."

He flashes his teeth and hands me the bag. "T'anks, sistah."

"I don't know why we haven't been talking more this summer. You and I have a lot in common," I say, spinning the marshmallow slowly over the fire.

"You were too busy trying fo' make up your mind about Kai," he says, leaning back in his chair. "And writing dat song of yours. You eva finish dat one yet?"

I kick my toes into the sand. "I'm still working on it. It changes a lot, depending on how I'm feeling. I don't know—I guess this summer has hit me in stages. Feeling lost, trying to escape, and finding a way to live again." I shrug. "And the lyrics change whenever I do. I guess I'm still trying to figure out what to write about."

"Why no write about dat?" Gareth offers.

I frown. "About being confused?"

"No. About da summer. About how you changed."

"I—I don't know. I guess I need to make sure I'm still done changing before I write a song like that."

I finish making Gareth a s'more and go back to strumming random melodies on the ukulele until it's time to cook the food. I get up to help Kai barbecue pineapple cubes and chicken legs. We talk like we're childhood friends and it feels so natural. I feel happy. Comfortable. Maybe even a little excited, because I feel more relaxed in my skin than I have in a long time.

Maybe my blue hair is more magic than I realized. Or maybe I'm just ready to grow. To change.

After we all eat, we play card games, share funny stories about each other, and spend a lot of time making fun of Jerrod now that his battery is dead and his phone has been forced out of his hands.

Eventually, when the stars are out and the air smells crisp with salt, we all cram ourselves into the tents and fall asleep.

If it weren't for the hundred roosters that wake me up at all hours of the night, I would have made it all the way until morning before remembering Lea is dead. It would have been the first time since the accident.

But in the darkness, in a tent on my own, I see her lying beside me, her nose inches from mine. Smiling. Telling me it's okay, that *everything is okay*, and to go back to sleep. And looking at her—seeing her right here next to me—doesn't hurt the same as it did before.

Maybe I'm going to be okay after all.

CHAPTER FORTY-SIX

When Sunday morning rolls around and it's time to leave the campsite, we all decide the weekend has been too much fun and we're not ready for it to end.

So instead of going home, we stop by Laniakea Beach, otherwise known as Turtle Beach. Kai shows me the sea turtles that come to shore to eat seaweed near the rocks. They're strangely docile, and Jerrod gets close enough that—if his phone had any battery left—he could've easily taken one of his beloved selfies with them.

Afterward we visit Chun's Reef and throw a Frisbee around near the water. Gareth tells me it's a good place for longboard surfing, if you stay away from the shallow end, which is filled with sea urchins. I help Hannah look for pieces of sea glass. She tells me she's been collecting them since her dad was first stationed here and that most of the ones she finds are teal, white, and turquoise. I find one that's a deep cobalt blue and she tells me I'm her lucky charm.

After that we stop off at a taco stand for a late lunch, and nobody seems to mind that we haven't had a working cell phone since yesterday.

And then we say good-bye. Hannah gives me a hug and says she hopes we can hang out again soon. Gareth throws me a high-five and offers to teach me how to surf, if I'm interested. And Jerrod tells me he's going to post all the photos from the weekend on Instagram and that he'll tag me in everything.

I get in the car with Kai, but he doesn't start the engine right away. He looks at me instead, with his half smirk and happy eyes.

I wrinkle my face at him and laugh. I don't need to say anything; this is the first weekend I've felt like myself in a long time. And knowing Kai, he probably wants to take some credit for it.

When he pulls the car back into our cul-de-sac, his dad practically throws himself out of the house and onto the sidewalk. By the time we're in the driveway, he's already at Kai's door.

"Why didn't you answer your phone?" he shouts.

Kai's face recoils. "We were camping—my battery died."

I expect him to yell—about the military, about surfing, about hanging out with me—but Mr. Yamada doesn't keep yelling. He looks straight at *me*.

I look back and forth between Kai and Mr. Yamada. "What?"

And then I hear Aunty Ani's door fall shut. I look up—she's making her way down the steps shakily.

Oh God. It's Mom. Something happened to Mom.

My stomach feels heavy and desperate. I shove the door open

and take a hurried few steps toward my aunt, who is gripping her sides like she's aching.

"Is she okay? What happened to her?" My voice is panicked. All I'm thinking is that Mom is dead and I was awful to her.

"What happened to—" Aunty Ani looks confused and shakes her head. "No, it's—" Her voice breaks away. She looks toward Mr. Watanabe's house like her heart is breaking.

She calls after me when I start running to his house, but I can't hear her. I can only hear my footsteps thudding against the pavement and up the steps. I tear the screen open and pound my fist against the door over and over again.

"Mr. Watanabe?" I'm shouting in a coarse, weary voice.

There's no answer. I skirt around the edge of the house, looking into every window. The living room is empty. The hallway is empty.

"Poi?" I call out hoarsely. I'm running around the back of the house, checking the dog run I helped build.

Where the fuck is that damn dog? Why isn't she barking and yapping and being her obnoxious guard dog self?

And where is Mr. Watanabe?

I come back to the front steps, and Aunty Ani is standing there with her hands up like she's trying to get me to slow down.

"Where is he?" I ask with so much fear in my throat.

"Calm down, okay? He's in the hospital. You didn't have a phone, so I couldn't call you. I tried to get in touch with Kai, but it kept going straight to voice mail." She reaches for me, and I realize I'm shaking like I'm standing in subzero temperatures.

Something powerful punches me in the gut. My rib cage feels brittle and weak, like my heart is about to roll out of it.

"What do you mean he's in the hospital?" It's my voice, small and empty.

She starts rattling on about chest pains and complications from an old surgery and his age and how the doctors are taking care of him, but I can't deal with it. I can't process it.

"Is he going to be okay?" My voice is a pebble tumbling to the bottom of an empty well.

Aunty Ani's eyes move back and forth. She pulls me close to her chest and hugs me. "I hope so, sweetheart. I hope so."

Angrily, I bare my teeth and sneer, pushing her away from me. "Who just leaves like that without saying good-bye? What a selfish bastard. What a giant pain in the okole."

I tear back through the gate, past Aunty Ani and Mr. Yamada and a worried Kai with his open arms desperate to comfort me, and I tuck myself away in my bedroom and close all the doors and walls and center myself in a place nobody can touch me.

CHAPTER FORTY-SEVEN

I'm sitting on the floor with a racing heart and an unimaginable migraine when I realize I don't know how many days it's been. The world feels dark again. I don't know how Hawaii can possibly be this dark, but it is.

Aunty Ani doesn't give up on trying to talk to me. She says she's not going to let me retreat into the darkness. She said she let it go on for long enough.

I want to tell her it's not her choice, but I'm too angry. At her, at Mom, at Mr. Watanabe. I'm even angry at Poi, for being in the care of some random family member who never visited instead of here, barking through the night and annoying the crap out of me. I wonder if I'll ever see that obnoxious, wonderful dog again.

He has to get better. He just has to.

Aunty Ani says a lot of other things too, about knowing I need Mom and Lea and being sorry I only have her, but most of it is white noise. Unintelligible, garbled white noise.

I stare at Mr. Watanabe's ukulele for a long time, thinking of how I haven't played since the camping trip. I thought I stopped being this angry, yet here I am, with the urge to break every one of my fingers just to prove how mad I am.

He can't die. He just can't.

It's late, but I can't fall asleep. I'm too busy staring at the ceiling, picturing the whirl of the fan from Mr. Watanabe's living room, thinking of all the memories I have of lying on the floor trying to feel whole. I didn't think I'd ever feel like a complete person again, but I was starting to.

I was trying.

Wasn't I?

I shove the covers away from me and find my flip-flops next to the welcome mat. I make my way next door, searching for Mr. Watanabe's spare key in a small fake rock he keeps hidden beneath the mock orange, and force my way into his living room.

It's so quiet in here. No barking, no records, no music. No Mr. Watanabe.

I flick the switch near the wall and slowly sink to the floor, lying back until my head is pressed into the hardwood boards. And with my arms spread like I'm making an angel in the snow, I watch the fan.

Around and around and around.

Is he going to die? Is he going to the place where Lea is?

Does a place exist for them at all?

I take a breath and close my eyes. There are no angels here. Only the demons that follow me everywhere.

A memory

I hear Lea's footsteps on the stairs. Even if Alex's car hadn't woken me up, I'd still have heard her. Lea might have the build of a ballerina, but she walks like she belongs on a football field.

She presses my door open and peers inside.

"Are you lost?" I say with my hand tucked under my pillow. "You have your own room now, remember?"

She giggles because she never notices right away when I'm in a bad mood. She thinks I'm being my normal grumpy self. Closing the door quietly behind her, she half skips toward my bed and collapses behind me. "I had the best night of my life."

I roll my eyes. "I'm trying to sleep. Tell me in the morning."

She gives out a melodic sigh. "I can't sleep. I'm too excited."

"It was just a date. You've been on a hundred dates."

"Not like this one." She pauses, and I can feel the joy build in her hesitation. "Alex kissed me."

I feel something horrible grow inside me. A horrible, ugly monster that wants to claw and swipe and tear at her happiness.

She leans away from me so she can sigh into the ceiling. "It was perfect. He wrote me this song on the guitar— it was so adorable—and then we had pizza at Luigi's, and ice cream. After that we played at the arcade for a while and then hung out on the playground swings like we were kids."

"That sounds dangerous," I say dryly.

Lea wraps her arm around me and squeezes. "Come on, talk to me. I want to know what you think."

"About what? About how irresponsible you're being?"

She pulls her arm away and sits up. "What's that supposed to mean?"

I sit up too, because I've started and now I can't stop. "We move houses, Mom finally has extra money, and you go around wasting it on pizza and ice cream and arcade games?"

She looks wounded, but I don't stop. I never do.

"Mom didn't work as hard as she did so you can go on a new date every Friday night," I say.

"That's harsh, Rumi. That's really fucking harsh."

"Well, it's true. I spent my whole life being poor too, you know. It's not like I had money for arcades and pizza and going out with guys."

"You could go out if you wanted to. Mom said—"

"Mom isn't going to tell you no. Not after she waited all these years to be able to spoil you. You're her baby, right? The good one. The happy one. And you're taking advantage of her."

I'm green, green, green from head to toe. But I can't stop. She's always had it so much easier than me, and it's not fair.

It's easier for Mom to love her.

It's easier for her to go out with her friends because Mom has money now and she doesn't have a little sister she's responsible for.

And it's easier for her to know who she wants to go out with because she's more sure of herself than I am. She's not confused like me, or working through things like me.

Life comes so much more naturally to Lea.

I can't help it—I'm jealous of how easy everything has always been for her. I'm bitter it hasn't always been as easy for me.

Lea scowls. "Why are you being so mean to me? What did I ever do to you?"

"Dad never wanted you. If you had never been born, he would've stayed. I wouldn't have had to grow up the way we did. I could've had piano lessons and summer camps and fucking pizza. But I didn't—none of us did—because of you. And you don't even understand what kind of sacrifice that is. Because you always had me growing up, when I needed my parents. I was a mom to you so you didn't have to miss out, but I missed out on everything. You ruined our family—you made it so Mom and me and Dad could never be together."

Lea scrambles off the bed full of fury and pain. "You take that back."

"No," I say.

She chews her lip. "It's my wish. I'm using my third wish. You take it back right now."

"I won't."

"A wish is a wish."

"Screw your wishes. Leave me alone."

I never took it back. We made up, but I never took it back. I didn't even apologize. Lea simply forgave me, in silence, like she always did.

I was an awful sister to her. Not all the time, but when I was, I was *really* awful.

Why did I say those things? Why was I always so mad at her? Why did I never tell her how much I really loved her? How it wasn't her fault I mothered her—I did it because I loved her and I wanted to protect her. When Dad left, I didn't run after him—I ran to Lea.

I should've told her that. It feels important now that she's gone.

Around and around and around goes the fan.

Just like my anger.

I hate this feeling. I hate not being able to take it all back. I hate not being able to give Lea her wish. I hate everyone leaving me, like I'm the poison that corrupted them all. I hate that right now, when I feel broken and empty and I need my sister more than ever, she isn't here for me to talk to.

I hate that I loved her so much I have to feel this kind of pain.

Around and around goes the fan.

And I scream and scream and scream, like I did the days after

Lea died, like I did the day I got to Hawaii, like I did the days after Mr. Watanabe went to the hospital, when I found myself alone all over again.

I scream to get the hurt out. I scream to be heard.

And then I see her.

Lea is standing above me, her face blossoming with kindness. She sits down next to me. I sit up so I can face her.

I should tell her I'm glad she's back. I should tell her I'm happy to see her, that I hope she never leaves me, that I'd rather have her ghost here with me than none of her at all.

But I say something else instead.

"I'm so *angry* at you."

Lea blinks carefully, her eyes waiting for me to finally tell the truth.

"I'm angry because you took Mom with you. You died and you should've left her to be with me. To take care of me. But you took her with you anyway. Why would you do that? Why would you leave me all alone?" My voice clips the air.

She reaches for my hands. I can almost feel them pressing against my skin, like a rush of cold air.

"I know it's not your fault, but I have to be angry. It's the only thing protecting my heart." I squeeze my fists together and push them into the floor. "That's why I can't cry. I'm too busy being mad at you and mad at Mom, because even when you stopped existing, she chose the grief of you over a life with me. And I'm worried . . . if I'm not mad at you . . . that you'll disappear for good. Because everyone I love disappears."

I twist my mouth, wondering if my anger is what's hurting me the most. I know I can't be mad forever, but how do I stop?

I want it to stop.

I look at her ghost. Is she listening? I hope she is.

"I'm sorry, Lea. I'm sorry I blamed you for Mom not loving me enough. I'm sorry I was so jealous of you. I'm sorry for every horrible thing I ever said to you. I'm sorry I was too selfish to give you your last wish."

She doesn't have to say a word—I already know Lea's forgiven me, wherever she is. Because that's who she was.

My stomach coils and tightens, and I shut my eyes to find enough strength to finish what I've started. "I'm sorry that you died and I got to live."

My words feel brittle. I look for Lea's ghost, but she's fading fast.

"Don't disappear. I need you."

But the shape of her continues to blur. I don't know how much longer I can keep her here with me.

I don't know how to stop being mad. I don't know how to turn off these feelings. I feel like my heart is *dying*.

Maybe I'm too weak to hold on to her.

Or . . .

Maybe it's just time.

I close my eyes and think of Lea. My sister, twirling around our room, strumming chords on her guitar, wrapping her arms around my neck and giggling like she was forever a child.

And she forever will be.

Because Lea's gone. She's really, really gone.

My nose tingles. I feel my chest tighten. And tears pool in my eyes.

I miss you.

A tear falls down my cheek.

Where did you go?

Two more follow.

Lea.

And then I feel all of it—the weight of her death, the crushing guilt, the suffocating jealousy, and the immense love I have for a sister I'll never see again.

Because I love her. I loved her in life and I love her in death, and that kind of love only comes around once in a lifetime.

Fuck romance—Lea was the love of my life. It was beautiful and horrible and messy and angry, but it was also the purest, most innocent kind of love I'll ever feel.

I wish I had protected her. I wish, when I had held her hand the night Dad left, that I had kept my promise and kept her safe.

The tears come, and they don't stop. I cry until my face is sore, and then I cough and choke on the floor because I feel like I'm suffocating.

And then I hear the footsteps. I bolt upright, tears covering my face like an extra layer of skin, and I see the blurry image of my mother.

"Mom," I gasp, my eyes burning. "Mom."

And then I'm on my feet and her arms are around me, and I don't stop crying, even when she buries my face back in her beautiful, wild, wavy hair and tells me it's all going to be okay.

CHAPTER FORTY-EIGHT

I'm standing beneath the whirling fan in Mr. Watanabe's living room when Mom tells me she's sorry for leaving.

She says she needed help, but she should never have made me feel so alone. She asks me to forgive her for causing more hurt and tells me that she loves me.

She promises to be stronger for me.

I'm still wrapped in Mom's arms when I tell her I'm so angry at her. At *everyone*.

She tells me that sometimes being angry is easier than letting the sadness in. She says anger attacks like a dagger; sadness is more like a wave.

I tell her that I don't know how to stop being mad. I don't know how to turn off these feelings—how to turn off the hurt.

Her nose is buried in my hair when she tells me I've been running from a wave and that I'm tired. She says it's time to stop running.

I cry until my face is swollen and my voice rips away.

*   *   *

I'm staring at my hands in the middle of the night, the light slipping through the leaves of the palm trees right outside the window, when I realize I don't recognize my hands anymore.

They aren't mine or Lea's. I don't know what that means.

I'm sitting with Mom and Aunty Ani at the table when the phone rings.

Mr. Watanabe is going to be okay. He's coming home soon.

I feel so relieved and exhausted I can barely hold my head up. I just let the tears fall onto the notebook beneath my nose, leaving teardrops on the pages of lyrics I still don't have the right words to finish.

I'm eating macaroni salad in the dining room when Mom brings me Lea's guitar. She asks if I could play her something. She says it helped her get better, to imagine what it would sound like to hear me play again.

I strum until my fingers hurt.

I'm sitting on the couch when I tell Mom the story of Lea's three wishes. I tell her about "Summer Bird Blue" and why it's so important that I finish it.

Mom's crying before I even finish the story. She presses her nose into my neck, and for a moment we're the same person, sharing the same grief over the beautiful soul we both lost.

*   *   *

I'm writing lyrics in my notebook when I hear a car pull up to Mr. Watanabe's house. Part of me wants to race outside, to go and see him and to make sure he's okay.

But the other part of me knows I'm not ready.

I need to say good-bye to my sister first.

I haven't spoken to Kai in weeks. I haven't even left the house.

I just write and write and write and write and . . .

CHAPTER FORTY-NINE

Mom and Aunty Ani sit on both sides of me like a protective sandwich. I think they're afraid I'll fly away again.

But I don't intend to go anywhere. I'm just glad I have my mom back.

She passes me a cup of tea from the coffee table. "It's the right temperature," she says. She was always good about that—reminding me when my drink was ready before I'd forget.

I take it from her and sip carefully. She's being gentle with me, and maybe I'm being a little gentle with myself, too.

Mom points to my notebook. "May I?"

I nod.

She pulls it into her lap and flips through the pages. It reminds me of how she used to read through our lyrics when we were younger, whenever she could find the time. She was always busy, but not too busy for me and Lea. Not too busy for our music.

She sees the letter I wrote her first. It's everything I wanted to say to her and everything I'll probably want to take back. But she reads it like she's soaking in every word, and at the end she nods like she understands. Like the words *make sense.*

And maybe they do. Maybe they're necessary for us to get past this.

When Mom gets to "Summer Bird Blue," she stops turning pages. I hear her breathing quicken, watch her press her fingers to her mouth, and look away when the first tear falls.

"You finished it," she says finally.

"It wasn't as hard as I thought," I say simply. "Turns out I've been living it. The words, the lyrics—some more literally than others, of course." I point to my fading blue hair.

"I like it," she says. "Lea would've liked it too."

And it makes me smile, thinking about how Mom knows Lea almost as well as I do.

She rests her cheek against my temple, and her curls spill from her shoulder. I want to reach out and touch them. I love the familiarity—the buttery smoothness of her skin, the grapefruit scent of her soap, the shimmery pink of her cheeks, and the way she is always, always warm. To me, Mom is *home.* "I'm sorry I wasn't here when you got your hair cut."

She's been apologizing for days. She's sorry she had to disappear for a while. She's sorry she wasn't there for me. She's sorry I had to mourn Lea all on my own. She's sorry she wasn't around more when we were kids. She's sorry she didn't force Dad to stay. And she's mostly sorry she's done so many things worth apologizing for.

"It's okay," I tell her, and it surprises me a little that I mean it. It's been bad, not having her around, but it hasn't been *all* bad. I took some steps on my own, even if they were wobbly and in the wrong direction.

But I have learned that I can survive this. That I *have* survived this. Even if there is still such a long way to go.

"Those two care about you a lot," Aunty Ani tells me when she's cooking saimin on the stove. I know who she's talking about— Kai and Mr. Watanabe. "Every time I see them outside they ask about you."

I lean against the wall, playing with the string of my pajama bottoms and staring at my bare feet. Mom's taking a shower, and it's strange how normal it feels to have her close by again. "Do you think he's mad at me?" I ask after a few seconds.

Aunty Ani looks puzzled.

"Mr. Watanabe. For not visiting him in the hospital."

She rests the wooden spoon on the counter and faces me. "Nobody would blame you fo' not wanting to be in a hospital after what you went through." She means the accident and losing Lea. I'm not in a hurry to step through the doors of a hospital again, even if I'm walking on my own two feet and not being pushed on a stretcher.

"Yeah, but"—I pause, chewing my lip—"I'm the only one who visits him. I'm the one who should've been there to keep him company."

"He has family in Hawaii."

"But not *close* family. If they cared about him, I'd have seen them at his house. I'd have seen photos of them *in* his house."

Aunty Ani shrugs. "Sometimes families are complicated. It doesn't mean they don't care."

I push my tongue to the side of my mouth and shake my head. "Mr. Watanabe is a good person. He doesn't deserve to be lonely all the time."

"You don't think maybe he likes being lonely?" she asks carefully.

"Some people like being alone, but nobody likes being lonely, even if they pretend they do," I say. "Besides, he likes having *me* around. Doesn't he?" I suddenly feel as if I'm searching for confirmation.

"I'm sure he does." She pauses. "I think sometimes grief finds grief. Maybe he felt comfortable around you in a way he didn't with his family."

I clench my teeth, considering her words.

She turns to me suddenly, like she needs me to listen carefully to what she's about to say. "I hope you know how much I care about you, Rumi. I know we lived far away from each other, but I love you. And even though I'm sorry about the way you came to Hawaii, I'm not sorry you were here. Ohana, right?"

Family. I nod. "I know. And thanks—for everything."

She smiles. I think she's trying to hold back her tears. She starts to stir the saimin again, but remembers something. "Oh, I almost forgot. He left something fo' you. Watch the stove?"

She disappears into the hallway, and when she comes back

she's holding one of Mr. Watanabe's records. The one with the guitar. The one that drew me to his front door that first night.

She hands it to me. "When his niece came to pick up Poi after he went to the hospital, she dropped this off. Said he wanted you to have it. I held on to it because I worried it would make you more upset, and then with your mom back . . ." She shakes her head apologetically. "I guess it slipped my mind."

"Why would he give me this?" I ask with a frown.

She offers me a small smile. "I'm not sure he was convinced he was going to make it. His niece told me he kept saying that you were his friend and that you'd be waiting fo' him. And . . . well, maybe he wanted you to have this, in case he didn't come home." She motions toward the single record. "He said you'd need it."

I don't say anything. I'm trying too hard not to cry.

"You no need worry whether he's mad at you or not. I think he's grateful fo' you. I think you brought him a lot of peace— more than he's had in years."

We eat dinner together, and afterward Mom and Aunty Ani make fresh tea, taking their cups out to the lanai to give me space. I sit on the couch for a long time, staring at the gift and wondering what I did to make Mr. Watanabe think I was worthy of such a present.

And as if some otherworldly presence were urging me to do so, I split the case open and slide the vinyl disk out of the packaging. A piece of paper falls out and floats to the ground.

I pick it up carefully, studying the handwriting I don't recognize but know is Mr. Watanabe's.

In neat, swooping letters written with black pen are the words: *If you get lost in the darkness, remember to follow the music. Thanks for reminding me to do the same.*

Even though I'm crying, I'm smiling, too.

CHAPTER FIFTY

Mom books us plane tickets to go back to Washington in a week. She says we've been hiding from our real lives for long enough, and it's time we face our empty home together.

It's going to be hard walking through our house and doing all the normal things we used to do, without Lea, but Mom says we have each other. She says we'll get through it together and that Lea would want us to live. She says we owe her that much—to be happy—because it's how she would have lived her life.

The next afternoon, I find myself wandering into my neighbor's yard. I can't leave Hawaii without saying good-bye. I wouldn't want to.

Poi starts barking before I reach the top step. Mr. Watanabe pushes the screen open and grunts like it hasn't been days at all.

"So, I don't know if you heard, but I'm going back to Washington soon," I say.

"I heard," he replies, as if it's simple—as if we don't have to make this harder than it needs to be.

I hold up the ukulele. "Thanks for letting me borrow this. It might have saved my life."

"You bettah keep it, if it's done all dat."

I hold the instrument close to my chest and smile.

He nods toward the living room. "You like mahi-mahi?"

We sit together at the table, eating lunch and listening to music, when I remember something. Something I forgot. Something I didn't fully understand.

A memory

The impact of the other vehicle against ours makes my head whip to the side. I don't have time to brace for it—it collides against us like metal punching metal, and then the world starts to spin.

I hear the noises—the glass and the crunching. The awful, awful noises.

And then the last sound I hear before the worst music of my life comes to a finish.

"Rumi."

My name. Someone calling my name. But it's not a shout, and it's not a whisper. It's the weak, desperate word of someone closing their eyes.

And it isn't Lea's voice at all.

I swallow the bite of white fish that's stuffed in my mouth and blink. And breathe. And feel the rush of cold through my nostrils.

"It was Mom," I say out loud.

Mr. Watanabe looks at me with a patience I've never seen him wear before.

"I thought Lea said my name right before I blacked out. But it wasn't her—it was my mom." My heart is stunned for a moment, the beating nonexistent.

"Your muddah loves you. I'm sure she was very worried about you." He speaks with more care than he usually does.

But why would she say my name? Why wouldn't she call out for Lea?

Maybe it means nothing. Maybe it means everything.

Maybe it simply means something to me.

A moment of clarity, if nothing else, where I will always know that my Mom loved me completely.

After dinner, I find Mom sitting on the steps near the front door, almost like she's waiting for me. Almost like she knows.

"Why didn't you tell me?" I sit beside her, the moon hovering above us like a soft lantern. "Why did you let me think Lea said my name?"

Mom gives me a weak smile. "I wondered if you'd ever remember—or if I should ever tell you the truth."

I wrap my arms around my knees and wait for her to explain.

She wipes a quiet tear away. "In some ways, I still feel responsible for the accident—like what happened was my fault. If only we'd left the house five minutes earlier, or five minutes later. If only we'd never left at all. If maybe I'd somehow paid more attention to the road, or taken an extra second before I hit the gas pedal."

"It's not your fault, though," I say.

"Thank you, Rumi. I know that, deep down." She shakes her head. "I loved you both the same. I love you equally. But I always worried about you in a way I didn't with Lea. And I guess that came out instinctively when the accident happened. I was worried about you, and when it turned out my other baby died, I felt horrible. I felt like—I don't know—like I'd made a choice and the universe answered."

My stomach turns, and my heart breaks all over again, but this time for my mother. "Oh, Mom . . ."

She lifts her head and tears spill down her brown cheeks.

"Why didn't you tell me?"

"At first because I was so ashamed. I didn't think you'd even heard me—I thought it would be a secret I'd carry for the rest of my life. And then you told me you thought it was Lea— how you thought she'd saved you in some way. And I guess I didn't want to take that away from you—that confirmation of how much your sister loved you. And she did, Rumi. She really, really did."

I chew my lip. "It would've been nice to know you loved me too. I felt like you abandoned me because your favorite daughter was gone."

"I know that now. And I'm so sorry. I shouldn't have let my grief swallow me up the way it did. I should've been there for you." She sniffs. "I guess I always felt like it was the two of you, you know? Rumi and Lea, my sweet, beautiful girls. You two loved each other so much—I guess the grief of knowing you lost each other was what killed me the most. I'm so sorry. I should've done better."

I rest my head on her shoulder and she kisses me, her sigh spilling into my hair.

"Please don't hate me," she whispers.

"I promise I don't. I never did—not really," I say. And then I tilt my head back to look at her. "Besides, Aunty Ani is actually pretty cool. It's been nice here."

Mom laughs. "I'm glad to hear it." After a while, she speaks again. "How would you feel about seeing a therapist when we get back home?"

I look up at Mom. "You think I still need to talk to someone? Even though you're back?"

"I do. I think it's important. And we could even go together, if you'd like that. I want us to both be healthy. I want you to have the best chance at healing you possibly can, and I think therapy is necessary," Mom says.

I nod because I believe her, and because I want things to be okay. "All right. I'll talk to someone."

"Together?" she asks.

"Together," I say.

Mom kisses my forehead again. I think she's making up for lost time.

I think it's going to be a long time before it feels normal without my sister. Maybe it never will. But I'll get through it. She'd want me to get through it. And I owe her that much—to be happy—because she wouldn't have wanted Mom and me to be sad. She'd want us to remember her, and keep going.

I can't let my grief swallow me up anymore. I have to be here, in the right now. *Alive.*

I strum the chords to "Summer Bird Blue" into the dark hours when the birds go to sleep and the stars light up the blackness. I sing until the sun starts to rise and I'm drowning in delirium. And I don't stop practicing, even when Mom and Aunty Ani laugh from the living room, where they're remembering to be sisters again.

I live for the music.

CHAPTER FIFTY-ONE

When Kai opens the door, he looks relieved. "I was wondering if you were ever going to stop by. I tried to visit you, but Aunty Ani said you needed some time."

I nod. "I did. But I'm all back to normal now."

He crinkles his nose. "Wait. Old you was *normal?*"

I snort. "Still as sensitive as ever. How have you been? I noticed your dad fixed the car window."

"I've been okay." He holds up his hand. There are a few scars where the stitches had been, but the bandages are gone. "Won't be long until I can surf again. Not that it matters much, since I'm leaving soon."

I bite the edge of my lip. "My aunt said you were leaving for boot camp in a few days."

"No judging, *friend*," he warns.

I laugh. "No judging."

His eyes flash with wild electricity. "I'm joining the air force."

I raise my eyebrows, and a grin spreads across my face. "Your dad must be livid. Good for you."

His laugh settles into a sigh. "I heard you're flying back to Washington tomorrow."

"I am," I say.

He looks down at the ground. "So I guess this is good-bye?"

I nod. "Yeah. I guess it is."

He motions toward the guitar in my hand. Lea's guitar. "What's that fo'? You goin' serenade me?"

I look down and nod. "Well, it is good-bye, after all."

He leans against the doorframe. "I have to admit, I pictured this a lot differently in my head."

I lift my gaze. "You pictured us saying good-bye?"

"No," he says. "I pictured the serenading. I thought there'd be moonlight. You'd be sitting in front of your window. I'd be leaning out of mine. And maybe there'd have been kissing at some point."

"I can tell my music meant a lot to you," I note dryly.

He straightens suddenly and twists his mouth. "Wait. You finished it, didn't you? 'Summer Bird Blue'?"

"I did." I pull the guitar in front of me. "You have a couple of minutes to spare? Kissing and moonlight not included."

"Of course I do." He pulls the door closed behind him and we both sit on his front step.

I clear my throat. "Okay. Well, you already know what this one is called."

I strum my fingers, the familiar sound of Lea's guitar filling the street like the scent of gardenias when I first landed in Hawaii. Mellow. Sweet. But with all the heart of an island.

I close my eyes and sing.

> *I woke up alone*
> *abandoned in this space you left.*
> *I tried to find you*
> *and fill the hole inside my chest.*
> *I wanted you to stay;*
> *I tried to find a way,*
> *and I did.*
> *I trapped you here*
> *with all my pain.*
> *We became a monster*
> *I couldn't explain.*
> *I needed you to stay;*
> *I had to make you stay,*
> *so I did.*
> *But the sun came up*
> *like you promised it would,*
> *and we were living in a cage*
> *cut off from the rest of the world.*
> *And I knew I had to set you free;*
> *I knew you couldn't stay with me.*
> *It's time.*
> *I know it's time.*

So I'm singing,
Good-bye, little bird,
I'll watch you fly into the blue.
And when the summer ends,
I'll fly with you.

When I look up, Kai is smiling, the electricity turned up full force in his eyes. And I know in my heart that I'll probably never see him again.

Some people are meant to be forever, like Lea and me. And other people come into your life for a reason—you help each other figure shit out and come to terms with complicated feelings that you can't process on your own.

And I'm okay with that. Kai has been a good friend. I'll always remember him and our time in Hawaii. And I'll always remember Mr. Watanabe and his obnoxious little dog, no matter what the future holds. But this has been a summer of good-byes—it was never about anything but good-byes.

Maybe there's something special in that. Something bittersweet and beautiful, all of these moments coming to an end.

"I love it. Your sistah would love it," he says.

I pull the guitar strap from my neck like I'm pulling off a piece of me. When I do, I feel lighter. "Thanks. I'm just glad it's finished. It needed to be finished, you know?"

"Yeah. I know." He curls the ends of his mouth into his signature smile. The corners of his eyes wrinkle. His freckle disappears. "I'm going to miss you, hapa."

"Yeah. I know," I say, setting the guitar down beside me. And then I lean in to him and wrap my arms around his neck, hugging him close like we're old friends saying good-bye forever. "Thanks for being so annoying all the time."

He hugs me back, his laughter tickling my neck.

When I pull away, I don't look at him again. I pick up Lea's guitar and go back inside to finish packing my suitcase and to spend more time with Aunty Ani before Mom and I go home.

Good-byes are hard. I've had to say way too many good-byes lately, and I think I'm finally ready for something else.

I think I'm ready to live.

A memory

The grass tickles the back of my legs, and I flick a dandelion so the white puff blows into the afternoon breeze.

Lea strums another chord on my old guitar.

"No, like this," I say, moving her fingers on the fret board.

She strums again and smiles when the notes don't clash. "I'll remember them eventually."

"I hope so. How cool would that be if you could play guitar? We could start a band. I'll play the keyboard," I say.

Her face lights up. "Would you really be in a band with me?"

"Of course," I say. "You're my best friend. I wouldn't be in a band with anyone *but* you."

Lea looks dizzy with excitement. "Maybe I could ask Mom for a guitar for my birthday. And Christmas—it could be two presents in one. So I don't have to keep borrowing yours. And you could keep teaching me how to play."

I nod. "That would be so cool. But you'd have to practice—you couldn't just quit on the band and change your mind."

She crosses her heart. "I'd never quit. And you couldn't change your mind either—you have to promise you'll always want to play music with me. You have to promise we'll do this forever. Because I'm not going to waste a birthday and Christmas present on a guitar if you are just going to change your mind."

I laugh. "I promise. We'll always play music together."

"Okay, I promise too."

We shake hands and laugh like the children we are, making promises we don't realize we can't keep, but making them anyway because we mean every word.

Because for Lea and me, music is the whole world.

ACKNOWLEDGMENTS

To my editor, Jennifer Ung—thank you for using your editorial magic to shape this book into what it is today. You always know exactly what to do to bring out the best in a story, and I feel like the luckiest author in the world to have worked with you on two books now. I'm so very grateful for your constant enthusiasm and excitement, and it is truly an honor to share this book with you!

To my agent, Penny Moore—thank you for always being in my corner, and for offering so much guidance, support, and wisdom. You already know I think you're a superhero, and I will shout about what a warrior you are until the end of time. I could not imagine being on this writing journey with anyone else!

An enormous thank you to the Simon Pulse team who've helped turn *Summer Bird Blue* into a real book—Mara Anastas, Chriscynethia Floyd, Liesa Abrams, Caitlin Sweeny, Alissa Nigro, Christian Vega, Amy Hendricks, Nicole Russo, Sam Benson, Christina Pecorale, Emily Hutton, Caitlin Nalven, Michelle Leo, Chelsea Morgan, and Sara Berko.

And to the incredibly talented Sarah Creech—thank you for once again designing a cover more beautiful than anything I could have ever imagined. You captured the heart of this story so perfectly and thoughtfully, and I get emotional every time I look at those adorable birds and remember what they represent.

A special thank you to Andrea Barzvi and Sandy Hodgman at Empire Literary for all of your time, hard work, and support this past year.

And an enormous amount of love and gratitude to Eric Smith, Brandy Colbert, S. K. Ali, Ashley Herring Blake, Samira Ahmed, Melissa Albert, Kelly Loy Gilbert, and Riley Redgate for being such generous and wonderful human beings.

To the readers, book bloggers, and booktubers who have championed *Starfish* and *Summer Bird Blue* from the beginning— thank you for making this experience so special. Every time a new reader picks up a book I've written, I feel like my dreams are coming true all over again. I'm so appreciative of all the time you spend promoting the books and authors you love.

To the readers who are finding my words for the very first time— thank you for reading this book. It means the absolute *world*.

A massive thank you to my writer friends Nicki, Lyla, Taylor, and Anisaa, who made the roller-coaster of being published a little less bumpy (and terrifying). And to my friends and family who have been so supportive—thank you for being the best hype-team I could ask for. And a special shout-out to my dad—thank you for reading so many early drafts of this book, and for sharing all your expertise on Hawaiian Pidgin. Your help has been invaluable!

And finally, to the three loves of my life—Shaine, Oliver, and my husband, Ross. You make up the center of my universe, and you'll always be home to me. Thanks for making every day better, brighter, and more brilliant than the last. I love you all times infinity.

ABOUT THE AUTHOR

Akemi Dawn Bowman is the author of *Starfish* and *Summer Bird Blue*. She's a proud Ravenclaw and *Star Wars* enthusiast, who served in the US Navy for five years and has a BA in social sciences from UNLV. Originally from Las Vegas, Nevada, she currently lives in Scotland with her husband, two children, and their Pekingese mix.